I POSE

My eyes are girt with outer mitts,
My ears sing shrill — and this I bless,
My finger-nails do bite my fists
In ecstasy of loneliness.
This I intend, and this I want,—
That, passing, you may only mark
A dumb soul and its confidante
Entombed together in the dark.
The hoarse church-bells of London ring,
The hoarser horns of London croak,
The poor brown lives of London cling
About the poor brown streets like smoke;
The deep air stands above my roof,
Like water to the floating stars;
My Friend and I — we sit aloof,
We sit and smile, and bind our scars.
For you may wound and you may kill —
It's such a little thing to die —
Your cruel God may work his will,
We do not care — my Friend and I, —
Though, at the gate of Paradise,
Peter the Saint withhold his keys,
My Friend and I -—we have no eyes
For Heaven ... or Hell ... or dreams like these

STELLA BENSON

2015 by Neo Editions (NEOEDITORIALBOOKS@GMAIL.COM).This book is a classic, and a product of its time. It does not reflect the same views on race, gender, sexuality, ethnicity, and interpersonal relations as it would if it was written today.

CONTENTS

I POSE 1
    PREFACE 1
    CHAPTER I 2
    CHAPTER II 200

PREFACE

Sometimes I pose, but sometimes I pose as posing.

CHAPTER I

There was once a gardener. Not only was, but in all probability is, for as far as I know you may meet him to this day. There are no death-bed scenes in this book. The gardener was not the sort of person to bring a novel to a graceful climax by dying finally in an atmosphere of elevated immorality. He was extremely thin, but not in the least unhealthy. He never with his own consent ran any risk of sudden death. Nobody would ever try to introduce him into a real book, for he was in no way suitable. He was not a philosopher. Not an adventurer. Not a gay dog. Not lively: but he lived, and that at least is a great merit.

In appearance the gardener was a fairly mediocre study in black and white. He had a white and wooden face, black hair as smooth as a wet seal's back, thin arms and legs, and enormous hands and feet. He was not indispensable to any one, but he believed that he was a pillar supporting the world. It sometimes makes one nervous to reflect what very amateur pillars the world seems to employ. He lived in a boarding-house in Penny Street, W. A boarding-house is a place full of talk, it has as many eyes as a peacock, and ears to correspond. It is lamentably little, and yet impossible to ignore. It is not a dignified foundation for a pillar.

The gardener was twenty-three. Twenty-three is said to be the prime of life by those who have reached so far and no farther. It shares this distinction with every age, from ten to three-score and ten.

On the first of June, in his twenty-fourth year, the gardener broke his boot-lace. The remains of the catastrophe dangled from his hand. String was out of the question; one cannot be decent dressed in string, he thought, with that touch of exaggeration common to victims of disasters. The world was a sordid and sardonic master, there was no heart in the breast of Fate. He was bereft even of his dignity, there is no dignity in the death of a boot-lace. The gardener's twenty-three years were stripped from him like a cloak. He felt little and naked.

He was so busy with his emotions that he had forgotten that the door of his room was open.

It was rather like the girl Courtesy to stand on the landing boldly staring in at a man sitting on his bedroom floor crushed by

2

circumstances. She had no idea of what was fitting. Any other woman would have recognised the presence of despair, and would have passed by with head averted.

But the girl Courtesy said, " Poor lamb, has it broken its boot-lace?" The gardener continued in silence to watch the strangling of his vanity by the corpse of the bootlace. His chief characteristic was a whole heart in all that he did.

A tear should have appeared in Courtesy's eye at the sight of him. But it did not.

"Give me the boot," she said, advancing into the room in the most unwomanly manner. And she knotted the boot-lace with a cleverness so unexpected — considering the sort of girl she was — that the difference in its length was negligible, and the knot was hidden beneath the other lace.

"Women have their uses," thought the gardener. But the thought was short-lived, for Courtesy's next remark was:

"There, boy, run along and keep smilin'. Somebody loves you." And she patted him on the cheek.

Now it has been made clear that the gardener was a Man of Twenty-three. He turned his back violently on the woman, put on his boot, and walked downstairs bristling with dignity.

The girl Courtesy not only failed to be cut to the heart by the silent rebuke, but she failed to realise that she had offended. She was rather fat, and rather obtuse. She was half an inch taller than the gardener, and half a dozen years older.

The gardener's indignation rode him downstairs. It spurred him to force his hat down on his head at a most unbecoming angle, it supplied the impetus for a passionate slamming of the door. But on the doorstep it evaporated suddenly. It was replaced by a rosy and arresting thought.

"Poor soul, she loves me," said the gardener. He adjusted his hat, and stepped out into London, a breaker of hearts, a Don Juan, unconscious of his charm yet conscious of his unconsciousness. " Poor thing, poor thing," he thought, and remembered with regret that Courtesy had not lost her appetite. On the contrary, she had been looking even plumper of late. But then Courtesy never quite played the game.

"I begin to be appreciated," reflected the gardener. "I always knew the world would find out some day . . ."

The gardener was a dreamer of dreams, and a weaver of many theories. His theories were not even tangible enough to make a philosophy, yet against them he measured his world. And any shortcomings he placed to the world's account. He wrapped himself in theories to such an extent that facts were crowded from his view, he posed until he lost himself in a wilderness of poses. He was not the victim of consistency, that most ambiguous virtue. The dense and godly wear consistency as a flower, the imaginative fling it joyfully behind them.

Imagination seems to be a glory and a misery, a blessing and a curse. Adam, to his sorrow, lacked it. Eve, to her sorrow, possessed it. Had both been blessed — or cursed — with it, there would have been much keener competition for the apple.

The million eyes of female London pricked the gardener, or so he imagined, as he threaded the Strand. He felt as if a glance from his eye was a blessing, and he bestowed it generously. The full blaze of it fell upon one particular girl as she walked towards him. She seemed to the gardener to be almost worthy. Her yellow hair suffered from Marcelle spasms at careful intervals of an inch and a half, every possible tooth enjoyed publicity. The gardener recognised a kindred soul. A certain shade of yellow hair always at this period thatched a kindred soul for the gardener.

He followed the lady.

He followed her even into the gaping jaws of an underground station. There she bought cigarettes at a tobacco stall.

"She smokes," thought the gardener. " This is life."

He went close to her while she paid. She was not in the least miserly of a certain cheap smell of violets. The gardener was undaunted.

"Shall we take a taxi, Miss?" he suggested, his wide eager smile a trifle damped by self-consciousness. For this was his first attempt of the kind. " They say Kew is lovely just now."

It was his theory that spoke. In practice he had but threepence in his pocket.

She replied, " Bless you, kid. Run 'ome to mammy, do."

Her voice sounded like the scent she wore. It had a hard tone which somehow brought the solitary threepence to mind.

The gardener returned at great speed to Penny Street.

It was lunch-time at Number Twenty-one. The eternal hash approached its daily martyrdom. Hash is a worthy thing, but it reminds you that you are not at the Ritz. There is nothing worse calculated to make you forget a lonely threepenny bit in your pocket.

The gardener had a hundred a year. He was apparently the only person in London with a hundred a year, for wherever he went he always found himself the wealthiest person present. His friends gave his natural generosity a free rein. After various experiments in social economy, he found it cheapest to rid himself of the hundred a year immediately on its quarterly appearance, and live on his expectations for the rest of the time. There are drawbacks about this plan, as well as many advantages. But the gardener was a pillar, and he found it easier to support the world than to support himself.

It was on this occasion that his neighbour at luncheon, unaware of his pillar-hood, asked him what he was doing for a living.

"Living," replied the gardener. He was not absolutely sure that it made sense, but it sounded epigrammatic. He was, in some lights, a shameless prig. But then one often is, if one thinks, at twenty-three.

"It's all living," he continued to his neighbour. "It's all life. Being out of a job is life. Being kicked is life. Standing's life. Dying's life."

The neighbour did not reply because he was busy eating. One had to keep one's attention fixed on the food problem at 21 Penny Street. There was no time for epigrams. It was a case of the survival of the most silent. The gardener was very thin.

The girl Courtesy, however, was one who could do two things at once. She could support life and impart information at the same time.

"I do believe you talk for the sake of talking," she said; and it was true. " How can dying be living?"

It is most annoying to have the cold light of feminine logic turned on to an impromptu epigram. The gardener pushed the parsnips towards her

5

as a hint that she was talking too much. But Courtesy had the sort of eye that sees no subtlety in parsnips. Her understanding was of the black and white type.

"Death is the door to life," remarked Miss Shakespeare, nailing down the golden opportunity with eagerness. 21 Penny Street very rarely gave Miss Shakespeare the satisfaction of such an opening. There was, however, a lamentable lack of response. The subject, which had been upheld contrary to the laws of gravitation, fell heavily to earth.

"Is this your threepenny bit or mine?" asked the girl Courtesy. For that potent symbol, the victim of its owner's absence of mind, in the course of violent exercise between the gardener's plate and hers, had fallen into her lap.

Whose idea was it to make money round? I sometimes feel certain I could control it better if it were square.

"It is mine," said the gardener, still posing as a philosopher. " A little splinter out of the brimstone lake. Feel it."

Courtesy smelt it without repulsion.

"Talk again," she said. " Where would you be without money?"

"Where would I be without money? Where would I be without any of the vices? Singing in Paradise, I suppose."

"If I pocket this threepenny bit," said Courtesy, that practical girl, " what will you say?"

"Thank you — and good-bye," replied the gardener. " It is my last link with the world."

Courtesy put it in her purse. " Good-bye," she said. " So sorry you must go. Reserve a halo for me.

The gardener rose immediately and walked upstairs with decision into his bedroom, which, by some freak of chance, was papered blue to match his soul. It was indeed the anteroom of the gardener's soul. Nightly he went through it into the palace of himself.

He took out of it now his toothbrush, a change of raiment, and Hilda. It occurs to me that I have not yet mentioned Hilda. She was a nasturtium in a small pot.

On his way downstairs he met Miss Shakespeare, who held the destinies of 21 Penny Street, and did not hold with the gardener's unexpected ways.

"Your weekly account . . ." she began.

"I have left everything I have as hostages with fate," said the gardener. "When I get tired of Paradise I'll come back."

On the door-step he exclaimed, " I will be a merry vagabond, tra-la-la . . ." and he stepped out transfigured — in theory.

As he passed the dining-room window he caught sight of the red of Courtesy's hair, as she characteristically continued eating.

"An episode," he thought. " Unscathed I pass on.' And the woman, as women must, remains to weep and grow old. Courtesy, my little auburn lover, I have passed on — for ever."

But he had to return two minutes later to fetch a pocket-handkerchief from among the hostages. And Courtesy, as she met him in the hall, nodded in an unsuitably unscathed manner.

The gardener walked, with Hilda in his hand. It became night. Practically speaking, it is of course impossible for night to occur within three paragraphs of luncheon-time. But actually the day is often to me as full of holes as a Gruyere cheese.

To the gardener the beginnings of a walk which he felt sure must eventually find a place in history were torn ruthlessly out of his experience. He was thinking about red hair, and all things red.

He hoped that Hilda, when she flowered, would be the exact shade of a certain head of hair he had lately seen.

"Hoping and planning for Hilda like a mother-to-be," he thought, but that pose was impossible to sustain.

Red hair.

He did not think of the girl Courtesy at all. Only her hair flamed in his memory. The remembrance of the rest of her was as faint and lifeless as a hairdresser's dummy.

It struck him that auburn, with orange lights in the sunlight, was the colour of heat, the colour of heaven, the colour of life and love. He looked round at the characteristic London female passer-by, the thin-breasted girl, with hair the colour of wet sand, and reflected that Woman is a much rarer creature than she appears to be.

He recovered consciousness in Kensington Gardens at dusk. He remembered that he was a merry vagabond.

"Tra-la-la . . ." he sang as he passed a parkkeeper.

People in authority seem as a rule to be shy of the pose. The parkkeeper was not exactly shy, but he made a murmured protest against the Tra-la-la, and saw the gardener to the gate with most offensive care.

In theory the gardener spent the night at the Ritz. In practice he slept on the Embankment. He was a man of luck in little things, and the night was the first fine night for several weeks. The gardener followed the moon in its light fall across the sky. Several little stars followed it too, in and out of the small smiling clouds.

The moon threaded its way in and out of the gardener's small smiling dreams. Oh mad moon, you porthole, looking up into a fantastic Paradise!

The gardener did not dream of red hair. That subject was exhausted.

When an undecided sun blinked through smoked glasses at the Thames, and at the little steamers sleeping with their funnels down like sea-gulls on the water with their heads under their wings, the gardener rose. He had a bath and a shave — in theory — and walked southward. Tra-la-la.

He walked very fast when he got beyond the tramways, but after a while a woman who was walking behind him caught him up. Women are apt to get above themselves in these days, I think.

"I'm going to walk with you," said the woman.

"Why?" asked the gardener, who spent some ingenuity in saying the thing that was unexpected, whether possible or impossible.

"Because you're carrying that flower-pot," replied the woman. "It's such absurd sort of luggage to be taking on a journey."

"How do you know I'm going on a journey?" asked the gardener, astonished at meeting his match.

"By the expression of your heels."

The gardener could think of nothing more apt to say than " Tra-la-la . . ." so he said it, to let her know that he was a merry vagabond.

The woman was quite plain, and therefore worthy only of invisibility in the eyes of a self-respecting young man. She had the sort of hair that plays truant over the ears, but has not vitality enough to do it prettily. Her complexion was not worthy of the name. Her eyes made no attempt to redeem her plainness, which is the only point of having eyes in fiction. Her only outward virtue was that she did not attempt to dress as if she were pretty. And even this is not a very attractive virtue.

She carried a mustard-coloured portmanteau.

"I know what you are," said the gardener. "You are a suffragette, going to burn a house down."

The woman raised her eyebrows.

"How curious of you!" she said. " You are perfectly right. Votes for women!"

"Tra-la-la . . ." sang the gardener wittily.

(You need not be afraid. There is not going to be so very much about the cause in this book.)

They walked some way in silence. The gardener, of course, shared the views of all decent men on this subject. One may virtuously destroy life in a good cause, but to destroy property is a heinous crime, whatever its motive.

(Yes, I know that made you tremble, but there are not many more paragraphs of it.)

Presently they passed a car, pillowed against a grassy bank. Its attitude, which looked depressed, was not the result of a catastrophe, but of a picnic. In the meadow, among the buttercups, could be seen four female hats leaning together over a little square meal set forth in the grass.

"Look" said the suffragette, in a voice thin with scorn.

The gardener looked, but could see nothing that aroused in him a horror proportionate to his companion's tone.

"Listen," said the suffragette half an octave higher.

The gardener listened. But all he heard was, " Oh, my dear, it was too killing . . ."

Then, because the chauffeur on the bank paused in mid-sandwich, as if about to rebuke their curiosity, they walked on.

"One is born a woman," said the suffragette. " A woman in her sphere — which is the home. One starts by thinking of one's dolls, later one thinks about one's looks, and later still about one's clothes. But nobody marries one. And then one finds that one's sphere — which is the home — has been a prison all along. Has it ever struck you that the tragedy of a woman's life is that she has time to think — she can think and organise her sphere at the same time. Her work never lets her get away from herself. I tell you I have cried with disgust at the sound of my own name — I won't give it to you, but it might as well be Jane Brown. I have gasped appalled at the banality of my Sunday hat. Yet I kept house excellently. And now I have run away, I am living a wide and gorgeous life of unwomanliness. I am trying to share your simplest privilege — the privilege you were born to through no merit of your own, you silly little boy — the privilege of having interests as wide as the world if you like, and of thinking to some purpose about England's affairs. My England. Are you any Englisher than I?"

"You are becoming incoherent," said the gardener. " You are enjoying a privilege which you do not share with me — the privilege of becoming hysterical in public and yet being protected by the law. You are a woman, and goodness knows that is privilege enough. It covers everything except politics. Also you have wandered from the point, which at one time appeared to be a picnic."

(Courage. There is only a little more of this. But you must allow the woman the privilege of the last word. It is always more dignified to allow her what she is perfectly certain to take in any case.)

"The picnic was an example of that sphere of which ' Oh, my dear, too killing . . .' is the motto. You educate women — to that. I might have been under one of those four hats — only I'm not pretty enough. You have done nothing to prevent it. I might have been an ' Oh, my dear ' girl, but thank heaven I'm an incendiary instead."

That was the end of that argument. The gardener could not reply as his heart prompted him, because the arguments that pressed to his lips were too obvious.

Obviousness was the eighth deadly sin in his eyes. He would have agreed with the Devil rather than use the usual arguments in favour of virtue. That was his one permanent pose.

A little way off, on a low green hill, the suffragette pointed out the home of a scion of sweated industry, the house she intended to burn down. High trees bowed to each other on either side of it, and a little chalky white road struggled up to its door through fir plantations, like you or me climbing the world for a reward we never see.

"I'm sorry," said the gardener. "I love a house that looks up as that one does. I don't like them when they sit conceitedly surveying their ' well-timbered acres ' under beetle brows that hide the sky. Don't burn it. Look at it, holding up its trees like green hands full of blessings."

"In an hour or two the smoke will stand over it like a tree — like a curse..."

When they parted the gardener liked her a little because she was on the wrong side of the law. There is much more room for the wind to blow and the sun to shine beyond the pale — or so it seems to the gardener and me standing wistful and respectable inside. It is curious to me that one of the few remaining illusions of romance should cling to a connection with that most prosy of all institutions — the law.

I forgot to mention that the gardener borrowed a shilling from the suffragette, thus rashly forming a new link with the world in place of the one he had relinquished to the girl Courtesy. The worst of the world is that it remains so absurdly conservative, and rudely ignores our interesting changes of pose and of fantasy. I have been known to crave for a penny bun in the middle of a visit from my muse, and that is not my fault, but Nature's, who created appetites and buns for the common herd, and refused to adapt herself to my abnormal psychology.

It was interesting to the gardener to see how easily the suffragette parted with such an important thing as a shilling. Superfluity is such an incredible thing to the hungry. The suffragette gave Holloway Gaol as her permanent address.

Thus accidentally bribed, the gardener, feasting on a cut from the joint in the next village, refrained from discussing women, their rights or wrongs, or their local intentions, with the village policeman. " She won't really dare do it," he thought.

(I may here add that I was not asked by a militant society to write this book. I am writing it for your instruction and my own amusement.)

The gardener did not sleep under a hedge as all merry vagabonds do — (Tra-la-la) — but he slept in the very middle of a large field, much to the surprise of the cows. One or two of these coffee-coloured matrons awoke him at dawn by means of an unwinking examination that would have put a lesser man out of countenance. But the gardener, as becomes a man attacked by the empty impertinences of females, turned the other way and presently slept again.

He washed next morning near to where the cows drank. He had no soap and the cows had no tumblers, — nothing could have been more elemental than either performance.

"I am very near to the heart of nature — tra-lala," trilled the gardener. But the heart of nature eludes him who tries to measure the distance. The only beat that the gardener heard was the soft thud of his own feet along the thick dust of the highway.

About the next day but one he came to a place where the scenery changed its mind abruptly, flung buttercups and beeches behind it, and drew over its shoulders the sombre cloak of heather and pines.

Under an unremarkable pine tree, listening to the impatient summons of the woodpecker (who, I think, is the feathered soul of the foolish virgin outside the bridegroom's door), sat a man. He was so fair that he might as well have been white-haired. His eyes were like two copper sequins set between white lashes, beneath white brows, in a white face. His lips were very red, and if he had seemed more detached and less friendly, he would have looked like harlequin. But he rose from his seat on the pine needles, and came towards the gardener, as though he had been waiting for him.

The gardener steeled himself against the stranger's first word, fearing lest he should say, "What a glorious day!"

But the stranger, making a spasmodic attempt to remove a hat which had been left at home, said, "My name is Samuel Rust, a hotel-keeper. Won't you come and look at my place?"

It was impossible for the gardener to do otherwise, for Mr. Samuel Rust's place framed itself in a gap in the woods to the right, and was introduced by a wave of its owner's hand.

"What a red place!" said the gardener.

"Of course. No other name is possible for it," said Mr. Rust.

The house was built of red brick that had much tangerine colour in it. The flowering heather surged to its very door-step. And thick around it the slim pine tree-trunks shot up, like flame, whispered flame.

The gardener smiled at it. If only Hilda might be the colour of those tree-trunks when she flowered.

Mr. Rust acknowledged the smile in the name of his red place. "It's an — inoffensive little hole," he said.

What he meant was of course, "It's a perfectly exquisite spot." What is becoming of our old eloquence and enthusiasm? The full-blooded conventions are dying, and we have already replaced them by a code of shadows. But whether the life beneath the code is as vivid as ever, remains to be seen. I think myself that manners are changing, but not man. In all probability we shall live to greet the day when "fairly decent " will express the most ecstatic degree of rapture.

The gardener was not intentionally modern. It is the tendency of his generation to be modern — it is difficult to believe that it has been the tendency of every generation from the prehistoric downwards. And it was the gardener's ambition to walk in the opposite direction to the tendency of his generation. He shared the common delusion that by walking apart he could be unique. This arises from the divine fallacy that man makes man, that he has the making of himself in his own hands.

I am glad that I share this pathetic illusion with my gardener.

So, as he thought the Red Place very beautiful, he said, " I think it is very beautiful."

But even so he was not sincere throughout. He posed even in his honesty. For he posed purposely as an honest man.

Of course you know that one of the most effective poses is to pose as one who never poses. A rough diamond with a heart of gold.

The first moment Mr. Samuel Rust heard the gardener say Tra-la-la he ceased to have a doubt as to the species of citadel he had invaded. " You are one of these insouciant wanderers, what?" he suggested. " A light-hearted genius going to make a fortune grow out of the twopence in your pocket. You got yourself out of a book. I think your sort make your hearts light by blowing them up with gas."

True to his code, he then feared that he had spoken with insufficient mediocrity, and blushed. A small circular patch of red, like a rose, appeared high up on either cheek, suddenly bringing the rest of his face into competition with his vivid lips.

"You are wrong about the twopence," said the gardener, " I have three halfpence."

"Come and see my Red Place," said Mr. Rust. " That is, if you're not bored."

Boredom and the gardener were strangers. One can never be bored if one is always busy creating oneself with all the range of humanity as model.

"This is an hotel," said the owner, as they approached the door. " It is my hotel, and it promised to make my fortune. So far it has confined itself to costing a fortune. When I remind it of its promise it puts its tongue in its cheek — what?"

The northern side of the Red Place was quite different in character from the side which first smiled on the gardener. This was because one essential detail was lacking — the heather. Fire had passed over the little space at some recent date in its sleepy history, and had left it sinister. Tortured roots and branches appealed from the black ground to a blue heaven. The surrounding pine trees, with their feet charred and blistered, and their higher limbs still fiercely red, still looked like flames now turned into pillars of delight in answer to the prayer of the beseeching heather.

"Is there anybody in your hotel?" asked the gardener, smoothing his hair hopefully — the young man's invariable prelude to romance.

"Nobody, except the gods," replied the host. " We sit here waiting, the divine and I. There is a blessing on the place, and I intend to make money out of it. You can see for yourself how wonderfully good it is. If people knew of the peace and the delight. . . . The table is excellent too — I am the chef as well as the proprietor. Our terms are most moderate."

"All the same you need advertisement," said the gardener, who, in unguarded moments, was more modern than he knew. "I can imagine most sensational advertising of a place with such a pronounced blessing on it. Buy up the front page of the Daily Mail, and let's compose a series of splashes."

"I am penniless," began Mr. Rust dramatically, and interrupted himself. " A slight tendency towards financial inadequacy — what?"

"I have three halfpence," said the gardener, but not hopefully.

"Come in for the night," begged the host. "I have twelve bedrooms for you to sleep in, and three bathrooms tiled in red. Terms a halfpenny, tout compris"

"Tra-la-la . . ." trilled the gardener, for as he followed his host the heather tingled and tossed beneath his feet, and the gods came out to meet him with a red welcome.

"You have nothing to do — what?" said Mr. Samuel Rust, when they were sitting in the high russet hall.

"We-ll . . ." answered the gardener, feeling that the suggestion of failure lurked there. "I am a rover, you know. Busy roving."

"To say that shows you haven't roved sixty miles yet. When you've roved six hundred you'll see there's nothing to be got out of roving. When you've roved six thousand you'll join the Travellers' Club and be glad it's all over."

"Six thousand miles . . ." said the gardener, as if it were a prayer. His heart looked and leapt towards the long, crowded perspective that those words hinted.

"You've never been to sea," continued Mr. Samuel. And the gardener discovered with a jerk that he was a blue man born for the sea, and that he had never yet felt the swing of blue water beneath his feet.

"No," he said, " I believe I must go there now."

And he jumped to his feet.

"If you stay here for the night," said Mr. Rust, to-morrow I'll suggest to you something that —? may possibly interest you to some slight extent."

With a clumsy blood-red pottery candlestick, which was so careless in detail as to seem to be the unconscious production of a drunken master-potter, the gardener found his room.

(I know it is a shock to you to find it bedtime at this point, but the gardener and I forgot to notice those parts of the day which I have not mentioned.)

He dreamt of red hair, redder than natural, as red as a sunset, seen at close quarters from Paradise. At midnight he awoke, in the clutch of perfectly irrelevant thoughts.

The room was a velvet cube, with the window plastered at one side of it, a spangled square. And the silken moonlight was draped across the floor.

"I am myself," said the gardener. "I am my world. Nothing matters except me. I am the creator and the created."

With which happy thought he returned to sleep again.

The Red Place lost its flame-like life at night. Night, that blind angel, has no dealings with colour, and turns even the auburn of the pine-trunks to cold silver. But before the gardener awoke again, the sun had roused the gods of the place to discover the theft of their red gold, and to replace it.

The gardener, as he trilled like a lark in one of the red-tiled bathrooms, was suddenly reminded that he was a merry vagabond.

"I must disappear," he thought. " No true vagabond ever says, ' Good-bye, and thank you for my pleasant visit.' "

So he prepared to disappear. From his bedroom window he could see, as he dressed, the pale head of Mr. Samuel Rust on a far fir-crowned slope, looking away over the green land towards London, waiting, side by side with the divine.

The gardener took three slices of dry bread from the breakfast which waited expectantly on a table in the hall, and went out. But under a gorse bush amongst the heather, he found some tiny scarlet flowers. He picked two or three, and returning put them on the breakfast plate of Mr. Samuel Rust. He put a halfpenny there too.

"Very vagabondish — tra-la-la . . ." he murmured tunefully, and studied the infinitesimal effect with his head on one side.

Then he disappeared. He did it straightforwardly along the open road, as the best vagabonds do, and he was pleased with his fidelity to the part.

Presently he recalled for the first time Mr. Samuel Rust's promise of a happy suggestion for that morning. For a moment he wondered, for a second he regretted, but he posed as being devoid of curiosity. This is a good pose, for in time it comes true. It eventually withers the little silly tentacles which at first it merely ignores. Curiosity needs food as much as any of us, and dies soon if denied it. And I am glad, for it seems to me that curiosity and spite are very closely akin, and that spite is very near to the bottom of the pit.

The memory of Mr. Rust's remark, however, kept the gardener for some moments busy being incurious. He was not altogether successful in his pose, for when the pallid owner of the Red Place stepped out of a thicket in front of him, he thought with a secret quiver, " Now I shall know what it was ...

"Taking a morning walk — what?" remarked Mr. Rust, achieving his ambition, the commonplace, for once in perfection.

"No," replied the gardener (one who never told a lie unless he was posing as a liar), " I was leaving you. I have left a smile of thanks and a halfpenny on your plate. You know I'm a rover, an incurable vagabond, and my fraternity never disappears in an ordinary way in the station fly."

It is rather tiresome to have to explain one's poses. It is far worse than having to explain one's witticisms, and that is bad enough.

"Come back to breakfast," said Samuel. "I can let you into a much more paying concern than vagabondage."

It is not in the least impressive to disappear by brute force in public, so the gardener turned back.

The gods did not run out to meet the returning vagabond, as they had run out to meet him arriving. The gardener did not look for them. He was too much occupied in thinking of small cramping things like "paying concerns" The expression sounded to him like a foggy square room papered in a drab marbled design.

"A paying concern does not interest me at all," he said, feeling rather noble.

"It won't as long as you're a merry vagabond. But your situation as such is not permanent, I think. Wouldn't you like to go and strike attitudes upon the sea?"

The gardener was intensely interested in what followed.

Mr. Samuel Rust was penniless, owing, as he frankly admitted, to propensities which he shared with the common sieve. But in other directions he was well supplied with blessings. He had, for instance, a mother. And the mother — well, you know, she managed to scrape along on nine thousand a year — what? The said mother, excellent woman though she was, had refused to finance the Red Place. She had not come within the radius of its blessing. She had no idea that it was under the direct patronage of the gods, and that it promised a fortune in every facet. Samuel had explained these facts to her, but she had somehow gathered the impression that he was not unbiased. In her hand she held the life of the Red Place, and at present held it checked. A little money for advertisement, a few hundred pounds to set the heart of the place beating, and Samuel Rust saw himself a successful man, standing with his gods on terms of equality. But his mother had become inaccessible, she had in fact become so wearied by the conversation of Samuel upon the subject that she had made arrangements to emigrate to Trinity Islands, somewhere on the opposite side of the world.

"And what is it to do with me?" asked the gardener, who suffered from the drawbacks of his paramount virtue, enthusiasm, and never could wait for the end of anything. " Do you want me to turn into an unscrupulous rogue and dog her footsteps because "

"You can have scruples or not as you choose," said Mr. Rust. "But rogue is a word that exasperates me. It's much the same as ' naughty-naughty,' and that is worse than wickedness. The wicked live on brimstone, which is at least honest; but the naughty-naughty play with it, which is irreverent. With or without your scruples, armed only with the blessing and the promise of this place, I want you to cross the Atlantic on the Caribbeania with my mother, and tell her what it is the gods and I are waiting for. That is — just try and talk the old lady round — don't you know. Any old twaddle would do — what?"

The gardener produced two halfpennies, one of which he placed on each knee.

"And the fare first-class is . . ." he said.

"I have a cousin whose only virtue is that he occasionally serves the purpose of coin," said Mr. Rust. "That is — I know a fellow I can bleed to a certain extent — what? He is the son of — well, a middling K-nut at the top of the shipping tree — what?"

The gardener had visions of an unscrupulous rogue, neatly packed into a crate labelled champagne, being smuggled on board the Caribbeania. Truly the pose had possibilities. The affair was, however, vague at present, and the gardener retained, whatever the role he was playing, an accurate mind and a profound respect for the exactness of words.

"Will he stow me away?" he asked.

"Not in the way you mean. But there'll be room for you on the Caribbeania. Come down to Southampton with me now. There's a train at noon."

"I have my own feet, and a good white road," replied the gardener in a poetic voice. "I'll join you in Southampton this evening."

"It's thirty-five miles," said Mr. Rust. "And the boat sails to-morrow morning. However . . . We haven't discussed the business side of the affair yet."

"And we never will. I'll take my payment out in miles — an excellent currency."

In spite of the distance of his destination, the gardener stood by his determination to go by road. A friendly farmer's cart may always be depended on to assist the pose of a vagabond. It would have been extremely hackneyed to approach the opening door of life by train. So he left his blessing with the Red Place, and shook the hand of its white master, and set his face towards the sea.

It was still early. The sun had set the long limbs of the tree-shadows striding about the woods; the gorse, a tamed expression of flame, danced in the yellow heat; the heather pressed like a pigmy army bathed in blood about the serene groups of pines. There was great energy abroad, which kept the air a-tingle. The gardener almost pranced along.

Presently he came to a woman seated by the roadside engrossed in a box of matches.

"You again" said the gardener to the suffragette, for he recognised her by her hat. There was a bunch of promiscuous flowers attached to her hat. They were of an unsuitable colour, and looked as though they had taken on their present situation as an after-thought, when the hat was already well advanced in years. A manage de convenance.

"Have you any matches?" was the suffragette's characteristic reply.

"I never give away my matches to people with political opinions without making the fullest enquiries," replied the gardener. " People are not careful enough about the future morals of their innocent matches in these days."

Forgetting the thirty-five miles, he sat down on the bank beside her, and began to refresh Hilda by splashing the water into her pot out of a tiny heathery stream that explored the roadside ditch.

"I can supply you with all particulars at once," said the suffragette in a business-like voice. "I am going to burn down a little red empty hotel that stands in the woods behind you. There is only one man in charge."

"You are not," said the gardener, descending suddenly to unfeigned sincerity.

"Certainly it is not the home of an Anti," continued the suffragette, ignoring his remark. "At least as far as I know. But you never can tell. A Cabinet Minister might want to come and stay there any time; there are good golf-links. I had hoped that the last affair, the burning of West Grove — a most successful business — would have been my last protest for the present. I meant to be arrested, and spend a month or two at the not less important work of setting the teeth of the Home Office on edge. But the police are disgracefully lax in this part of the world, and though I left several clues and flourished my portmanteau in three neighbouring villages, nothing happened. I do not like to give myself up, it is so inartistic, and people are apt to translate it as a sign of repentance. But the little hotel is a splendid opportunity."

One of the drawbacks of posing yourself is that you are apt to become a little blind to the poses of others. Also you must remember that women, and especially rebellious women, were an unexplored continent to the gardener.

"You are not going to take advantage of the opportunity," said the gardener, refreshing Hilda so violently that she stood up to her knees in water.

"I've heard the caretaker is constantly out . . ." went on the suffragette.

"Possibly," admitted the gardener. "But if the house were twenty times alone, you should not light a match within a mile of it. How dare you — you a great strong woman — to take advantage of the weak gods who can't defend themselves."

The great strong woman crinkled her eyes at him. She was absurdly small and thin.

"Well, if you won't lend me any matches, I shall have to try and do with the three I have. I am going to reconnoitre. Good-morning."

There is nothing so annoying as to have one's really impressive remarks absolutely ignored. I myself can bear a great deal of passing over. You may with advantage fail to see my complexion and the cut of my clothes; you may be unaware of the colour of my eyes without offending me; I do not care if you never take the trouble to depress your eyes to my feet to see if I take twos or sevens; you may despise my works of art — which have no value except in the eyes of my relations; you may refuse to read my writings — which have no value in any eyes but my own, — all these things you may do and still retain my respect, but when I speak you must listen to what I say. If you don't, I hate you.

The gardener felt like this, and the retreating form of the suffragette became hateful to him. Somehow delightfully hateful. " Come back," he shouted, but incredible though it may seem, the woman shrugged one shoulder at him, and walked on towards the Red Place.

It was most undignified, the gardener had to run after her to enforce his will. He arrived by her side breathless, with his face the colour of a slightly anaemic beetroot. It is very wrong of women to place their superiors in such unsuperior positions.

I hope I do not strike you as indulging my suffragettism at the expense of the gardener. I am very fond of him myself, and because that is so, his conceit seems to me to be one of his principal charms. There is something immorally attractive in a baby vice that makes one's heart smile.

The gardener closed his hand about the suffragette's thin arm.

"You will force me to take advantage of my privilege," he said, and looked at his own enormous hand.

The suffragette stood perfectly still, looking in the direction she wanted to go.

"Turn back," said the gardener. But she made a sudden passionate effort to twist her arm out of his grasp. It was absurd, and very nearly successful, like several things that women do.

The gardener's heart grew black. There seemed nothing to be done. No end could be imagined to the incident. His blue sea future dissolved. He pictured himself standing thus throughout eternity, with his hand closed around the little splinter of life she called her arm. Time seemed to pass so slowly that in a minute he found he knew her looks by heart. And yet he was not weary of them. I suppose the feeling he found in himself was due to a certain reaction from the exalted incident of the blue and golden young lady who had divined the loneliness of the threepenny bit. For he discovered that he did not so very much mind hair that had but little colour in it, and that he found attractive a pointed chin, and an under lip that was the least trifle more out-thrust than its fellow.

"Do you know why I want to stop you?" he said at last.

"Yes."

"Why?"

"Because you are not a woman, and don't understand."

"Because I am a man, and I understand."

She was silent.

"Do you know what I mean?"

"Yes."

"You don't. I mean that I am a man, and I am not going to let you go, because you must come with me to the uttermost ends of the earth."

"Why?"

"Because I love the shape of your face, you dear little thing."

The gods should not be disturbed. Also there was something very potent in the impotent trembling of her arm. There was an unnaturally long pause. Then she turned round.

"Let us discuss this matter" she said, and gave him her portmanteau to carry. The gardener loosed her arm and walked beside her. Silence and a distance of a yard and a half were maintained between them for some way.

The gardener was gazing in blank astonishment at that ass, the gardener of three minutes ago. Into what foolery had he not plunged?

If I could always be the Woman I Am, I should be a most rational and successful creature. It is the Woman I Was who makes a fool of me, and leaves me nervous as to the possible behaviour of the Woman I Shall Be.

There was something in the way the suffragette's neck slipped loosely into her collar which took a little of the sting out of the gardener's regrets. But the little plain eyes of her, and the aggressive manners of her, and the misguided morals of her — that was the sequence in which the gardener's thoughts fell into line.

As for the suffragette, her heart, in defiance of anatomy, had gone to her head, and was thundering rhythmically there. She was despising herself passionately, and congratulating herself passionately. How grand

— she thought: how contemptible — she thought. For she was a world's worker, a wronged unit seeking rights, a co-heritor of the splendour of the earth, a challenger, a warrior. And now, quite suddenly, she discovered a fact the existence of which she had seldom, even in weak moments, suspected. She found that — taken off her guard — she was a young woman of six-and-twenty.

"How laughable," she thought — and did not laugh — "I'm as bad as the ' Oh my dear ' girls."

"Now," she said at last, " what did you mean by that?"

"Only that you look like a good friend," replied the gardener, who, poor vagabond, was blushing furiously. "Mightn't we be friends?"

"I am a friend to women," said the suffragette slowly. "I'm a lover of women. But never of men. I wouldn't stir an inch out of my way for a man. Unless I wanted to."

"And do you want to?"

She looked at the gardener's profile with the eyes of the newly discovered young woman of six-and-twenty. Hitherto she had seen him only with the militant eyes of armed neutrality. She looked at the rather pleasing restlessness of his eyes, and the high tilt of his head. His eyes were not dark with meaning, as the eyes of heroes of novels should be, they were light and quick. The black pupils looked out fierce and sharp, like the pupils of a cat, which flash like black sparks out of the twilight of its soul. The gardener's eyes actually conveyed little, but they looked like blinds, barely concealing something of great value.

Presently the suffragette said: "Can you imagine what you feel like if you had been running in a race, and you had believed you were winning. The rest were miles behind wasting their breath variously: and then suddenly your eyes were opened, and you saw that you had been running outside the ropes of the course, for you were never given the chance to enter for the competition."

"Good," said the gardener enthusiastically. " So you're tired of running to no purpose, and you're coming back to the starting-place to begin again.

"No," said the suffragette, as firmly as though she had the muscular supremacy and could start back that moment to pit her three matches against the gods. " Never. There's no such thing as running to no purpose. It's excellent exercise — running, but I'll never run with the crowd. There are much better things than winning the prize. There's more of everything out here — more air, more light, more comedy, more tragedy. Also I get there first, you know. When you get the law-abider and the church-goer in a crowd, they increase its moral tone, but they lessen its power of covering the ground."

"Personally I never was inside," said the gardener, who had a natural preference for talking about himself. "But then I am building a path of my own."

"Anyway, what did you mean originally?"

The gardener blushed again. He showered rest on himself. " Only that we might walk into Southampton as friends. And if we liked it. . . . Besides I owe you a shilling, and you'd better keep an eye on your financial interests. My boat sails to-morrow. You know, it is a nice shock to me to find that a militant suffragette is human at all. When I held your arm, I was surprised to find it was not iron."

"Did you say your boat sailed to-morrow?"

"I should have said, Our boat sails to-morrow."

"There's no time to walk. We'll hire a car in Aldershot."

So at sunset, side by side, they arrived in sight of Southampton's useful but hackneyed sheet of water.

Even then they had no plans. In youth one likes the feeling of standing on empty air with a blank in front of one.

The suffragette paid for the car without question. "I am quite well off," she excused herself, as they traversed the smug and comfortless suburbs of the town. " Has that shilling I lent you to invest brought in any interest?"

"I hate money," posed the gardener; "But I have a profession, you know. I am a gardener."

"And where is your garden?"

"I have two. This is one " — and he held up Hilda, who was looking rather round-shouldered owing to the exertions and emotions of the day — " and the world is the other. It also happens that

I have had three months' training in a horticultural college."

The gardener did not talk like this naturally, any more than you or I do. But in addition to his many other poses he posed as being unique. Unfortunately there is nothing entirely unique except insanity. Of course there are better things than insanity. On the other hand, it is rather vulgar to be perfectly sane.

The suffragette went to an hotel, and the gardener went to meet Mr. Samuel Rust at their appointed meeting-place.

Mr. Rust looked even more colourless against the brownness of the town than he had seemed against the redness of his place. He wore town clothes, too, and one noticed them, which is what one does not do with a well-dressed man. The ideal, of course, is to look as if the Almighty made you to fit your clothes. There are a great many unfortunates whose appearance persists in confessing the truth — that the tailor made their clothes to fit them.

Mr. Samuel Rust, however, was not self-conscious. He escaped that pitfall, but left other people to be conscious of his appearance for him.

"Come along," he said, skipping up to the gardener like a goat, or like a little hill. " I've sounded my cousin on the telephone, and the outlook is not otherwise than middling hopeful. He's promised, in fact, to ship you on board the Caribbeania. The question is — what as? What can you do?"

"I am a gardener — in theory."

"Unfortunately only facts are shipped on Abel's line."

"Then all is over. For I am just a sheaf of theories held together by a cage of bones. There is no fact in me at all."

"Don't be humble. It's waste of time in such a humiliating world."

"I'm not humble " — the gardener indignantly repudiated the suggestion. " I'm proud of being what I am. I am more than worthy of the Caribbeania"

"Then come and prove it," said Mr. Rust, and dragged the gardener passionately down the street.

The gardener found himself placed on the doorstep of an aspiring corner house. Mr. Samuel Rust stood on a lower step with his back to the door. It is part of the code of shadows to pretend, when you have rung the bell, that you do not care whether the door is opened or not.

The gardener, following the code of the socially simple, stood with his nose nearly touching the knocker, and his eyes glued to the spot where the head of the servant might be expected to appear. It therefore devolved on him to draw Mr. Rust's attention to the eventual appearance of a blackfrocked white-capped answer to his summons.

"Ah!" exclaimed Samuel, " Mr. Abel in?" The maid, with fine dramatic feeling, stepped aside, thus opening up a vista, at the end of which could be seen Mr. Abel advancing with both hands outstretched.

When people shake hands with both their hands and both their eyes and all their teeth, and with much writhing of the lips, you at once know something fairly important about them. They have acquired the letter of enthusiasm without its spirit, and their effect on the really enthusiastic is like the effect of artificial light and heat on a flower that needs the sun.

The gardener became as though he were not there. All that he vouchsafed to leave at Mr. Rust's side in the library of Mr. Abel was a white and sleepy-looking young man, standing on one fourteen-inch foot while the other carefully disarranged the carpet edge. The gardener was not shy, though on such occasions he looked silly. He was really encrusted in himself; loftily superior to Mr. Abel and his like he hung, levitated by the medium of his own conceit, at a level far above Mr. Abel's house-top.

Fortunately Mr. Abel and Mr. Rust both took his aloofness for the sheepishness to be expected of one of his age.

"This is the instrument of my designs, and the victim of your kindness, Abel," remarked Mr. Rust. " He doesn't always look such an ass. He is a gardener, by profession."

" In theory," added the gardener, whose armour of aloofness had chinks. There is something practical about this inconsistent young man which he has never yet succeeded in smothering, and to this day, though he poses as being superbly absent-minded, his mind is generally present — so to speak — behind the door.

"In theory," repeated Mr. Abel, ecstatically amused. He made it his business to shoot promiscuous appreciation at the conversation of his betters, and though his aim was not good, he was at least gifted with perseverance. If you shoot enough, you must eventually hit something. Hereafter he kept his profile agog towards the gardener, a smile hovering round that side of his mouth in readiness for his guest's next sally.

One pose in which the gardener has never approached is that of the wag, and he made renewed efforts to unhook his mind from this exasperating interview.

"Is there any opening for a gardener on the Caribbeania?" asked Mr. Rust.

"A gardener . . ." said Mr. Abel, looking laboriously reflective. "We have no gardener as yet on board."

"But is there a garden?" asked Mr. Samuel Rust acutely.

"A garden," repeated Mr. Abel, ruminating intensely. "There is the winter garden. And a row of geraniums on the promenade deck. And some trellis work with ivy. Yes, there is certainly a garden."

"Then the thing is settled," said Mr. Rust, and at these hopeful words the gardener rose loudly from his chair.

"Wait a moment," said Mr. Abel in the same voice as the voice in which Important Note is printed in the Grammar Book. " What about the salary?"

There was no reply and no sensation. The gardener was yearning towards the door.

"Of course . . ." said Mr. Abel. " The position is not one of any responsibility, and therefore could hardly be expected to be a paying one. Your passage out . . ."

"I wouldn't touch money. I hate the feel of it," said the gardener abruptly. That threw Mr. Abel into a paroxysm of humour.

On the door-step the gardener did a heroic thing. He turned back and found Mr. Abel in the hall, completely recovered from his paroxysm.

"What about " began the gardener, with the suffragette in his mind. " Dangerous to lose sight of her," he thought.

"What about what?" asked Mr. Abel, and was again very much amused by the symmetry of the phrase. He was a bright-mannered man.

The gardener's new pose lay suddenly clear before him.

"What about my wife?" he asked. He was rather pleased with the sensation he made.

"Your wife?" exclaimed Mr. Rust and Mr. Abel in duet (falsetto and tenor).

"What on earth did you do with her last night?" continued Samuel solo.

"Can't she ship as stewardess?" asked the gardener.

Poor suffragette! But in the eyes of men one woman is much the same as another. Every woman, I gather, is a potential stewardess. This is woman's sphere when it takes to the water. The gardener thought he knew all about women. All her virtues he considered that she shared with man, but her vices he looked upon as peculiarly her own.

"The boat sails to-morrow," Mr. Abel observed reproachfully. " The stewardesses have been engaged for weeks."

"Why can't you leave her behind, what?" asked Mr. Rust. "Women do far too much travelling about nowadays. There's such a thing as broadening the mind too far, you know. Sometimes, like elastic, it snaps. A lot of women I know have snapped."

"Yes," said the gardener. "But it would be better for England if I took her away."

This spark nearly put an end to the career of Mr. Abel. He squeezed the gardener's hand in an agony of appreciation.

"I won't go without her," said the gardener, rather surprising himself. He gave Mr. Abel no answering smile. He was too busy reproaching himself.

"Abel," implored Mr. Rust. "I simply can't let old Mrs. Paul go without some one to keep the Red Place in her line of thought. This is obviously the man for the job. My career hangs on you. Be worthy. That is — be a sport, now, what?"

"I'll find your wife a berth," said Mr. Abel, accompanying each word with a dramatic tap on the gardener's arm. " The boat is not full."

"Settled," exclaimed Mr. Samuel, and after that, of course, escape followed. The idea of dinner together hovered between the two as they emerged into the principal street, but as both were penniless, the idea, which originated chiefly in instinct, died.

The gardener went to call on the suffragette. He was conscientious in his own way, and fully realised that the woman had a right to know that she was now a wife, and, if not a stewardess, an intending passenger on a boat bound immediately for the uttermost ends of the earth.

He found the suffragette, looking sad, playing a forlorn game of solitaire in forlorn surroundings in the little hotel sitting-room. With her hat off she looked not so ugly, but more insignificant. Her hair seemed as if it would never decide whether to be fair or dark until greyness overtook it and settled the question. It had been tidied under protest, and already strands of it were creeping over her ears, like deserters leaving a fortress by stealth. The room was papered and ceiled and upholstered in drab, there were also drab photographs of unlovable bygones on the walls, and some drab artificial flowers in a drab pot on the table.

There are some colour schemes that kill romance. Directly the gardener felt the loveless air of the place, he plunged headlong into the cold interview. Like a bather who, on feeling the chill of the sea, hastens desperately to throw it around him from head to foot.

"I have been telling lies," said the gardener.

"I have been crying," said the suffragette.

They each thought that it was thoughtless of the other to be so egotistical at this juncture. There is nothing that kills an effect so infallibly as a collision in conversation.

"I have been telling lies," said the gardener, " about you."

"I have been crying — about you."

(These women . . .)

The gardener took a deep breath, recoiled for a start, and ran upon his subject.

"I have told them that you are my wife, and that you are coming with me on the Caribbeania, sailing to-morrow morning for Trinity Islands."

"Told who . . . Caribbeania . . . Trinity Islands . . ." gathered the suffragette, with a woman's instinct for tripping over the least essential point. And then she interviewed herself laboriously on the subject. There was ample motive for a militant protest, and that was a comfortable thought. She was justified in throwing any article of the drab furniture at the gardener's sharp and doubtful face. This creature had put himself in authority over her without the authority to do so; he had decided to lead her to Trinity Islands, whereas her life's work lay in England. This cold and curious boy had twisted off its hinges the destiny of an independent woman. She had hitherto closed the door of her heart against to-morrow. She had momentarily liked the idea of having a friend who loved the shape of her face, especially as he was leaving the country to-morrow. The unconventionality of the friendship had crowned as an ornament a life of dreadful refinement. She had meant to step for a moment from the lonely path, and now she found that her way back was barred — by this impenetrable trifle. It was infuriating. But the suffragette searched in vain for a trace of real fury in her heart. She tested the power of words.

"It is infuriating," she said.

"Yes," said the gardener, not apologetically. "I quite see that."

But she did not see it herself — except in theory.

"All the same," said the gardener, " you are an incendiary, not exactly a woman. Can't two friends, an incendiary and a horticultural expert, go on a voyage of exploration together? Mutual exploration?"

"One can be alone in couples," thought the suffragette. " It would be studying loneliness from a new angle. My life has been a lifeless thing, run on the world's principles; I shall try a new line, and run it on my own principles."

But, as I may have mentioned, she was a woman, so she said: " What is to prevent my going back to that house in the woods now, and burning it down — if I ever meant to do it?"

"Me," said the gardener.

"But you can't sit there with your eyes pinned to me until the boat sails."

"Unless you give me your word as a World's Worker that you will not leave the hotel, I shall stay here, and so will you."

For quite a long time the suffragette's upbringing wrestled with all comers, but it was a hopeless fight from the first. There is no strength in the principles created out of a lifeless past. Besides, the woman of six-and-twenty was very much flattered and fluttered, whatever the militant suffragette might be.

"I will come with you on your exploration tour," she said, and her voice sounded like the voice of the conqueror rather than the conquered. "I will give my word as a — woman without principles that I will not leave Southampton except to go on board the Caribbeania"

The gardener left her, he felt innocently drunk. He made his way out of the amethyst light of electricity, into the golden light of the outskirts of the town, and thence into the silver light of the uncivilised moon. On the beach the tide was receding, despite the groping, grasping hands of the sea, which contested every inch of the withdrawal. The gardener stumbled upon the soft solidity of the sand above high-water mark, and slept the sleep of the thoroughly confused. He dreamt of a pearl-and pink sea, and of unknown islands.

I need hardly say, after all this preamble, that the suffragette and the gardener sailed next day on the Caribbeania for Trinity Islands.

Mr. Samuel Rust, for some time before the boat started, was conspicuous for a marked non-appearance on the wharfs edge.

The gardener, who had a vague feeling that tears should be shed in England on his departure, stood feeling a little cold at heart on the starboard side of the main deck, looking at the tears that were being shed for other people.

The suffragette, who was under the impression that her hand was against all men, stood bleakly on the port side, looking at the hydro-aeroplanes leaping self-consciously about the Solent in seven-league boots. She was proud to stand thus aloof and unhampered on the threshold of a novelty. The pride she had in her independence was one of her compensations. This is a world of compensations, and that is what makes it the hollow world it is sometimes. So seldom do we get the real thing that in this age we congratulate ourselves upon our compensations. Mr. Samuel Rust made a late and dramatic appearance upon the gangway after the first bell of preparation for departure had been rung. His hat, inspired by the prevalent aviation craze, blew away. But Mr. Rust's thoughts were occupied with other things than the infidelity of hats. He passed the gardener without noticing him, and with restrained fervour addressed a square elderly woman, who stood leisurely on the deck, surrounded by an officious maid, like a liner being attended to by a tug.

Mr. Samuel Rust did not seem like the sort of person who would have had a mother. He gave the impression of having been created exactly as he stood, with one stroke of the Almighty Finger, and not gradually evolved like you or me. You could imagine the gardener, for instance, at every stage of his existence. You could picture those light bright eyes under those scowling brows looking out of lace and baby-ribbons in a proud nurse's arms. You could see him as the fierce little schoolboy, with alternately too much to say and too little. You could imagine him as an old man, with that thick hair turned into a white strong flame upon his head, and those already deep-set eyes blazing out of hewn hollows above his abrupt cheek-bones. But Mr. Samuel Rust seemed to have no past and no future.

He addressed the woman who, contrary to appearances, had played an important part in the creating of him.

" I couldn't let you go without saying good-bye to you, Mrs. Paul," he said.

" Of course you couldn't," said Mrs. Rust, and the words seemed shot by iron lips from above a chin like a ship's ram.

Something that might have usurped the name of a kiss passed between them, and Mr. Samuel hurried to the impatient gangway. As he passed the gardener he winked earnestly, conscious of his mother's eyes on the back of his head. The gardener, feeling delightfully unscrupulous and roguish, made no sign.

The vulgarly tuneful swan-songs of Cockney emotion trailed from the deck to the wharf and bade again. The sound was like thin beaten silver, becoming thinner as the distance increased. There were tears among the women on land, and the shivering water blurred the reflections of the crowd until they looked as though they were seen through tears. The last song fainted in the air, the crowd on the wharf ceased to be human, and became a long suggestion of many colours, a-quiver with waving handkerchiefs.

The gardener looked at Mrs. Paul Rust. There was a tear following one of the furious furrows that bracketed her hyphen of a mouth.

The south of England is a land that reluctantly lets her deserters go. For full twelve hours she stands on tiptoe on the sea-line, beckoning their return. The gardener watched the land and felt the sea for long hours. He felt no regret at having forsaken one for the other. For the moment he prided himself on heartlessness, or rather on intactness of heart, for he had left none of it behind. He was proud of the fact that he loved no one in the world. He prided himself on his vices more than on his virtues. There seems something more unique in vice than in virtue.

The gardener had the convenient sort of memory that is fitted with water-tight doors. His mind conducted a process by which the past was not kept fresh and green, nor altogether left behind, but crystallised and packed away on shelves in a business-like manner. He could label it and shut it away without emotion. He shut away England now, and rejoiced to do so. Poor grey silly England that I am so glad to leave and so glad to see again . . .

The gardener turned presently to look for his garden, and found — the girl Courtesy.

Her brilliant and magnetic hair.

Her broad face with the abrupt flush on the cheeks, that was an inartistic accompaniment to the red of her hair, and looked as if Nature had become colourblind at the moment of giving Courtesy her complexion.

She herself looked herself — simple yet sophisticated.

"To think of seeing you here," she said. " Who would have thought it." The gardener was one of those who are never surprised without being thunderstruck. He was very thorough in habit, and drank every emotion to its dregs.

His manners fell in ruins about him. His hat remained upon his head. His words remained somewhere beneath his tongue.

"I got a sudden invitation from a cousin in Trinity Island," explained Courtesy. "And Dad gave me my passage out as a birthday present. I gave the threepenny bit to a porter, so I hope you don't want it back. Have you kept a halo for me in this Paradise?"

"There is the glassy sea," replied the gardener, recovering. "And the halo is just flowering. It is exactly the colour of your hair."

"I hope the sea will be as you say," said Courtesy, " for I'm a shockin' bad sailor."

And at that moment the sea ceased to be totally glassy. You could suddenly feel the slow passionate heart of the sea beating.

Courtesy did not look at the change in this poetic light at all. She hurried along the deck and disappeared.

Even if you are a good sailor there is, apart from a natural pride in your sailorship, little joy about a first day on board. The climate of the English seas is not adapted to ocean travel. If I could steam straight out of Southampton Harbour into the strong yet restrained heat that I love, if I could glide from the wharf — mottled with regrets — straight to the silver and emerald coasts of a certain land I know, where the cocoanut palms lean out over the strip of immaculate sand, to see their reflections in the opal mirror of the sea, I think I should love the first day as much as I love its successors. And yet I would not have the voyage shortened by a minute.

I wonder why nobody has ever brought forward as a conclusive Anti-suffrage argument the fact that more women are sea-sick than men on the first day of a sea-voyage. I can so well imagine the superb line the logic of such a contention would take. If the basis of life is physical ability, and if physical ability depends upon the digestion, then must the strong digestion only constitute a right to citizenship. To the wall with the weak digestion.

Mrs. Paul Rust and the suffragette were the only women who scaled the heights of the dining saloon for that evening's meal. Mrs. Rust looked supremely proud of her immunity from sea-sickness; all the men looked laboriously unaware that such a thing as sea-sickness existed; the suffragette looked frankly miserable. The gardener was obliged to remind himself casually from time to time that there was no pose that included sea-sickness.

But any disastrous tendency he might have had to give too much thought to his inner man was checked by the appearance of Mrs. Paul Rust, the fortress he was there to besiege. She was a truly remarkable woman to look at. The absence of her hat revealed a surprise. Her hair was dyed a forcible crimson. And it might have been mud-coloured like mine for all the self-consciousness she showed. It was so profoundly remarkable that for a time one's attention was chained to the hair, and one forgot to study the impressive general effect, of which the hair was only the culminating point. Mrs. Rust's only real feature was her chin, but no one ever realised this. Her eyes and nose were too small for her face, and seemed to fit loosely into that great oval; her mouth was only redeemed by the chin that shot from beneath it. Altogether she would have been sufficiently insignificant-looking had it not been for her hair. She proved the truism that the world takes people at their own valuation.

It is always a surprise to me when a truism is proved true. I have come across the rock embedded in these truisms several times lately to my cost. And each time it bruises my knuckles and shocks me. It almost makes one wonder whether, after all, the ancients occasionally had their flashes of enlightenment.

The world thought of Mrs. Paul Rust what she thought of herself. It is so often too busy to work out its own conclusions.

Of a modest woman with a heavy jaw, the world would have said, " A dear good creature, but dreadfully underhung." Of a well-chinned woman with dyed hair, it said, " There goes a strong character." The hair did it, and the hair was dyed by human agency. Providence had no hand in the making of Mrs. Rust's forcible reputation. Nowadays we leave it to our dressmaker, and our manicurist, and our milliner, and our doctor, and our vicar, to make us what we are. This is an age of luxury, and it is so fatiguing to assert a home-made personality. Shall I go to my hairdresser and say, " Here, take me, dye me heliotrope. Make an influential woman of me "?

The gardener did not quail before the terrifying outer wall of Mrs. Rust's fortress. Believing as he did that man makes himself, and that the pose of victor is as easy to assume as any other, he was unaware of the reality of the word ' defeat' Whether woman also makes herself, I never fully understood from the gardener at this stage. But I gathered that woman takes the roles that man rejects.

The gardener, as a protégé of Mr. Abel, who, on the Caribbeania, was respected because he was not personally known, found himself treated a la junior officer, streaked with a certain flavour of second-class passenger, but distinctly suggesting ship's orchestra. He was allowed to have his meals in the first-class saloon, he was occasionally asked about the weather by lady passengers, and the captain and officers looked upon him good-naturedly, as a sort of example of poetic licence.

It seemed a good thing when dinner was over. One had proved one's courage, and the strain was past. The suffragette, who had given a proof rather of obstinacy than of courage, retired weakly to- her cabin. And the gardener stood on deck and looked at the sea, while the moon followed the ship's course with her eyes. A table companion, an Anglican priest, with a weak chin and piercing eyes, came and leaned upon the rail at the gardener's side.

"You smoke?" he asked, and you could hear that he was very conventional, and that he believed that he was not.

A man-to-man sort of man.

"No," said the gardener, and added, " I have no vices.

He said this sort of thing simply to exasperate. The pose of indifference to the world's opinion is apt, sooner or later, to lead to the pose of wilful pricking of the world's good taste. The gardener had a morbid craving for unpopularity; it was part of the unique pose. Unpopularity is an excellent salve to the conscience; it is delicious to be misunderstood.

The priest did not appear exasperated. He was tolerant. The man who aims at unlimited tolerance, as a rule, only achieves the absorbent and rather undecided status of spiritual blotting-paper. But he is a dreadfully difficult man to anger.

I hate talking to people who are occupied in reminding their conscience: " After all this is my sister, albeit, a poor relation. I must be tolerant." Then they pray for strength, and turn to me, spiritually renewed, with a brave patient smile.

This was the priest's pose. " You have no vices?" he said, in a slow earnest voice. " How I envy you!"

The gardener was more concerned with the varied conversation of the sea. Each wave of it flung back some magic unspeakable word over its shoulder as it ran by. But he answered the priest:

"You don't really envy me, you would rather be yourself with virtues than me without vices."

The priest smiled the inscrutable smile of the vague-minded. " You have a very original way of talking. You interest me. Yerce, yerce. Tell me what you were thinking about when I came up."

The gardener did so at once. Sometimes his imagination weighed heavily upon his mind, and he expanded, regardless of his listeners.

I was thinking about the things I saw," he said. Things that I often see before I have time to think. Snapshots of things that even I have never actually imagined. Do you know, wonders crash across my eyes like a blow, when I am thinking of something else. Ghosts out of my enormous past, I suppose. There was a very white beach that I saw just now, with opal-coloured waves running along it, and a mist whitening the sky. There were very broad red men in grey wolf-skins, standing in the water, dragging dead bodies from the sea. There were little children, blue and thin, lying dead upon the beach. I know the way children's ribs stand out when they are dead. I have never seen a dead child, except those . . ."

"You ought to write fiction, yerce, yerce," said the priest. " You have a very strong imagination."

"I have," admitted the gardener. "But not strong enough to control these visions that besiege me.

The priest, who had preached more and known less about visions than any one else I can think of, was constrained to silence.

Next morning the gardener found his garden. He saw it under varied aspects and at varied angles, for a gold and silver alternation of sun and shower chequered the Atlantic, and inspired the Caribbeania to a slow but undignified dance, like the activities of a merry cow. The high waves came laughing down from the high horizon, and curtseyed mockingly at her feet.

There was a bay tree in a tub on either side of the entrance to the garden, and the gardener, as he stood between them, surveying his territory, slid involuntarily from one to the other and back again, as the world wallowed. The garden was conventionally conceived, by a carpenter rather than a gardener. Grass-green trellis-work, which should belong essentially to the background, here usurped undue prominence. Arches in the trellis-work, looking to the sea, gave bizarre views, now of the heavy hurried sky, now of the panting sea. Hanging drunkenly from the apex of each arch was a chained wicker basket, from which sea-sick canadensis waved weak protesting hands. A few creepers, lacking sufficient initiative for the task set before them, clawed incompetently at the lowest rungs of the trellis. A row of geraniums in pots shouted in loud brick-red at the farther and more sheltered end of the garden. It was impossible to tolerate the thought of Hilda associating with those geraniums. She was a very vulnerable and emotional soul, was Hilda. Deep orange is a colour beyond the comprehension of the vermilion and vulgar. A few sodden-looking deckchairs occupied the gardener's territory, and repelled advances. But on the farthest sat the suffragette. She was crying.

If you have ever crossed the Bay of Biscay while weakened by emotion, you will not ask why she was crying.

The gardener dropped his pose between the bay trees, and did something extraordinarily pretty, considering the man he was. He sat on the next deckchair to hers, and patted her knee.

"My fault . . ." he said. " My fault . . ."

Of course he did not really believe that it was his fault, but it was unusually gracious of him to tell the lie.

The suffragette turned her face from him. She had cried away all her vanity. Her hair was lamentable, her small plain eyes were smaller than ever, and her nose was the only pink thing in her face.

"I'm very morbid," she said. "And that at any rate is not your fault."

Don't let's think either about you or me," said the gardener, and it would have been wise had he meant it "We have all our lives to do that in, and it is a pity to do it in the Bay. When one's feeling weak, it's easier to fight the world than to fight oneself."

The suffragette was a grey thing, a snake-soul. To the eye of a grey soul there is something forbidding about the many colours of the universe, and you will always know snake-people by their defensive attitude. It is an immensely lonely thing to be a snake, to have that tortuous spirit, with no limbs for contact with the earth. And yet the compensation is most generous, for there are few joys like the joy of knowing yourself alone.

In cubes of blue, in curves of mauve.

They spotted up my firmament;

And with my sharp grey heart I strove

To stab the colours as they went.

"Lou-la . . ." they said — "Lou-la, a thing

At war without a following."

"Lou-la . . ." they cried — and now cry I —

"At war without an enemy . . ."

"I can't think how you dare to speak out your imagination," said the suffragette. " Most people hide it like a sin."

He was always willing to be the text of his own oratory.

"Imagination is my Genesis, and my Book of

Revelations," he answered. " There is nothing with more power. It is stronger than faith, for it can really move mountains. It has moved mountains, it has moved England from my path and left me this clear sea."

The suffragette walled herself more securely in. "I have no imagination at all," she lied, and then she added some truth: " I am very unhappy and lonely."

"The other day . . ." said the gardener, " you were happy to be independent and alone."

"That's why I'm now unhappy to be independent and alone. You can't discover the heaven in a thing without also tripping over the hell. I like a black and white life."

"Don't think," said the gardener suddenly, and almost turned the patting of her knee into a slap. "It's a thing that should only be done in moderation. Some day you won't be able to control your craving for thought, and then you'll die of Delirium Tremens."

"It's not such a dangerous drug as some," smiled the suffragette. " I'd rather have that craving than the drink craving, or the society craving, or the love craving."

"Better to have nothing you can't control."

"You hypocrite I You can't control your imagination."

"You're right," said the gardener after a pause. He was a curiously honest opponent in argument. Besides, she had stopped crying, and there was no special reason for continuing the discussion. Also Mrs. Paul Rust at that moment appeared between the bay trees.

Mrs. Rust's hair looked vicious in a garden, beside the geraniums, which were at least sincere in colour, however blatant.

"Is this private?" she asked. There was something in the shy look of the garden, and in the reproachful look of the gardener, that made the question natural.

"No," said the gardener. " This is the ship's garden."

"Good," said Mrs. Paul Rust.

She always said " good " to everything she had not heard before. To her the newest was of necessity the best. Originality was her ideal, and as unattainable as most ideals are. For she was not in the least original herself. She was doomed for ever to stand outside the door of her temple. And " good " was her tribute of recognition to those who had free passes into the temple. It owned that they had shown her something that she would never have thought of for herself. For nothing had ever sprung uniquely from her. Even in her son she could only claim half the copyright.

The suffragette tried to rearrange her looks, which certainly needed it. There are two sorts of women, the women before whom you feel you must be tidy and the women before whom such things don't matter. Mrs. Rust all her life had belonged to the former, all her life what charm she had, had lain in the terror she inspired.

For the first time the gardener questioned himself as to his plan of attack. Hitherto he had pinned his faith to inspiration. He had left the matter in the hands of his private god, Chance. His methods were very simple, as well as bizarre. His mind was a tortuous path, but he followed it straightforwardly, and never looked back. To do him justice, however, I must say that he searched his repertoire for a suitable point of conversational contact with Mrs. Rust. Finding none, he dispensed with that luxury.

"I am the ship's gardener," he said, smiling at his intended victim.

Mrs. Rust was broad, and the deck-chair was narrow. It was some time before a compromise between these two facts could be arrived at, so the remark came upon her at a moment of some stress.

"Now, then, what was that you were saying?" she asked at last, in an unpromising voice.

The gardener, who was very literal in very small things, repeated his information, word for word, and inflection for inflection. "I am the ship's gardener."

Mrs. Rust grunted. She showed no tolerance for the thing that was not sensational. Nor had she any discrimination in her search for the novelty. Still, energy is something.

"But I am only ship's gardener in theory," persisted the gardener. " In practice I don't even know where the watering-can is kept."

"Then you are here under false pretences," retorted Mrs. Rust a little more genially, for his last remark was not everybody's remark.

"I am," said the gardener, suddenly catching a fleeting perspective of the path to her good graces.

"Good," said Mrs. Rust, and turned her little bright eyes upon him.

When she opened her eyes very wide, it meant that she was on the track of what she sought. When she shut them, as she often did, it meant that she did not understand what was said. But it gave the fortunate impression that she understood only too well. She was instinctively ingenious at hiding her own limitations.

It was the end of that interview, but a good beginning to the campaign.

The sea to some extent recovered its temper within that day. Towards the evening, when slate and silver clouds, with their backs to the Caribbeania, were racing to be the first over the horizon, the garden was invaded by passengers, racing to be the first over the boundary of sea-sickness. The silence of the unintroduced at first lay, like a pall, along the deck-chairs, but a mutual friend was quickly found in Mothersill, whose excellent invention was represented in every work-bag. The bright noise of women discussing suffering rippled along the garden. Abuse of the Caribbearners stewardesses sprang from lip to lip. It was a pretty scene, and the gardener turned his back on it, and went below to water Hilda.

The gardener's cabin, which was impertinently shared by a couple of inferior souls, was as square as a box, and furnished with nautical economy. The outlook from its porthole was as varied in character as it was limited in size. At one moment one felt oneself the drunken brain behind the round eye of a giant, staring into green and white obscurity; at another one blinked, as a mist of spray like shivered opal spun up over one's universe; again one enjoyed an instantaneous glimpse of the flat chequered floor of the Atlantic; and at rare intervals the curtain of the sky slid over the porthole, and the setting sun dropped across the eye like a rocket.

Hilda sat wistfully on the recess of the porthole, leaning her forehead against the glass. She had a bud, chosen to match Courtesy's hair. Just as Hilda's stalk was necessary to hold her bud upright, so Courtesy herself was necessary to support the conflagration of her hair on the level of the onlooker's eye. Both were necessities, and both were artistically negligible.

The gardener looked around the cabin. There is something depressing about other people's clothes. There is something depressing in an incessant attack on one's skull by inanimate objects. There is something depressing in a feeling of incurable drunkenness unrelieved by the guilty gaiety that usually accompanies such a condition. There is something depressing about ocean life below decks at any time. The gardener and Hilda sat in despair upon the hardhearted thing that sea-going optimists accept as a bed.

"Of course I don't want to go home," the gardener told himself.

Hilda, poor golden thing of the soil, had no doubts as to what she was suffering from. But the gardener wondered why despair had seized him. Until he remembered that the spirit of the sea walks on deck alone, and is never permitted by the stewards to' enter the cabins. He climbed the companion-way, like a tired angel returning to heaven after a stuffy day on earth. He came upon Courtesy making a bad shot at the door that leads to the Promenade deck.

"Come and sit in the garden," he said in a refreshed voice.

On deck, a few enterprising spirits were playing deck quoits against the elements. The general geniality whose rule only lasts for the first three days of a voyage was reigning supreme. Young men were making advances to young ladies with whom they would certainly quarrel in forty-eight hours' time, and young ladies were mocking behind their hands at the young men they would be engaged to before land was reached. The priest, with an appearance of sugared condescension, was showering missiles upon the Bullboard as though they were blessings. (And they were misdirected.) The inevitable gentleman who has crossed the Atlantic thirty times and can play all known games with fatiguing perfection, was straining like a greyhound on the leash towards the quoits which mere amateurs were usurping. Captain Walters, who has a twin brother on every liner that ever sailed, was brightly collecting signatures for a petition to the Captain concerning a dance that very evening.

The gardener, with unusual cordiality, gave the reeling Courtesy his arm, as they threaded the maze of amusements towards the garden.

There was only one deck-chair unoccupied. It was labelled loudly as belonging to some one else, but Courtesy, always bold, even when physically weakest, advanced straight upon it. It was next to the suffragette's. And the gardener became for the first time aware of a cat in a bag, and of the fact that the cat was about to emerge.

The suffragette was the sort of person next to whom empty chairs are always to be found. She had plenty to say, and what she said was often rather amusing, but it was always a little too much to the point, and the point was a little too sharp. She had a certain amount of small talk, but no tiny talk. She was not so much ignored as avoided. She had altogether missed youth, and its glorious power of being amused by what is not, correctly speaking, amusing. Her generation thought her " brainy," it was very polite to her. Do you know the terrible sensation of being invariably the last to be chosen at Nuts in May? This was the suffragette's atmosphere. My poor suffragette! It is so much more difficult to bear the snub than the insult. Insult is like a bludgeon thrown at the inflated balloon of our conceit. With the very blunt force of it we rebound. But the snub is a pin-prick, which lets our supporting pride out, and leaves us numb and nothing. I always feel the insult is founded on passion, while the snub springs from innate dislike.

"May I introduce Miss Courtesy Briggs . . ." began the gardener, hoping for an inspiration before the end of the sentence. " Miss Courtesy Briggs . . ."

Both women looked expectant.

"Miss Courtesy Briggs . . . my wife."

"O Lor'!" said Courtesy, and then, with her healthy regard for conventions, remembered that this was not the proper retort to an introduction.

"When you left Penny Street, a week ago . . ." she said to the gardener, as she shook the suffragette's hand, "you didn't tell me you were engaged."

"I wasn't," said the gardener.

Courtesy dropped the subject, because it was hardly possible to continue it. She was not the girl to do what was conventionally impossible. Besides the bugle was sounding to show that dinner was within hailing distance. Courtesy was a slave of time. Her day was punctuated by the strokes of clocks. Her life was a thing of pigeon-holes, and if some of the pigeon-holes were empty they were all neatly labelled. She was the sort of person who systematically allowed ten minutes every morning for her prayers, and during that time, with the best intentions, mused upon her knees about the little things of yesterday. It is a bold woman that would squeeze Heaven into a pigeon-hole.

Theresa stopped in front of the gardener's chair. Theresa's surname had been blown away from her with the first Atlantic wind. So had the shining system in her yellow hair. So had most of her land conventions. She was not a thing of the ocean, but a thing of the ocean liner. She had immediately become Everybody's Theresa. I could not say that everybody loved Theresa, but I know that everybody felt they ought to.

"Captain said no dance this evening," said Theresa, in her telegraphic style. " Too much sea on. Doctor said broken legs. But I went and wheedled. Called the Captain Sweet William. Dance at nine."

The dance was at nine. There were no limits to what Theresa could do — in her sphere.

A proud quartermaster was superintending the last touches of chalk upon the deck, when the gardener and the suffragette led the exodus from the dining-saloon.

In Paradise I hope I shall be allowed a furious walk around a windy rocking deck at frequent intervals throughout eternity. I know of nothing more poetic, and yet more brilliantly prosaic. At such moments you can feel the muscles of life trembling by reason of sheer strength.

The suffragette and the gardener walked so fast that the smoke from the suffragette's cigarette lay out along the wind like the smoke behind a railway train. The strong swing of the sea threw their feet along. There was a moon in the sky and phosphorus in the sea.

But there are people who go down to the sea in ships, and yet confine their world to the promenade-deck. The heart of Theresa's world, for instance, was the shining parallelogram, silvered with chalk, on the sheltered side of the deck. Theresa, looking extremely pretty, was superintending the over-filling of her already full programme.

"Mustn't walk round like that," she said in the polite tones that The Generation always used to the suffragette. " Must find partners, because the orchestra will soon begin to orch."

"We are not dancing," said the gardener. One always took for granted that the suffragette was not dancing.

"If you will dance," said Theresa, " I will give you number eight." She assumed with such confidence that this was an inducement, that somehow it became one.

"Thank you very much," replied the gardener. "I'll ask Courtesy Briggs for one, too."

The suffragette sat down upon an isolated chair.

"May I have a dance?" asked the gardener of Courtesy. "I can't dart or stagger, only revolve."

"I was sea-sick only three hours ago," retorted Courtesy with simplicity. "But I have a lot to talk to you about, so you can have number one. And we'll begin it now."

But the orchestra was still idling in the melancholy manner peculiar to orchestras. Why — by the way — is there something so unutterably sad in the expression of an orchestra about to play a jovial one-step?

"I do want to know about your marriage," pursued Courtesy, whose curiosity was a daylight trait, like the rest of her characteristics. " When did it happen, and where did you meet her, and why did you have a wedding without me to help?"

"I met her — on the way to Paradise," said the gardener, posing luxuriously as an enigma. " We got married on the way too. It was a no-flowers-by-request sort of wedding, otherwise we would have invited you."

"But I can't understand it," said Courtesy. "Only a week ago you were snivelling over a broken bootlace."

The gardener's pose had a fall. He might have expected that Courtesy would trip it up.

The violins, relieving their feelings by a preliminary concerted yell, settled down to a lamentation in ragtime.

The gardener danced rather well, as his mother had taught him to dance. Courtesy danced rather well, after the manner of The Generation. But the Caribbeania danced better than either. She reduced them to planting their four feet wide and sliding up and down. The ship's officers, with their lucky partners, leaning to the undulations of the deck, like willows bending to the wind, showed to immense advantage. They evidently knew every wave of the Atlantic by heart. But among the remaining dancers there was much unrest. Captain Walters, who was accustomed to be one of the principal ornaments of a more stationary ballroom, at once knocked his partner down and sat upon her. Theresa and a subaltern slid helplessly at the mercy of the elements into a forest of chaperons. The gardener and Courtesy leaned together and clung, with a tense look on their faces.

I dare not say what angle the deck had reached when the orchestra, with an unpremeditated lapse into a Futurist style of melody, broke loose, and glided in a heaving phalanx to join the turmoil. The piano, being lashed to its post, remained a triumphant survivor, calmly surveying the fallen estate of the less stable instruments.

"I am not enjoying myself a bit," said Courtesy, as she disentangled a violin from her hair, and strove to dislodge the 'celloist from his position on her lap. The gardener disliked agreeing with any one, but he seemed by no means anxious to continue dancing. The orchestra also seemed a little loth to risk its dignity again at once, and even Theresa, though still plastered with a pink smile, was retiring on the arm of her subaltern to a twilit deck-chair.

In the distance, among her rows of empty chairs, the suffragette was smiling. She had watched the dancing with that half-ashamed sort of amusement which some of us feel when we see others making fools of themselves. And because she smiled, the priest came and sat beside her. He considered himself a temporary shepherd in charge of this maritime flock, and you could see in his eye the craving for souls to save. He had hardly noticed the suffragette until her smile caught his eye, but directly he did notice her he saw that she was not among the saved. He therefore approached her with the smile he reserved for the wicked.

"Very amusing, is it not?" he said.

Now the suffragette liked to see the young busy with their youth, but because she was a snake she could not bear to say so. Especially in answer to " Very amusing, is it not?"

So she said, " Is it?" and immediately cursed herself for the inhuman remark. Some people's humanity takes this tardy form of hidden self-reproach after expression, and then it strikes inward, like measles.

"Well, that's as it may be, yerce, yerce," said the priest, who was so tolerant that he had no opinions of his own, and had hardly ever been guilty of contradiction. " That is your husband, is it not?" he added, as the gardener extricated himself from the knot of fallen dancers.

The suffragette actually hesitated, and then she said, " Yes," and narrowly escaped adding, " More or less."

"A most interesting young man," said the priest, who, with the keen eye of the saver of souls, had noticed the hesitation.

"Naturally he interests me," said the suffragette.

"He is so original," continued the priest. " Even his occupation strikes one as original. A gardener on an ocean liner. The march of science, yerce, yerce. Most quaint. I suppose you also are interested in Nature. I always think the care of flowers is an eminently suitable occupation for ladies."

"Perhaps," she admitted. "But I am not a lady. I am a militant suffragette."

The priest's smile changed from the saintly to the roguish. " Have you any bombs or hatchets concealed about you?" he asked.

"I wish I had," she replied. I fully admit that her manners were not her strong point. But the priest persisted. He noted the absence of any answering roguishness, and recorded the fact that she had no sense of humour. True to his plastic nature, however, he said, " Of course I am only too well aware of the justice of many of women's demands, yerce, yerce. But you, my dear young lady, you are as yet on the threshold of life; it is written plain upon your face that you have not yet come into contact with the realities of life."

"In that case it's a misprint" said the suffragette. "I am twenty-six."

"Twenty-six," repeated the priest. "I wonder why you are bitter — at twenty-six?"

"Because I have taken some trouble not to be sweet," she said. " Because I was not born blind."

As a matter of fact she had been born morally short-sighted. She had never seen the distant delight of the world at all.

49

The priest did not believe in anything approaching metaphor. He considered himself to be too manly. So he deflected the course of the conversation. "And your husband. What are his views on the Great Question?" (A slight relapse into roguishness on the last two words.)

"I have never asked him. I know he does not believe in concrete arguments from women. Though he approves of them from men." She fingered a bruise on her arm.

"The arguments about women's lack of physical force are the most incontrovertible ones your cause has to contend with," said the priest. " Say what you will, physical force is the basis of life."

"I think it is a confession of weakness."

"There is something in what you say," said the priest. He did not really think there was, for he had taken no steps to investigate. He was busy thinking that this was an odd wife who did not know her husband's views on a question that obsessed her own thoughts.

The gardener had by now extracted Courtesy from the tangle, and was steering her towards a chair.

"Your husband appears to know that young lady with the auburn hair," said the priest. "He knew her before he came on board, did he not?"

"Apparently he did," said the suffragette. "I didn't."

She was providing him with so many clues that he was fairly skimming along on the track of his prey. When he left her he felt like a collector who has found a promising specimen.

"Altogether on the wrong lines," he told himself, and added, " Poor lost lamb, how much she needs a helping hand "; not because he felt sorry for her, but because word-pity was the chief part of his stock-in-trade.

Next morning the Caribbeania had flung the winds and waves behind her, and had settled down to a passionless career along a silver sea under a silver sky, — like man, slipping out of the turmoil of youth into the excellent anti-climax of middle life.

Similes apart, however, the Caribbeania was now so steady that an infant could have danced a jig upon her deck. Several infants tried. Amusements rushed upon her passengers from every side. A week passed like a wink. Hardly were you awake in the morning before you found yourself pursuing an egg round your own ankles with a teaspoon. Sports and rumours of sports followed you even unto your nightly bunk. Everybody developed talents hitherto successfully concealed in napkins. Courtesy found her life's vocation in dropping potatoes into buckets. She brought this homely pursuit to a very subtle art, and felt that she had not lived in vain. Not that she ever suffered from morbid illusions as to her value. The gardener brought to light a latent gift for sitting astride upon a spar while other men tried with bolsters to remove him. The suffragette, when nobody was looking, acquired proficiency in the art of shuffling the board. When observed, she instinctively donned an appearance of contempt. Mrs. Paul Rust settled herself immovably in a chair and applauded solo at the moments when others were not applauding. The priest, looking in an opposite direction, clapped when he heard other hands being clapped, in order to show the kind interest he took in mundane affairs.

While occupied thus, one day, he found himself next to Courtesy. That determined lady had her back to a Whisky and Soda Race then in progress, and looked aggrieved. She had been beaten in the first heat, whereas she was convinced that victory had been her due. Courtesy suffered from all the faults that you and I — poetic souls — cannot love. She was greedy. She was fat. She could not even lose a race without suspecting the timekeeper of corruption. All the same, there was something so entirely healthy and human about her, that nobody had ever pointed out to her her lack of poetry, and of the more subtle virtues.

The priest, who had also never been able to lose a game without losing his temper too, sympathised with Courtesy, and employed laborious tact in trying to lead her thoughts elsewhere.

"Trinity Islands are your destination, are they not, yerce, yerce?" he said.

"Yes," replied Courtesy. " And I wish this old tub would buck up and get there."

"You have reasons of your own for being very anxious to arrive?" suggested the priest archly.

"Nothing special that I know of," answered Courtesy. " I'm only an ordinary globe-trotter."

Frankly, she was being sent out to get married. But this, of course, was among the things that are not said. Her father had become tired of supporting a daughter as determined to study art in London as she was incapable of succeeding at it. He had accepted for her a casual invitation from a cousin for a season in the Trinity Islands. The invitation was so very casual that Courtesy had appreciated the whole scheme as a matrimonial straw clutched at by an over-daughtered parent. But her feelings were not hurt. She had bluff, tough feelings.

"How curious that you should have found former friends on board I " said the priest. " How small the world is, is it not?"

"Yes, isn't it?" assented Courtesy, whose heart always warmed towards familiar phrases. " And so odd, too, him being married within the week like this."

The priest pricked up his ears so sharply that you could almost hear them click. " So quickly as that?" he encouraged her.

"Yes, when he left: the private hotel where he and I were both staying just over a fortnight ago, he was not even engaged. He says such quaint things about it, too. He says he picked her up on the way to Paradise."

The mention of Paradise confirmed the priest's worst suspicions. But " Yerce, yerce . . ." was his only reply to Courtesy.

Late that night the priest walked round and round the deck trying to peer into the face of his god, professional duty. His conscience was as short-sighted as some people's eyes, and he was often known to pursue a shadow under the impression that he was pursuing his duty.

"Of course I must warn the Captain," he said. " And that bright young lady who unconsciously gave me the news. And Mrs. Rust, who encourages that misguided young man to talk. And Mrs. Cyrus Berry, who lets her children play with him. As for the woman — I always think that women are the most to blame in such cases."

Although he was altogether narrow his limits were indefinite, except under great provocation. He had not strength enough to draw the line anywhere. " Wicked " was too big a word for him; and although he believed that the gardener and the suffragette were in immediate danger of hell-fire, he could only call them " misguided." This applies to him only in his capacity as a priest. In his own interests he was very much more sensitive than he was in the interest of his God.

Sometimes I think that angels, grown old, turn into enemies to trap the unwary. The angel of tolerance was the great saviour of history, but now he saps the strength of every cause. Either I Am Right, or I May Possibly Be Right. If I may only possibly be right, why should I dream of burning at the stake for such a very illusory proposition? But if I am right, then my enemy is Wrong, and is in danger of hell-fire. That is my theory. My practice is to believe that belief is everything, and that I may worship a Jove or a stone with advantage to my soul. Belief is everything, and I believe. But if my enemy believes in nothing, then I will condemn him. Why should I be tolerant of what I am convinced is wrong?

The priest, in the dark, found some one clinging round his knees. A woman — a little woman — wrapped so tightly in a cloak that she looked like a mummy. Her face was grey, and her lips looked dark. Her hair lay dank and low upon her brow, and yet seemed as if it should have been wildly on end about her head. The whole of her looked horribly restrained — bound with chains — and her eyes, which should have given the key to the entreaty which she embodied, were tightly shut. For five seconds the priest tried to run away. But she held him round the knees and cried, " Save me, save me!"

Nobody had ever come to the priest with such a preposterous request before.

"Let me go, my good woman," he said, audibly keeping his head. " Be calm, let me beg you to be calm."

She let him go. But she was not calm.

It was very late, and the deck-chairs had been folded up and stacked. As the woman would not rise to the priest's level, he saw nothing for it but to sink to hers. They sat upon the deck side by side. He felt that it was not dignified, but there was nobody looking. And otherwise, he began to feel in his element. Here was a soul literally shrieking to be saved.

"What is it? Tell me. You have sinned?" he asked.

"Certainly not," replied the woman in a hard thin voice. "I have never deserved what I've got. It seems to me that it's God who has sinned."

"Hush, be calm," the priest jerked out. " Be calm and tell me what has upset you so much."

The woman began to laugh. Her laughter was absurdly impossible, like frozen fire. It lasted for some time, and the world seemed to wait on tiptoe for it to stop. It was too much for the priest's nerves, and for his own sake he gripped her arm to make her stop. She was silent at once. The grip had been what she needed.

"Now tell me," said the priest.

She paused a little while, and seemed trying to swallow her hysteria. When she spoke it was in a sane, though trembling voice. "I am not Church of England, sir, but you being a man of God, so to speak, I thought ... I am suffering — terribly. There's something gnawing at my breast . . . I've prayed to God, sir; I've prayed until I've fainted with the pain of kneeling upright. But he never took no notice. I think he's mistaken me for a damned soul . . . before my time. Why, I could see God smiling, I could, and the pain grew worse. I've been a good woman in my time; I've done my duty. But God smiled to see me hurt. So I prayed to the Devil — I'd never have believed it three months ago. I prayed for hell-fire rather than this. The pain grew worse . . ."

"Have you seen the doctor?"

"Oh, yes. And he said the sea-voyage would do me good. He couldn't do nothing."

"Poor soul!" said the priest, and found to his surprise that he was inadequate to the occasion. " Poor soul, what can I say? It is, alas, woman's part to suffer in this world. Your reward is in heaven. You must pin your faith still to the efficacy of prayer. You cannot have prayed in the right spirit."

"But what a God — what a God . . ." shouted the woman with a wild cry. " To hide himself in a maze — and me too distracted to find out the way. Why, my tears ought to reach him, let alone my prayers. I've sacrificed so much for him — and he gives me over to this . . ."

"This is terrible, yerce terrible," said the priest. " My poor creature, this is not the right spirit in which to meet adversity. Put yourself in God's hands, like a little child . . ."

The woman dragged herself suddenly a yard or two from him. " Oh, you talker — you talker . . ." she cried, and writhed upon the deck.

"Listen," said the priest in a commanding voice. "Kneel with me now, and pray to God. When we have prayed, I will take you to the doctor, and he will give you something to make you sleep."

"I won't touch drugs," said the woman. "And I don't hold with that young doctor in brass buttons. If I pray now with you, will you promise that I shall be better in the morning?"

"Yes," said the priest. It was spoken, not out of his faith, but because that seemed the only way to put an end to the scene. And when he prayed, in a musical clerical voice, he prayed not out of his heart, but out of his sense of what was fitting.

The stars bent their wise eyes upon the wise sea and bore witness that the priest's prayer never reached heaven's gate.

"Now you feel better, do you not?" he asked, when he had said all that had occurred to him, and intoned a loud Amen, as if to give the prayer an upward impetus.

"No," sobbed the woman.

"Who are you? What is your name?"

"I am Elizabeth Hammer, Mrs. Rust's maid," she replied, and staggered in a lost way into the darkness of the companionway.

"To-morrow it will be better," the priest called after her. And wished that he could think so.

The world smiled next morning, when the sports began again. Elizabeth Hammer was invisible, probably concealed in some lowly place suitable to her position. The sea was silver, the sky blazed blue, the sun smiled from its height, like a father beaming upon his irresponsible family. Mrs. Paul Rust looked incredible in a pale dress, designed for peculiarity rather than grace; pink roses sprigged it so sparsely as to give the impression of birth-mark afflictions rather than decorations. I am not sure whether the feather in her hat was more like an explosion or a palm tree. The gardener rolled upon a deck-chair with three children using him as a switchback railway. Theresa was smiling from her top curl down to her toes. Even the suffragette was talking about the transmigration of souls to the fourth officer. Everything on the surface was highly satisfactory, and, on board ship, nothing except the surface matters a bit.

The priest had a leaky mind. He never poured out all that was in it, but he could not help letting a certain proportion of its contents escape. He paused in his daily walk of thirty times round the deck, and found a seat beside Mrs. Paul Rust

"Your maid seems to be in a shocking state of health," he said.

"She suffers from indigestion," replied Mrs. Rust. " Some fool of a doctor has told her that she has cancer. She has quite lost her head over it."

"At any rate she appears to be in great pain," said the priest, who considered that indigestion was rather too unclothed a word for ordinary use. " And pain is a terrible thing, is it not?"

"No," said Mrs. Rust.

"You mean that you consider it salubrious for the soul?"

"No," said Mrs. Rust.

"Then I wonder in what way you consider pain desirable?"

Mrs. Rust, who had meant nothing beyond contradiction, shut her eyes and looked immovably subtle. The priest changed the subject He had a real gift for changing the subject.

"Have you made the acquaintance of that dark young man who acts as the ship's gardener?" he asked.

"An excellent young man," said Mrs. Rust, immediately divining that the priest did not approve of him.

"Yerce, yerce, no doubt an excellent young man," agreed the priest mechanically. "But I have reason to believe that his morals are not satisfactory."

"Good," said Mrs. Rust.

"I do not think he is really married to that aggressive young woman he calls his wife."

"Good," said Mrs. Rust. She did not approve of such irregularities any more than the priest did, but she disapproved of disapprobation.

The priest, being constitutionally incapable of argument, and yet unable to broaden his view, was left wordless. But an interruption mercifully rescued him from the necessity of attempting a reply.

Elizabeth Hammer, Mrs. Rust's maid, appeared at the companion door. Her eyes were fixed hungrily upon the sea.

There was a race about to be run, and the starter stood ready to say the word. But Elizabeth Hammer brushed past him and walked across the empty strip of deck. She climbed the rail as though she were walking upstairs, and dropped into the sea.

"Hammer," barked Mrs. Rust hoarsely, as she heard the splash. That word broke the spell. A woman shrieked, and Captain Walters shouted, " Man Overboard."

The suffragette was not a heroine. What she did was undignified and unconscious. The heroine should remove her coat, hand her watch to a friend, send her love to a few relations, and bound gracefully into the water. The suffragette, fully clothed, tumbled upside down after Elizabeth Hammer. No noble impulse prompted her to do it. She did not know of her intention until she found herself in the water, and then she thought, " What a fool!" She could not swim. The Caribbeania looked as distant as heaven, and as high. She felt as if she had been dead a long time since she saw it last. She paddled with her feet and hands like a dog, her mouth was full of water and of hair. She had never felt so abased in her life, she seemed crushed like a wafer into the sinking surface of the nether pit. For centuries she wrestled with the sea, sometimes for years and years on end a wave tore at her breath. She never thought of Elizabeth Hammer.

"This is absurd," she thought, when eternity came to an end, and she had time for consecutive thought. She felt sure her eyes were straining out of their sockets, and tried to remember whether she had ever heard of any one going blind through drowning. Then she cried, and remembered that her head must be above water, if she could cry. She knew then that there was some one on her side in the battle. The sea seemed to hold her loosely now, instead of clutching her throat. She had a moment to consider the matter from the Caribbeania" point of view, and to realise what a pathetic accident had occurred. It dawned upon her that her own hand, wearing her mother's wedding ring, was just in front of her, holding the cord of a neat white life-buoy. " Caribbeania " painted in black on the life-buoy seemed like a wide mad smile. " This Is absurd, " bubbled the suffragette. "I shall wake up in a minute now. It's the air makes one sleepy. " And then she thought of something else for ages and ages, and could not find out what she was thinking of, though she tried all the time.

On the promenade deck of the Caribbeania the gardener stood dumb with enormous astonishment. His soul was dumb, his limbs were numb, his mental circulation was stopped. He had a sort of impression that the Atlantic had been suddenly sprinkled with a shower of women, but he could only think of one drop in the shower.

"How red her face was as she went under — and what a dear she is!"

The Caribbeania had flung the two women behind her, and swept upon her way, only for a second had the red face of the suffragette floated like a cherry upon the water beside the black wall of the ship. The fourth officer had flung a life-buoy. Theresa had fainted. There was a black cork-like thing a thousand miles away which the fourth officer said was the head of one of the women. The Caribbeania, checked in her scornful attempt to proceed uncaring, was being brought round in a circle. A boat was being lowered.

There was a long silence on the promenade deck.

Presently — "Is it — her?" asked Courtesy in a husky voice by the gardener's side.

"Of course," answered the gardener. Elizabeth Hammer had found the sleep she sought without recourse to drugs.

Everybody watched the distant boat receive the thin small warrior out of the grasp of the sea, and then sweep in wide circles on its search for Elizabeth Hammer.

The dream ended. The boat drew alongside. The suffragette, who had to some extent collected herself, made a characteristic attempt to step unassisted from the boat. It failed. Everybody had come down to the main deck to gratify their curiosity. The suffragette was carried on deck, though she obviously supposed she was walking. She looked somehow out of proportion to the elements with which she had battled.

"You poor lamb," said Courtesy, looking very dry and motherly beside her. " How do you feel? I'm coming to help you into bed."

"I am perfectly well, thank you," said the suffragette.

"Why did you jump overboard if you couldn't swim?" asked the fourth officer, who was young and believed that there are always reasons for everything.

"It was a mistake," said the suffragette testily, and was led below by Courtesy and a stewardess.

Tongues were loosened. Everybody reascended to the upper deck to vent their sympathy on Mrs. Paul Rust.

She had remained in her chair, because she felt that any other woman would have retired below after witnessing the suicide of an indispensable part of her travelling equipment. But she could not control her complexion. Her face was blue-white like chalk, beneath her incongruous hair. She would reply to no questions, and the priest, after making several attempts to create for himself a speaking part in the drama, was obliged to abandon his intention as far as she was concerned, for lack of support. He turned to the gardener, whose stunned mind was now regaining consciousness.

"I do indeed congratulate you on the rescue of your — your wife," said the priest. " Yerce, yerce. As for that other poor soul, I was afraid she might make some attempt of the sort. She was suffering from some internal complaint, and had lost control of herself. Of course she had confided in me — yerce, yerce. I was so fortunate as to be able to say a few words of comfort. Perhaps it was a merciful release. But I hope she was prepared at the last. I hope that in that awful moment she thought upon her sins."

"I hope so too," said the gardener. " It is good to die with a happy memory in the heart."

The general impression was that Elizabeth Hammer had made a mistake, poor thing. She was the subject of much conversation but little conjecture. The big problem of her little mind was not so much buried as never unearthed. She had made a mistake, poor thing. That was her epitaph. The suffragette was of course a heroine. She was a heroine for the same reason as Elizabeth Hammer was a poor thing — because nobody had analysed her motives. It would have been heresy to suggest that the heroine's motive had been pure hysteria. She had done a very useless thing in a very clumsy way, but because it had been dangerous she was promoted to the rank of heroine.

"I have been a damn fool," mourned the suffragette, writhing profanely on her bunk.

"Nonsense," said Courtesy briskly. " You have been frightfully brave. It was only hard luck that you couldn't save the woman."

"But I didn't try. I had forgotten all about her until this moment."

"Nonsense," repeated Courtesy, busy with a hot-water bottle. " You were splendid. We didn't know you had it in you."

The suffragette laughed her secret laugh, which she kept hidden beneath her militant exterior. The sort of laughter that flies, not unsuitably, in the very face of tragedy.

"This is a change," she said.

"What is?"

"To be respected."

"My dear gal, we all respected you all along. Personally I always told them: ' Mark my words,' I said, (that gal's got brains.' "

"Yes, I expect they needed to be told."

"Nonsense," said Courtesy. " For the last five years," said the suffragette, " I have followed my conscience over rough land. I have been suffragetting industriously all that time. And every one laughed behind their hands at me. Not that I care. But to-day I have been a fool, and they have promoted me to the rank of heroine."

"Nonsense," said Courtesy. " You're not a fool. And surely you never were a suffragette."

"I am a militant suffragette," said the suffragette proudly. " It takes a little courage and no hysteria to march through the city with drunk medical students waiting to knock you down at the next corner; and it takes hysteria and no courage to fall by mistake into the Atlantic."

"You quaint dear," said Courtesy, who had not been giving undivided attention to her patient's remarks. "I do believe you've got something in you besides brains after all. There now, you must try and sleep. Pleasant dreams. And if you're a good gal and wake up with some roses in your cheeks, you shall have your husband to come and have tea with you."

"No," said the suffragette. " Don't call him that."

Courtesy wrenched the stopper of the hot-water bottle tightly on, as though she were also corking up her curiosity.

As she went upstairs Courtesy discovered that she quite liked the suffragette — from a height. For a person suffering from brains, and from a mystery, and from political fervour, and from lack of physical stamina, the woman was quite surprisingly likeable.

On deck, Courtesy's friendly feeling was immediately put to the test. Mrs. Paul Rust beckoned her to her side.

"That woman who jumped into the water after Hammer . . . she is quite well again, of course?" It was rather difficult for Mrs. Rust to put this question, because the most obvious form was, " How is she?" and that would have been far too human.

"She'll be all right," said Courtesy. " And even if she wasn't she wouldn't say so. She keeps herself to herself. You've torn a button off your coat. Shall I sew it on for you? You'll miss your maid."

"I shall not," said Mrs. Rust. " She was a fool to behave in that way. Nothing but indigestion."

"You shouldn't speak hardly of the dead," said Courtesy, indomitably conventional.

"Stuff and nonsense," retorted Mrs. Rust, and closed her eyes in order to close the subject. " That young woman . . ."

"I shall call her the suffragette," said Courtesy. "She says she is one, and she looks like one."

"At any rate, the priest tells me she is not married to the ship's gardener. Is that so?"

"It's not the priest's business. Nor mine either."

"You would drop her like a red-hot coal if she were not married."

"Time enough to decide that later. I don't approve of irregularity, of course. Marriage after all is an excellent idea."

That turned the balance successfully in the suffragette's favour. " You are wrong," said Mrs. Rust. "Marriage is an idiotic institution. It must have been invented by a man, I feel sure. It is like using ropes where only a silken thread is necessary."

"O Lor'," said Courtesy.

Mrs. Paul Rust decided to reach the truth by interrogating the gardener. She always tried to approach a mystery by the high-road, rightly considering that the high-road is the most untrodden way in these tortuous days.

"Come here," she called to the gardener, when Courtesy disappeared to see if her patient was asleep.

"Is that young woman who foolishly jumped into the sea — your wife?" she asked.

The gardener had resisted hours of siege on the subject. He was tired. Besides he instinctively understood Mrs. Rust.

"In some ways she is," he replied, after rather a blank pause.

"Good," said Mrs. Rust.

"Is that young man who owns a little red hotel in the woods in Hampshire your son?" asked the gardener, suddenly face to face with an opportunity.

"In some ways he is," replied Mrs. Rust inevitably, without a smile.

The gardener became more and more inspired. " Because if you are his mother, I am his friend, and you may be interested to know that I put your point of view clearly before him when I met him last. He told me that you were unwilling to treat his hotel as an investment, and I said, ' Why should she? f I said, ' You may take it from me that she won't.' "

"Then you had no business to take my intentions for granted," retorted Mrs. Rust. "What the dickens did you mean by it?"

"I told him . . ." continued the gardener, almost suffocating in the grasp of his own cleverness, " that obviously you could take no notice of so vague a scheme. Ninety-nine women out of a hundred, I said, would do as you were doing."

"You had better have minded your own business," interrupted Mrs. Rust wrathfully. " And you had better mind it now. I shall do exactly what I like with my money, no matter what the other ninety-nine women would do."

"I was afraid you would be annoyed by my speaking like this," said the gardener humbly. " It is only natural."

"Stuff and nonsense. Do you know that the priest is shocked by his suspicions about you and your suffragette?"

"I don't mind," said the gardener. " Being a priest, I suppose he is paid to be shocked sometimes. I don't object to being his butt."

"Good," said Mrs. Rust. " Then you don't continue to assert that she is your wife."

"I can't be bothered to continue to assert it," said the gardener.

"Good," said Mrs. Rust.

The gardener felt that the reward of the successfully unscrupulous rogue was within his reach. Lying in a good cause is a lovely exercise. The warm feeling of duty begun surged over him. He had justified his presence on board the Caribbeania, he had been true to Samuel Rust. The suffragette was not drowned. The blue sea was all round him. There was little else to be desired.

"I shan't be an unscrupulous rogue a moment longer than I can help," thought the gardener. "I shall pose as being good next. We will be married on landing."

Courtesy at that moment returned and said, "Your wife would like you to come and have tea with her."

"Don't leave us alone," begged the gardener of Courtesy as they went below. "I don't know how to behave to heroines."

He was obviously at a loss when he reached the suffragette's cabin. He had never seen her with her hair down, and that upset him from the start.

He shook her gently but repeatedly by the hand, and smiled his well-meaning young smile. He did not know what to say, and this was usually a branch of knowledge at which he was proficient.

"Did you know that Captain Walters won the sweep yesterday on the Captain's number?" he asked.

"Don't be a donkey," said Courtesy. There was a genial lack of sting about Courtesy's discourtesies, which kept her charm intact through all vicissitudes. " She doesn't want to hear about the sweep. Let her be just now. She's busy pouring out your tea."

For in the same spirit as the nurse allows a convalescent child to pour out tea from its own teapot, Courtesy had encouraged the suffragette to officiate. The headquarters of the meal, on a tray, were balanced upon the invalid's bunk. It was not a treat to the suffragette, who loathed all the details of Woman's Sphere, but for once she did not proclaim the ungracious truth.

"I'm sorry," she said nervously. "It's years since I did anything of this sort. But I don't know whether you take milk and sugar."

The gardener distrustfully eyed the hot water with vague aspirations towards tea-dom that dripped into his cup.

"I don't take either milk or sugar, thank you," he said, " I like my troubles singly."

"Naughty boy," said Courtesy, helping herself generously to cake. " You are beastly rude. And you're a naughty gal, too, you suffragette. You ought to know how your husband likes his tea."

"But he's not my husband," said the suffragette.

The gardener sat with a bun arrested half-way to his mouth. He had lived a self-contained existence, and had never before had a pose of his dismantled by an alien hand. The experience was most novel. He liked the suffragette more and more because she was unexpected.

"Nonsense," said Courtesy. " You're feverish. You'll tell me what you'll be sorry for, in a minute."

"It's true; and I'm far from sorry for it," said the suffragette. "It's almost too good to be true, but it is. I'm still alone. But because he thought I was a menace to England's safety, he brought me away — by force."

"Perfectly true," corroborated the gardener.

"You babies," said Courtesy. "It's lucky for you it's only me to hear you."

"It's not a secret," said the gardener. " I've just been talking about it to Mrs. Rust."

"And what did she say?" asked Courtesy and the suffragette together.

"She said, ' Good.' "

At that moment the voice of Mrs. Rust was heard in the passage outside. "Miss Briggs."

Courtesy ran clumsily from the cabin.

"That button," said Mrs. Rust. " You said you would . . . Myself I never can remember which finger I ought to wear my thimble on, or at what angle the needle should be held . . ."

Anybody else, arrived within three feet of the suffragette's door, would have thrown a smile round the corner. But Mrs. Rust did not. She did possess a heart, I am told, but a heart is such a hackneyed thing that she concealed it.

"What do you intend to do when you get to Trinity Islands?" asked the suffragette.

"I don't know what we shall do," replied the gardener. "I hate knowing about the future. I am leaving it — not to fate, but to my future self."

"Don't you believe in fate?"

"No. I believe in myself. I believe I can do exactly what I like."

"And what about me? Can't I do exactly what I like? Do you think you can do exactly what you like with me?" asked the suffragette militantly.

"So far I seem to have succeeded even in that."

She laughed.

After a pause he said suddenly, "Iama brute to you, you dear, unaccommodating little thing. Somehow my will and my deed have got disconnected in my dealings with you. It is curious that having such good intentions I should still remain the villain of the piece. Yet I meant — if ever I had a woman — to make up to her for all I have seen my mother go through."

"When you have a woman — perhaps you will . . ." said the suffragette. "You must wait and see."

"Come up and see land," shouted Courtesy, running in with a semi-buttoned coat in her hand.

The gardener shot up the companion-way, and, behold, the gods had touched the sea, and fairyland had uprisen.

A long vivid island, afire in the ardent sun. Its mountain was golden and eccentric in outline, its little town and fortresses had obviously been built by a neat-fingered baby-god out of its box of bricks. The tiny houses had green shutters and red roofs. There was no doubt that the whole thing had only been created a minute or two before, it was so neat and so unsullied. It was nonsense to call the place by the name of a common liqueur, as the quartermaster did, any one could see it was too sudden and too faery to have a name or to make a liqueur. There was something very exciting in the way it had leapt out of a perfectly empty sea, and in the way it sped over the horizon, as if shrinking from the gaze of the proud Caribbeania.

It passed. The gardener had looked at a dream. Courtesy had looked at good dry land. Captain Walters had looked at the monastery from which the liqueur emanated. Mrs. Rust had not looked at all. It is surprising that there should be so much difference in the material collected by such identical instruments as one pair of human eyes and another.

Islands are gregarious animals, they decorate the ocean in conveys. The Caribbeania, her appetite for speed checked, began to stalk them with bated breath.

"We'll be going through the Hair's Breadth tomorrow at seven," said the Captain, in a fat, self-congratulatory voice, as though he had himself created the channel he referred to. " You must all get up early to see her do it."

There are few penances easier than early rising on board ship. There are no inducements to stay upon the implacable plane that is your bunk, in the hot square cube that is your cabin. Your ear is tickled by the sound of the activities of food in the saloon outside; you can hear the sea singing in a cheerful, beckoning way past your inadequate porthole. You emerge from your cabin and find men in pyjamas, and ladies in flowered dressing-gowns and (if possible) thick pig-tails, or (if impossible) pleasing head-erections of lace, sitting in rows at sparkling tables, and being fed by stewards with apples and sandwiches. There is scarcely ever any need to remind the voyager by sea about the tiresome superiority that distinguishes the ant.

The Captain, therefore, had a large audience ready for his sleight-of-nerve feat of threading the Hair's Breadth. He looked very self-conscious on the bridge.

Land climbed slowly down the spangled sloped sea from the horizon. There seemed to be no gap in the quivering line of it. Presently, however, as if it had quivered itself to pieces, the line was shattered. Silver channels appeared beckoning on every side. The Caribbeania, blind except to her duty, headed towards the least likely-looking channel of all. The most ignorant passenger on the ship could have told the Captain that he was running into certain destruction. Many longed to take command, and to point out to the Captain his mistake. Like a camel advancing foolhardily upon the needle's eye the Caribbeania approached. Her speed was slackened, she went on tiptoe, so to speak, as if not to awaken the gods of ill-chance, but there was nothing faltering about her. She thrust her shoulders into the opening.

(It would be waste of time to inform me that in nautical language a ship has no shoulders.)

You could have whispered a confidence to the palm trees on either side — except that you would have been afraid to draw enough breath to do so, for fear of deflecting the ship an inch from her course.

Courtesy was, as usual, bold. She spoke in quite an ordinary voice. " Why, look, there's a man with hardly anything on, paddling! How killing! He's the colour of brown paper!"

"You'll soon be dead in Trinity Islands if you find that killing," snapped Mrs. Rust. " The Captain evidently doesn't know his business. We're at least six feet nearer to this shore than the other."

The first of Trinity Islands heaved before them quite abruptly when they had traversed the channel. The land seemed to have been petrified in the act of leaping up to meet them. I think the wind had changed upon it at a moment of grotesque contortion. My nurse used always to warn me that this climatic change might fatally occur when my anatomical experiments became more than usually daring.

Green woods had veiled the harsh shapes of the hills. Palms waved their spread hands upon the sky-line. A tangle of green things tumbled to the water's edge. Far away to the right a faint blessing of pearl-coloured smoke and a few diamonds flung among the velvet slopes of the hills hinted at the watching windows of Port of the West. Shipping clustered confidentially together on either side of the Caribbeania, like gossips commenting jealously on the arrival of a princess of their kind. The entering liner shook out little waves like messages to alight on the calm shore.

The whole scene looked too heavy to be painted on the delicate sea. It was absurd to think that that pale opal floor should be trodden by the rusty tramp-steamers, the tall red-and-black sailing ships, the panting tugs, the blunt and bloated coal-tenders laden with compressed niggerhood. There were broad-headed catfish, and groping jellyfish in the water, and they alone looked fashioned from and throughout eternity for the tender element that framed them.

The suffragette, who had risen from her berth, contrary to the advice of Courtesy and of the doctor, looked at the first of Trinity Islands with her soul in her eyes and a compressed adoration in her breast.

For there was a silver sea, silver mist enclosing the island, and a silver shore shining through the mist. Silver, of course, is idealised grey — grey with the memory of black and white refined away. Silver is the halo of a snake-soul.

The day was mapped out in so many ways by the different passengers of the Caribbeania, that, from their prophetic descriptions, you could hardly recognise it as the same slice out of eternity. There were globe-trotters, eager to trot this tiny section of the globe in hired motor-cars, others anxious to buy souvenirs in Port of the West all day, others nervously determined to call upon the Governor in search of a Vice-regal luncheon, others without imagination desirous of fishing for catfish from the poop, and a very few who dared to avow their intention of spending the day in absorbing cold drinks on the verandah of the King's Garden Hotel.

In theory the gardener wished to lie upon a chair on the shady side of the deck, with a handkerchief over his face all day. Such a course would have been flattering to his dignity and to his worship of aloofness. In practice his unquenchable energy and that of the suffragette were too much for him. He was vividly stirred by the strange land. The clawlike hands of the palms beckoned him.

Following the suffragette, he bounded on to the first launch as eagerly as though he were not a man of theory. Behind him bounded Courtesy, and behind her Mrs. Paul Rust strove to bound. Courtesy, the gardener, and the suffragette sat squeezed in a row upon a dirty seat in the launch. Mrs. Rust, because sitting in a squeezed row was against her principles, stood. By these means she kept many men-passengers standing in wistful politeness during the whole journey of three miles to the shore.

The bay swept its wide arms farther and farther round them. The palm trees on the promontories on either side of the town looked no longer beckoning, but grasping.

"Oh, isn't it good!" said the gardener, thrilling so that Courtesy and the suffragette, by reason of compressed propinquity, had to thrill too. He took the suffragette's hand violently, and waggled it to and fro. " Isn't it fine . . ." and he jumped his feet upon the deck.

"You babies," said Courtesy. For the suffragette, even though she did not jump her feet, was jumping her eyes, and obviously jumping the heart in her breast. Most unorthodox for a snake.

"We shall run head foremost into the wharf," said Mrs. Rust in a final voice. " What a pity it is that sailors never know their work."

"Yes, isn't it," agreed the gardener, as if he had been longing to say something of the sort. " Extraordinary. Fine. Won't it be fine if we run head foremost into the wharf, and sink, to be sealed up in this blue jewel here!"

He tried to pat the bay with his hand.

"Closed in the heart of it," said the suffragette,

'c like flies in amber."

"I shouldn't like it at all," sniffed Courtesy.

"Not like flies in amber," said the gardener. " Because flies spoil the amber."

"Well, you and I wouldn't exactly decorate the sea," remarked the suffragette.

"Look at those cannibals waiting for us," said Courtesy. " My dears, I'm simply terrified."

The cannibals received them from the launch with the proverbial eagerness of cannibals. In the first three minutes of their arrival on land the travellers could have bought enough goods to furnish several bazaars had they been so inclined. The suffragette, by tickling the chin of a superb blue and yellow bird, was considered to have tacitly concluded a bargain with the owner as to the possession of it, and there was much discussion before she was disembarrassed of her unwelcome protégé. The gardener bought two walking-sticks in the excitement of the moment, before he remembered that he was devoid of money. The owner of the walking-sticks, however, kindly reminded him of the one-sidedness of the purchase, and he was obliged to borrow from the suffragette.

The town, like a brazen beauty feigning modesty, was withdrawn a little from the wharves. There was a dry-looking grass space with goats as its only gardeners. This the party crossed, and the sensitive plant ducked and dived into its inner remoteness as they passed. The streets in front of them, hot and glaring, pointed to the hills, like fevered fingers pointing to peace which is unattainable.

The main street received them fiercely. The heat was like the blaring of trumpets. The trams were intolerably noisy, clanking, and rattling like a devil's cavalry charge. Black, shining women, with the faces of bull-dogs — only not so sincere — swung in a slow whirlwind of many petticoats up and down the street, with vivid burdens of fruit piled in ochre-coloured baskets on their heads. Little boys and girls, with their clothes precariously slung on thin brown shoulders, and well aired by an impromptu system of ventilation, ran by the gardener's side, and reminded him of the necessity of quatties and half-pinnies, even in this paradise of the poor, where sustenance literally falls on your head from every tree in the forest.

"This is exhausting," said Mrs. Paul Rust, forced by extreme heat into a confession of the obvious. " Policeman, where can we get a cab?"

"Yes, please, missis," replied the policeman, who was tastefully dressed in white, by way of a contrast to his complexion.

"Nonsense, man," said Mrs. Rust. "I repeat, where can a cab be found?"

"No, please, missis," replied the policeman, acutely divining that his first answer had been found wanting.

"You fool," said Mrs. Rust, another unoriginal comment wrung from her by the heat.

The policeman understood this, and giggled bashfully in a high falsetto.

"Missis wanta buggy?" asked a tobacconist, with a slightly less dense complexion, from his shop door. " Policeman nevah understand missis, he only a niggah."

The gardener, as ever prone to paint the lily, hurried into the breach. " Ah yes, of course, we white men, we always hang together, eh?"

It was The Moment of that tobacconist's life. The gardener all unawares had crossed in one lucky stride those bitter channels that divide the brown man from the black, the yellow man from the brown, the white man from the yellow, and the buckra, the man from England, from all the world.

Three buggies suddenly materialised noisily out of Mrs. Rust's desire. They were all first upon the scene, as far as one could judge from the turmoil of conversation that immediately arose on the subject. The gardener tried to look firm but unbiased. The three women stood and waited in a state of trance.

The sun was working so hard at his daily task in the sky, that one could almost have pitied him for being called to such a flaming vocation in this flaming weather.

Finally, Mrs. Rust awoke and, entering the nearest buggy, shook it to its very core as she seated herself and said, " King's Garden Hotel."

She could hardly have been recognised as the Mrs. Rust of the Caribbeania. You could see her pride oozing out in large drops upon her brow. Her hat was on one side, and completely hid her sensational hair, but for one flat wisp, like an interrogation mark inverted, which reached damply to her eyebrow.

The buggy horse, which consisted of a few promiscuous bones, badly sewn up in a second-hand skin, was more than willing to pause until the rest of the party should be seated, and even then seemed desirous of waiting on the chance of picking up yet another fare. It was, however, reminded of its duty by its driver, and turned its drooping nose in the direction of the King's Garden Hotel.

When they reached that heavenly verandah, they felt for a moment as though they were suffering from delusions. The Caribbeania seemed to have arrived on shore bodily. A long vista of familiar profiles rocked cheek by jowl, nose beyond nose, from end to end of the verandah. There was Theresa, who had made no secret of her intention of accompanying Captain Walters " for a lark " on a visit to a Trinity Island Picture Palace. There was the priest, who had expressed a determination (which nobody had tried to alter) to explore the famous botanical gardens all by himself all day. There was the fourth officer, who had left the Caribbeania inspired by a vision of a long walk to a sandy beach with a bathe at the end of it. There was the captain, who had set out to buy his wife a stuffed alligator as a silver-wedding present.

That cool strip of green rocking-chairs had acted on them all like a spider's web, with the manager of the King's Garden sitting in the middle of it, murmuring cool things concerning drinks in an iced voice. Exquisite white linen suits of clothes, the only blot on whose spotlessness was the nigger inside them, ambled up and down the line, like field-marshals reviewing the household cavalry, armed humanely with lemon squashes and whiskies and sodas.

The gardener, Mrs. Rust, the suffragette, and Courtesy enlisted in this force, and sat in a state of torpor only partially dispelled by luncheon, until Mrs. Rust began to look herself again. Her hat straightened and elevated itself to its normal position, and perched upon her hair like a nest of flowers on a ripe hay-field. The curls dried up like parsley after rain.

Little by little the other tourists regained consciousness, and with much show of energy set forth to the nearest buggy stand.

At about five, Courtesy, who was never happy unless she was moving with the crowd, became restless.

"Let's take a buggy and go back to the wharf," she suggested.

"We will hire a four-wheeler and return to the pier," said Mrs. Rust in a contradictory voice.

Buggy or four-wheeler, there was only one sort of vehicle to be found in Port of the West. They manned the nearest conveyance and quibbled not over its title.

"It would be frightful if we missed the boat," tto said Courtesy, who always said the thing that everybody else had already thought of saying, but rejected.

For the Caribbeania had begun raking the atmosphere with hoarse calls for its dispersed passengers.

But at the wharf the launch was still fussily collecting the mails.

There was a flame-coloured azalea leaning gorgeously out of the shade of the eaves of a customs house. It was Courtesy's colour — so obviously hers that Courtesy herself unconsciously answered its call.

"Ou — I say, that colour," she said, and ceased, because she could not voice the echo that streamed from her heart to the azalea's. It bent towards her like a torch blown by the wind.

"It's autumn," said the gardener. " And that azalea is the only thing that knows it on the island."

"Good," commented Mrs. Rust. "AH this green greenhouse rubbish has no sense ..." she waved her hands to the palm trees that plaited their fingers over the sky in the background.

"Autumn, I think . . ." began the gardener, addressing the azalea, " autumn runs into the year, crying, ' I'm on fire, I'm on fire . . .' and yet glories all the while; just as I might say, ' This is passion, this is passion . . .' and so it is passion, and pain as well, but I love it . . ."

"What a funny thing to say!" said Courtesy.

"Do you say that sort of thing by mistake, you quaint boy, or do you know what you're talking about?"

"My lips say it by mistake," said the gardener. "But my heart knows it, especially when I see — a thing like that. Otherwise, why should I have become a gardener?"

He looked round for the suffragette to see if she had caught this spark out of his heart, and whether the same torch had set her alight. She was not there.

"Come now, everybody," said Courtesy. " The launch'll be starting in a minute."

"But the suffragette's not here," said the gardener.

There was an instant's blank as heavy as lead.

"Stuff and nonsense," said Mrs. Rust. "I can't wait here all day. If she wants to moon around and miss the boat, let her. I am going."

She gave a hand each to two niggers, and sprang like a detachable earthquake into the launch.

"I think I ought to wait," said Courtesy. " She's a little shaky after yesterday, and you're such an irresponsible boy, gardener. She may have fainted, while we were looking the other way. Or she may be in that crowd buying souvenirs."

The gardener looked in the crowd for that well-known round hat with the faded flowers. But he knew that she would never buy a souvenir.

"You jump in, gardener. I'll wait," said Courtesy. " Perhaps there'll be another launch."

"Lars' launch, missis, please," said one of the mariners of the vessel in question.

"Come at once, girl," said Mrs. Rust's harsh voice from the stern.

Courtesy wavered.

Mrs. Rust made a great effort. She became extremely red. " Don't you understand, girl, you must come?" she shouted. "I can't spare you . . . I like you . . ." She cleared her throat and changed her voice. " Can't sew . . . buttons . . . companion . . . large salary . . ."

But the first part of the sentence reached Courtesy's sympathy She jumped into the launch.

The gardener stood on the hot wharf, and his heart turned upside down. His plans were stripped from him once more by this disgracefully militant creature who had broken into his life. He hovered on the brink of several thoughts at once.

"The little fool. The dear little thing. The little devil."

He ran round the customs house. He felt convinced that it was interposing its broad person between him and his suffragette. He could almost see it dodging to hide her from his sight.

"I shall find her in a minute," he thought. " I'm a lucky man." He thought that his hopes were pinned to the probability of arriving on the Caribbeania in time.

On the brown grass space there were only the goats. The gardener was astonished not to see the fleeing form of a woman making for the town. Things can be done very quickly if they must. The gardener was at the corner of the main street before he had time to think another thought. He looked back, and saw in one fevered glance the launch only just parting from the shore.

"Have you seen a lady in white with a brown hat?" he asked of a policeman.

"Yes, please, sah."

"Which way?"

The conversation was from beginning to end above the policeman's head. But such a very hot buckra man must be humoured. At random the policeman pointed up the main street. The gardener was indeed a man of luck, for that was the right direction.

The main street on a fiery afternoon was as long as eternity, but in certain states of mind a man may bridge eternity in a breath, and not know what he has crossed.

He was on the race-course. He looked back and the launch was approaching the Caribbeania in the far-off bay, like a dwarf panting defiance at a giant.

When he was half-way across the race-course, he saw a white figure surmounted by a brown straw hat, in the Botanical Gardens, in the shade of a banyan tree.

The suffragette had lighted a cigarette in a laborious attempt to appear calm, but she pressed her hand to her breast as though she had been running.

"I'm not coming," she shouted, when he was within shouting distance.

He vaulted the railing of the race-course, and the railing of the garden. " What a bore!" he said. " Then I must stop too."

"Why?" she asked.

Very far off, the launch was nestling at the side of the Caribbeania.

"For reasons I cannot be bothered to repeat to you."

She veiled herself in a cloud of smoke.

"You know," he added, " this is a repetition of the Elizabeth Hammer episode. Pure hysteria. Darling."

There was an appreciable pause.

"Why, you're right. So it is," said the suffragette.

"Come on," shouted the gardener. " We can catch it yet."

"If I come," she said, "it will be strong, not weak."

"Of course," said the gardener. " Come on."

"It would be much easier to stay here."

"Oh, much," panted the gardener. " Come on, come on."

So they ran, and on the way back they discovered how interminable the main street was, and how relentless is the sun of the West Atlantic.

But when they reached the wharf, the launch was still clinging to the liner. "A guinea," shouted the suffragette, who was experiencing the joys of very big-game hunting, " to the boatman who can get us up to the Caribbeania before she starts."

She spoke in the voice of one accustomed to speaking in Trafalgar Square, and everybody understood her. A boat practically cut the feet from under them before she had finished speaking, and in it they splashed furiously out into the bay.

"We shall catch it," said the gardener, rowing energetically with one finger. " I'm a man of luck."

He was posing as one who would not utter a reproach. It was a convenient pose for all concerned. When they were about halfway, the suffragette said, " You know — it takes a little courage to admit hysteria."

"Of course it does, my dear," said the gardener. "I wouldn't have done it for the world."

Presently they were within bare shouting distance of the whale which had threatened to make Jonahs of them. A liner's farewells are like those of a great many women I know, very elastic indeed.

"You'll do it," shouted a voice from the high boat-deck.

They did it. The Captain shook his finger at them from the bridge.

"What happened?" asked Courtesy, meeting them on the main deck with a shawl to put round

.the suffragette. Some women seem to think that a shawl, or a hot bath, or a little drop of sal-volatile are equal to any emergency under the sun.

"She didn't know that was the last launch," said the gardener, still posing as the magnanimous defender.

"Yes, I did," said the suffragette.

"She was buying a souvenir round the corner," persisted the gardener.

"No, I wasn't," contradicted the lady. "I made up my mind not to come back to the Caribbeania."

"Ou, I say, how killing of you!" said Courtesy. "But he changed your mind?"

"No. I overcame it."

"You quaint mite," said Courtesy.

The gardener's pose momentarily ended here, for he was stricken with whirling of the head and sickness, after running in the sun. Although there was a touch of martyrdom about it, it was not a dignified ending to a really effective pose. He had to seek the comfort of Hilda in his cabin.

Hilda had three flowers now, and they had cost her her independence, for she leaned upon a stick. But among her round green leaves she held up bravely her trinity of little gold suns.

The gardener being thus removed, Courtesy and the suffragette sat on the promenade-deck, and discussed the day. The suffragette was astonished to find herself in this position, being addressed as " my dear," by a contemporary. " Just like a real girl," , she thought, for as she had never passed through the mutual hair-brushing stage with other girls, she always expected to be hated, and never to be loved. She found it rather delightful to have Courtesy's hand passed through her arm, but she also found it awkward, and hardly knew how to adjust her own arm to the unaccustomed contact. The very small details of intercourse are very hard indeed to a snake, though pleasant by reason of novelty.

"So you didn't want to come back, and he bullied you?" said Courtesy, frankly inquisitive. " After all, my dear, that's what women are for."

"It is not I " shouted the suffragette. " Women are not born with a curse on them like that. I chose to come back; I made a great effort, and came."

"O Lor'!" said Courtesy, and tactfully changed the subject. Courtesy's tact was always easily visible to the naked eye. "My dear, I must tell you what a killing interview I had with old Mrs. Rust. She clutched my arm when I got into the launch — think of that, my dear — and presently she said in a gruff sort of frightened voice, as if she was confessing a crime, ' Miss Courtesy, I refuse to part with you; you are what I have been looking for; you are not to pay any attention to anybody else — do you hear? I forbid it.' I screamed with laughter — on the quiet, you know. I said, ' Do you want me to be a substitute for Hammer, Mrs. Rust? ' ' No,' she said. "Hammer was only a stopgap; I was keep the position open for a person like you. I will give you two hundred a year if you will promise to stay by me as long as you can bear me ' — and then she shouted as if she had made a mistake, and thought that noise could cover it — ' I mean as long as I can bear you!"

"So what did you answer?" asked the suffragette.

"My dear, two hundred a year — what could I say?"

"But what were you originally going out to Trinity Island for?" asked the suffragette. "To visit relatives, weren't you? What will they say?"

"Oh, they won't say anything — to two hundred a year. I was really only coming out as a globetrotter. I loathe colonial relations."

The matrimonial motive was the skeleton in Courtesy's cupboard.

"But wasn't it killing, my dear?"

"Very killing," agreed the suffragette gravely. She felt like one speaking a foreign tongue.

And then it occurred to Courtesy that she was squeezing the arm of one who, after all, had a criminal disregard of convention. She withdrew her arm, and proceeded to try and storm that house which she considered to be built on sand'

"I wish I could understand what you are up to, my dear?" she said. "Can't I persuade you to leave that naughty gardener, or to marry him? You needn't run away, or drown yourself or anything, just say to him, 'This won't do' I should be frightfully glad if I could feel you were all right. Why don't you get married on landing?"

"We don't want to," said the suffragette, who was too inexperienced in the ways of The Generation to feel offended. " We neither of us ever pretended to want to."

"Ou yes, of course I know the catchwords. I know you just came together as friends, and didn't see any harm in it."

"But we didn't come as friends — we came as enemies."

"Yes," said Courtesy, with a furrowed brow. "But really, my dear, enemies don't do these things."

"They do. We do."

"But, my good girl, you must know — you can't be as innocent as all that."

"Great Scott, no!" said the suffragette. " I'm not innocent!"

"Then am I to conclude," said Courtesy, suddenly frigid, "that you fully realise the meaning of the life you are leading?"

"You are to conclude that," said the suffragette, in a voice of growing militancy. "I realise its meaning much more fully than you do. I shall leave the gardener directly it becomes convenient to me to do so. For an utter stranger his behaviour has certainly been insufferable."

"O Lor'!" exclaimed Courtesy, falling back upon her original line of defence. "An utter stranger... I must go and button Mrs. Rust into her evening gown."

There is something very annoying to a woman in being accused of innocence. The suffragette was quite cross.

For the next two days the Caribbeania threaded her way cautiously between shore and shore. The horizon was frilled with palm-embroidered lands. Dry, terrible-looking beaches, backed by arid brown hills, marred the soft character of those calm seas. It was as if the Caribbeania saluted the coast of South America, and South America turned her back upon her visitor. At two or three ports in that forbidding land the boat touched. Drake had passed that way, and had left his ill-gotten halo upon the coast, but that was the only life of the land. The flat, dead towns seemed brooding over flat, dead tragedies.

It was almost a relief to the travellers when the last night fell, and the ship was enclosed in darkness and its trivial insularity. There was a great dance that night. Captain Walters called it the Veterans' dance, because the chalked deck was thick with noncombatants, who had determined to cast care aside and join with youth, because after all it was the last night, and one would never meet any of these people again. As a matter of fact, there was no youth to be joined, for youth sat out and began its farewells.

Half a dozen hours is not an over-large allowance of time for farewells between people who have known each other three throbbing ocean weeks.

The suffragette actually danced with the chief engineer. He always danced with ladies who could not find partners, being a conscientious young man of forty-two, with a brand-new bride at home. The suffragette knew well that by his courtesy she was branded as one undesired, and she laughed her in- visible cynical laugh.

I think men are akin to sheep as well as to moo' keys, and the theory only needs a Darwin to trace the connection, I have yet to meet the man who, where women are concerned, does not follow in the track of others of his kind. I think that very few men conceive an original preference for a woman unbiased by the public tendency.

Directly the gardener saw the suffragette dancing with the chief engineer, he wondered why he was not dancing with her himself, although she danced rather badly. The gardener felt a mysterious call to go and monopolise her directly she was at liberty.

"I'm glad you have come to talk to me," said the suffragette. " Because I shall go on shore early tomorrow, and should like to say good-bye to you."

"Good-bye?" questioned the gardener.

"You didn't really expect me to stay with you, did you?" she asked.

"Yes," said the gardener, and thought how peaceful and how stupid life would be without her. "I shan't dream of letting you go." And even while he said it, he experienced the awful feeling of being powerless to make his words good. He realised for the first time how indispensable to a man's sight are soft straight hair that has never committed itself to any real colour, and a small pointed face, and quick questioning eyes. But there was something indescribable, peculiar to the suffragette, that made it impossible to humble oneself before her. She was anything but a queen among women; no man had ever wished to be trodden under her feet, though they were small and pretty. Plain people often have pretty hands and feet, a mark of Nature's tardy self-reproach.

To any other woman, the gardener might have said, " Please, my dear . . ." with excellent results' He had a good voice with a tenor edge to it, and he could pose very nicely as a supplicator. But not to the suffragette.

"I have not brought you all this way just to let you return to your militant courses," he said, with a sort of hollow firmness. "I owe a duty to Trinity Island, after all, now that I have imported you."

The suffragette smiled and said she was tired and would go to bed — good-bye.

The gardener said Good-night.

The Caribbeania and the first ray of the sun reached the Island simultaneously next morning.

When the gardener came on deck at half-past seven he found himself confronted by the town of Union, backed by its sudden hills. The Caribbeania, like a robber's victim, ignominiously bound to the pier, was being relieved of its valuables. The air was thick with talk. On the pier the over-dressed representatives of British rule, in blue serge and gold braid, rubbed shoulders with the under-dressed results of their kind tyranny, in openwork shirts and three-quarters of a pair of trousers.

"Your wife went off early," said the fourth officer to the gardener. "I asked her whether she were eloping all by herself, and she said you knew all about it."

"Thanks," said the gardener curtly.

You will hardly believe me when I tell you that his first conscious thought after this announcement was that he had no money to tip the steward with. The suffragette meant a good deal to him, and among the things she meant was temporary financial accommodation.

I hope that you have noticed by now that he was not a money-lover, but a steward was a steward, and this particular steward had been kind in improvising a crutch for Hilda. Any assistance from the suffragette was, of course, taken as temporary: independence was one of the gardener's chronic poses. He meant to change it from a rather hollow dream into reality on arriving on the Island; he supposed that he would be able to turn his brains into money. He considered that no such brain could ever have landed at Union Town. Its price in coin, which had been rather at a discount in the stupid turmoil of London, would be instantly appreciable under this empty sky. His pose on the Island was to be The One Who Arrives, in capital letters.

He went down to his cabin to pack his little luggage. He had nothing beloved to pack now; men's clothes seem to be inhuman things without a touch of the lovable, and they were all he had. For Hilda was dead. For the last week of her life she had been a little concrete exclamation of protest against her unnatural surroundings. One born to look simply at the sun, from the shelter of a whitewashed cottage wall, with others of her like jostling beautifully round her; a fantastic fate had willed that she should reach the flower of her life in a tipsy cabin, with a sea-wind singing outside the thick glass against which she leant. The gardener had given her a sailor's grave somewhere near the spot in the Spanish Main to which I hope the spirit of Drake clings, for his mother-sea received him there. It was hardly a suitable ending for Hilda, but it was the best available.

The gardener set himself to put his scanty property together stealthily, and creep from the boat, that the stewards might not see him go. He had an imposed horror of ungenerosity. To him, as to most men, the tip was more of a duty than the discharge of a debt. He suffered keenly for a while from the discovery that there was no escaping from the stewards to-day, they were stationed with careful carelessness at every corner. Presently the siege was raised unexpectedly by the arrival of the boot-boy with a note.

"The lady left it, sir."

It contained a five-pound note, and it was addressed in the suffragette's small defiant handwriting.

Of course the hero of a novel should have thrown the whole missive into the sea. He should have struck an attitude and explained to the admiring boot-boy that such gifts from a woman could only be looked upon as an insult. But you must remember the gardener considered that the fortunes of the Island were at his feet. And he would not have gone so far as to pose at his own expense — not to speak of the steward's. He put the note in his pocket, and went to the purser for change.

When his duties were discharged, he came on deck to collect any plans that might be in the air. It is a most annoying fact that theories will not take the place of plans. In theory you may be The One Who Arrives, but in practice you have to think about passing the customs and finding a cheap hotel and getting yourself a sun-helmet. I think the world has an antipathy to heroes; it certainly makes things very hard for them.

On deck Courtesy was sitting calm and ready. Her plans had been made for three days. She had only just stopped short of writing a time-table for the hourly career of herself and Mrs. Rust throughout their sojourn on the island. She had a genius for details.

"The suffragette has disappeared," said the gardener. A disarming frankness was one of his weapons.

"I'm jolly glad," replied Courtesy. "I believe you owe that to me, you naughty boy. I gave her a bit of my mind about it the other day."

The gardener uttered no reproaches. He felt none. For he had learnt by now that the suffragette would never be affected by a bit of anybody's mind.

"What are you going to do?" asked Courtesy. "We are going to the St. Maurice Hotel for four days — Father Christopher told us of it — and at mid-day on Saturday we go up to the hills for a fortnight, and then we hire a car and tour round the Island, staying twenty-four hours at Alligator Bay."

"I'm going to look for work," said the gardener.

"Sugar or bananas?"

"Neither. Head-work."

"Stuff and nonsense," said Mrs. Rust. "Nobody on the Island ever uses their head except to carry luggage on."

"That's why I shall find work. There's no competition in my line."

"You funny ..." giggled Courtesy. "Isn't he quaint, Father Christopher?"

For the priest was passing on his twenty-second circuit of the deck.

"Very droll, no doubt," said the priest in the voice of a refrigerator, and continued to pass. He was very much annoyed with the gardener's soul.

The gardener waited till he came round again before saying to Courtesy, " Besides, I have to look for the suffragette."

"I hope you won't find her this time," said Courtesy. " Will you come to tea with us one day, and tell us which of your searches seems most hopeful. You see, now the suffragette's gone, you are respectable for the moment, and I needn't be afraid for Mrs. Rust's morals."

When Courtesy giggled, her hair laughed in the most extraordinary way. Everything she did was transmuted into something wonderful by that halo of hers.

"I'll come to-day, if I may," said the gardener, who had never mastered the art of social diffidence. " You'd better have me to-day, for I hope I shan't be respectable to-morrow."

Courtesy did not want him to-day. In her code there was only one programme for the first day in a strange land. It was made up of a visit to the principal church, the principal shop, the principal public gardens, and to a few " old-world relics of the past." It did not include ordinary five-o'clock tea with a familiar figure. But, on the other hand, her invincible conventionality made it impossible for her to evade the gardener's suggestion. Courtesy was content to suffer for her convictions. At any rate, you will notice that Mrs. Rust was not consulted.

You may come," Courtesy said. " At five. We are due back from the cathedral at a quarter to."

Probably the reason why Mrs. Rust submitted to Courtesy's tyranny from the first was that no other woman in the world would have done so.

The land reeled under the gardener's feet as he arrived. The only comfort in parting with the sea after a long intimacy is that for the first day or two the land follows the example of its sister element. The gardener found more difficulty in walking straight along Union High Street than he had experienced along the deck of the Caribbeania.

The morning was yet very young when he put his little luggage down at the bamboo-tree arch of a house that proclaimed itself ready to receive boarders at moderate terms. He relied much on impulse, and the little house, which was lightly built on its own first story, so to speak, beckoned to him. But only in theory, for when he mounted the flight of wooden steps, and, through the open door, saw the dirty living-room, seething with gaudy trifles, he knew that in practice it was better suited to his means than to his mind.

However, he had rung the bell. One has to pay penalties for acting on impulse. A woman with black wire hair, a face the colour of varnished deal, and a pale pink dressing-gown, appeared. Luckily she transpired to be the hostess before the gardener had voiced the fact that he mistook her for a drunken housemaid.

"I want a room here," began the gardener, who had never wanted anything less in his life. But the three pounds lay very light in his pocket.

"We can give you one," said the lady, and took his portmanteau. She could have given him several, but not one worth having. She conducted him through one or two doors that led from the livingroom. Each showed a less attractive bedroom than the one before, but the cheapest was barely within the range of prudence, as far as the gardener's pocket was concerned. In a leaden voice, proceeding from a heart of lead, he concluded a bargain for the temporary possession of the least inviting. And when it was done, and the portmanteau deposited drearily in the middle of a dirty linoleum floor, he discovered that time had been standing still, and that it was hardly nearer five o'clock than before.

It was the first time he had realised the four thousand miles that lay between him and the kindly grey pavements of Penny Street. He remembered the look of the London lamps reflected in the slaty mirrors of London streets . . . the smile of the ridiculous little griffin who sits on a pedestal at the top of Fleet Street, playing the 'cello with his shield . . . the shrugging shoulders of St. Paul's on tiptoe on the peak of Ludgate Hill . . . the dead leaves blowing down the Broad Walk, in the rain . . .

There is no pose that saves you from that awful longing for the things that are no longer yours, and which you hated while you possessed.

"I said I was enough for myself. And I am not," said the gardener, and hid his face in the mosquito net

Strange things in barbaric colours made the garden outside a whirlpool. Sometimes these things say to you: " You are a very long way from home "; and you exult, and think This is Life. But sometimes they say again: " You are a very long way from home "; and you cry out, and think This is Worse than Death.

Now there are moral drawbacks about the posing habit. But there are also advantages, though possibly none deserved. For after three minutes of despair the gardener straightened himself, blinked, and began putting his spare shirt into a drawer that would not shut. He was posing as One Who was Seeing Life, and who was Making the Best of it. The vision that inspired this brave pose was the ghost of a pair of small haggard eyes, set in a short pointed face, eyes that cried easily and never surrendered. A thin unbeautiful ghost with clenched fists, and in the air, the ghost of a low and militant voice.

"I am not enough," the gardener admitted. "But together, we are enough."

He whistled a comic song tentatively. The Englishman never whistles or sings to suit his feelings.

He dies to the tune of " Tipperary," or goes to his wedding humming the " Dead March in Saul."

There was no more life to be seen in that hot little room, even by one fixed in an optimistic pose. He emerged into the sitting-room, and through an opposite and open door he could see the pink dressing-gown, containing his landlady, heaving sleepily under a mosquito net. One of her bare feet was drooping under the net. At this he had to swallow down London again violently, and remember that he was Seeing Life, and that he was Luckier than Most.

Did you know that the surest way of ensuring luck is to be sure that you are lucky?

"Now I will find my suffragette," he said, standing between the bamboos at the gate. And he expelled an entering misgiving that he was perhaps presuming on his luck.

It was curiously cool in the shade of the high cactus hedge that ran along one side of the way. A fresh breeze, like the unbidden guest at the wedding, conscious that it was not attired in character, crept guiltily in from the sea. The sun, which would have disclaimed even distant relationship with the cool copper halfpenny that inhabits English skies, fretted out the black shadows across and across the white street. The gardener thought painfully of many glasses of cold water that he had criminally wasted in England. He stiffened his long upper lip, and tried to look for new worlds instead of remembering the old.

He went into the Botanical Gardens, and sat on a seat opposite the mad orchids. I think the Almighty was a little tired of His excellent system by the time He came to the orchids, so He allowed them to fashion themselves. For they are contrived, I think, and not spontaneously created like the rest.

On the other end of the seat were two children, so blessedly English that for a moment the gardener smelt Kensington Gardens. The girl wore very little between her soft neck and her long brown arms and legs, except a white frill or two, and a passion flower in her sash. The boy, more modest, was encased in a white sailor suit. Both were finished off at the feet with sandals.

Hardly had the gardener sat down when he was regretfully aware that he had sat by mistake on a pirate-ship in mid-ocean. The two commanders looked coldly at him from their end of the treasure-laden deck, and there was an awkward silence which somehow left the impression that much exciting talk had immediately preceded it on that vessel.

"I beg your pardon," said the gardener. "I forgot to tell you that I am the prisoner you seized when you captured your last prize. There was a desperate resistance, but in spite of heavy odds, you overcame me."

The boy, because he was a boy, looked for a second towards his mahogany-coloured Nana, who was staring an orchid out of countenance farther up the path. The girl, because she was a girl, looked neither right nor left, but straight at the gardener, and said: "All right then. But you mustn't let your feet dangle into the sea. And you must be very frightened."

The gardener restrained his feet, and became so frightened that the whole vessel shook. The boy continued to look doubtful, until his sister reminded him in a hoarse whisper: "It's all right, Aitch, we were wanting somebody to walk the plank."

In providing a willing villain, the gardener was supplying a long-felt want in pirate-ships. So thoroughly did he do his duty that when he was finally obliged as a matter of convention to walk the walking-stick blindfolded, and die a miserable death by drowning in the gravel-path, the pirate-ship seemed to have lost its point.

"Let's betend," said the lady-pirate, " that Aitch and me are fairies, and we touch you with our wand and you turn into a speckled pony."

"Greatscod, no," said Aitch; for there are limits to what a fellow of seven can betend in company. " Don't let's have any fairying, my good Zed. Let's betend we're just Aitch and Zed, and we'll show the prisoner the Secret Tree."

So they set off, and the Nana, who might as well have been a Nanning-machine for all the individuality she put into her work, trotted behind them.

The Secret Tree was one of those secrets that remain inviolate because it occurs to nobody to lay them bare. It was an everyday little palm tree, exquisitely bandaged by Nature in cocoanut matting; it was very fairy-like, and when you looked up at its fronds in their infinite intersections against the sky, you saw a thrill, like the thrill you see on a cornfield curtseying in the wind, or in the light moving across watered silk. In one of the folds of the palm tree's garment a White Pawn, belonging to Aitch, had made his home. He lived there for days at a time — the gardener was told with bated breath — and the park-keeper never knew he was there. At night he saw the fireflies light their lamps, and heard the swift slither of the fearful scorpion; once he had reported an adventure with a centipede three times his own size. That pawn was the epitome of People Who Stay Up Late At Night, and Are Not Afraid of the Dark. A super-grown-up.

On their way to the garden gate, each child held a hand of the gardener, and the automatic Nana walked behind. As they came out into the main street, the gardener thought that the houses looked like skulls — so white they were, and so soulless, and their windows so black and empty.'

"Greatscod," said Aitch, " what is happening to the church steeple?"

For it was reeling in front of them, to the tune of a paralysing open roar from underground.

Behind them the automaton blossomed madly into life, Nana fled shrieking back into the garden.

Those two things happened, one by one, like sparks struck out of a flaming experience. Then everything happened at once, and yet lasted a lifetime. There seemed not a second to spare, and yet nothing to be done.

The gardener felt unspeakably terrified, his mother earth shot away from under him, truth was proved false. He discovered that he had seized Aitch and Zed, one under each arm; and later on — his memory having vaulted the blank — he found that he was lying on them in the gutter, and that Aitch was yapping like a dog. Zed was crying, " Mother, Mother." And the gardener, with a quick vision of some one watering a cool English herbaceous border, also said, " Mother, Mother."

After a while a green beetle ran past his eye, and he recalled the moment, and raised himself upon his hands and knees. A fire of pain burnt him suddenly, and he turned his head and saw a pyre of twisted iron posts heaped upon his legs.

The air was thick with strange sounds, muffled as if from a gramophone. Some one quite near, but unseen, was shouting, " Oh, Oh," as regularly as a clock's chime. There was a rending wheeze behind them, and the gardener looked round in time to see a palm tree sink with dignity into a trench that had been gashed at its feet. But that might have been a dream.

He felt absolutely sick with horror. His head seemed as though it were all at once too big for his skin. His whole being throbbed terribly in a sort of echo of the three throbs that had laid life by the heels.

Yock — Yollock — Yollock. A pounce, and then two shakes, like a terrier dealing with a rat. Why had one ever trusted oneself to such a risky crumb of creation as this world? The gardener lost himself in littleness. And presently found that he had insinuated himself into a sitting position, and was feeling very sick indeed.

"That was an earthquake," remarked Zed, with the truly feminine trick of jumping to foregone conclusions. And she burst into tears, wailing still, " Mother, Mother."

"It is funny we should both have thought of her," observed the gardener, forgetting that there was room for more than one mother in this tiny world. His eyes were fixed on a thin and fearful stream of blood that was issuing from between two bricks in the mass of miscellany that had once been a house. "Blood — from a skull?" he thought, and fainted.

For centuries his mind skirted round some enormous joke. It was so big that he could not see its point, and then again it was so little that he lost it. At any rate it was round, and turned with a jovial hum.

Later on he was aware of the solution of a problem which he felt had been troubling him all his life. What colour was the face of a nigger pale with fright? It was several colours, chiefly the shade of a wooden horse he had once loved, but mottled. But the whites of the eyes were more blue than white, they shone like electric light. With an effort he fitted the various parts of his mind together.

"Hullo, constable," he said in a voice he could not easily control. " This is a pretty business, isn't it?" And he tried to rise, and to whistle a bar or two, in an effort to assume the pose of the hero who trifles in the face of death. But he could not rise. He was pinned to the pavement by a leg that seemed somehow to have lost its identity.

It is not in the least romantic to be hurt. There is something curiously dirty in the feeling of one's own pain, and in the sight of one's own blood, though wounds in others are rather dramatic.

Now Courtesy was a person who, without ever trying to be sensational, was often unexpected by mistake. Coincidence seemed to haunt her. Out of the hundred streets that lay shattered in Union Town that afternoon, she chose the one in which the gardener lay, and, accompanied by the priest, she bore down upon that unheroic hero, laden with brandy and bandages. The gardener saw her large face, frank as a sunflower, between him and the yellow sky.

The priest was quite obviously a saviour. You could see in his eye that he was succouring the wounded. You could hear in his voice as he addressed the terrified hotel porters who followed him that he was busy rising nobly to an emergency.

"Why, gardener," said Courtesy, in the tones of one greeting a friend at a garden party. "You here? I was wondering what had become of you. Now what's the matter with you?"

She poured him out some brandy, as though it were the ordinary thing for a lady to offer to a friend in the street. And the gardener's world regained its feet, he wondered why he had been so frightened.

"Poor little mites," said Courtesy to Aitch and Zed. " They won't forget this in a hurry, will they?"

There is something very comforting in the utterly banal. That is why the instinct is so strong in good women to make you a cup of tea, and poke the fire, when you are crossed in love.

"But if she had been the suffragette . . ." thought the gardener. He knew quite well that the thing would not have been so well done, had it been the suffragette. He was fully aware that the operation of having his leg put into improvised splints, and of being lifted upon a door, would have been much more painful, had it been accomplished by the little nervous hands of the suffragette, instead of the large excellent hands of Courtesy.

It is discouraging to those of us who have spent much money on becoming fully efficient in first aid and hygiene and practical economy and all the luxuries of the modern female intellect, to find how perfect imperfection can seem.

"Thank you — you little darling," said the gardener with his eyes shut, when, after a few spasms of red pain, he was safe upon the door. White-dad hotel porters stood like tombstones at his head and feet.

"Lor' bless you," said Courtesy. " Take him to the St. Maurice, porter. It's the only place left more or less standing, I should think."

"It is not," said the priest. " Excuse me, Miss Briggs, there are thousands in this stricken town in need of our help, and I should prefer that only the gentler and worthier of the sufferers should come under that roof. There are many excellent restingplaces where our friend here would be far more suitably placed. You ought to know his character by now, and you must think of your own good name."

"Rot," said Courtesy. " What do his morals matter when he's broken his leg?"

"Remember you are also succouring these innocent children," persisted the priest. " Would you have them under the same roof?"

"Rot," repeated Courtesy. " The roof'll be all right."

"Dose little children . . ." said the policeman suddenly. "He covahed dem when dat house was fallin'. Verree brave gentleman. I chahnced to be runnin' by. ..."

"Of course he did," said Courtesy. " The St. Maurice, porter." And seizing Aitch and Zed each by a hand, she started the procession.

The High Street looked as if one side of it had charged the other with equally disastrous results to both. At different points in it, fire and heavy smoke were animating the scene. Distracted men and women panted and moaned and tore at the wreckage with bleeding hands. A little crying crowd was collected round a woman who lay nailed to the ground by a mountain of bricks, with her face fixed in a glare of terrible surprise. By the cathedral steps the dead lay in a row, shoulder to shoulder, with the horrid uniformity of sprats upon a plate. Courtesy lifted up Zed and called Aitch's attention to the healthier distress of a little dog, which ran around looking for its past in the extraordinary mazes of the present.

The gardener, swinging along painfully upon his door, opened his eyes and saw the fires. To his surprise he recognised the house which could boast the highest flames. Its wall had fallen to disclose the shattered remains of the rooms in which the gardener had lately wrestled with despair. The bamboos and the gorgeous garden watched unmoved the pillar of fire that danced in their midst. There was no sign of the wire-haired woman.

But only one thought came to the gardener's mind on the subject. " Why she will see that. It is a beacon from me to her."

As a matter of fact she did not.

A pretty woman, crying in a curious laughing voice, ran into Courtesy's arms. " My little babies . . ." she quavered. " What a catastrophe. I don't know where my husband is. There is a grand piano on my bed."

"This is my mother," said Aitch.

"Come along to the St. Maurice," said Courtesy. "That's where I am taking your babies to. Our piano there is still in its proper place."

So they all followed the gardener.

"Somebody must go and find a doctor," said Courtesy at the door of the St. Maurice. She looked suggestively at the priest.

But he replied, " I wash my hands of the matter, Miss Briggs. I consider this to be a judgment on that young man."

"A judgment?" wept the mother of Aitch and Zed. " Why, what has he done?"

"He saved the lives of your babies," replied Courtesy. " And anyway, a judgment needs a surgeon just as much as a simple fracture."

"Yerce, yerce, only don't ask me to help," said the priest. "I prefer to succour those deserving of help." And he went out into the street again. He seemed wedded to the word succour. It is a pose word, and fitted him exactly. Nothing but an earthquake could have made this worm turn. But the effect of the disaster on the priest was an obstinate certainty that there was a Jonah in the case, and that, as heaven was never to blame, the wicked were entirely responsible.

"Oh, Lor'," said Courtesy. " I'll have to go for a surgeon myself."

"I'll go with you," cried the mother of Aitch and Zed, whose name, for the sake of brevity, was Mrs. Tring. "I don't know what has become of my Dally " (who was her husband).

"Somebody must sit with the gardener," said Courtesy, when she came back from a successful search for an intact bed, into which, with the help of a housemaid, she had inserted the gardener.

"I will sit with him," said the harsh voice of Mrs. Rust, as she rose from a seat where she had been sitting with an enormous paper bag held in a rigid hand. "I refuse to run about the streets with brandy. All the old cats are doing that."

"Why, Mrs. Rust," observed Courtesy, whose conventionality was not quite so striking after an earthquake as it had been upon the comparatively stable Atlantic. "I had clean forgotten that you existed."

"Good," said Mrs. Rust. "I was buying mangoes when the incident occurred. Perhaps the gardener would like a mango."

"Perhaps he would. I am so glad to see that you don't take the same view about the gardener as the--"

"I never take the same view," barked Mrs. Rust. "Show me the boy's room."

So the gardener saw that poisonous hair advance along a shaft of sunlight that intruded through the broken shutter. " Your jug and basin are broken," said Mrs. Rust. "Disgraceful."

"Oh, there are several things broken in this town," he said feverishly. "Windows and necks and a heart or two."

Mrs. Rust sat deliberately on a chair and burst into tears.

"I was buying mangoes," she sobbed stormily, " from a black man with bleached hair. And the whole of a shop-front fell out on him. One bride hit my toe. I looked at the man through a sort of cage of fallen things. It was as if — ■ one had trodden on red currants."

"What did you do?" panted the gardener. " How fine to live in a world where things happen."

"I ran away," said Mrs. Rust shakily. "I didn't pay for the mangoes."

"I would rather have had this happen," said the gardener after a pause, " and have broken my leg, than have had an ordinary day to meet me on Trinity Island."

After another pause, he added: "But I have lost the suffragette. And that is another matter."

"Was she killed?" asked Mrs. Rust, steeling herself against the commonplace duty of condolence.

"Certainly not," replied the gardener. " She is a militant suffragette."

"Good," said Mrs. Rust

"How good the world is," said the gardener, " to provide such excellent material. The sea, and the earthquake, and a fighting woman to love. Just think — an earthquake — on my first day. I am a man of luck."

"You have broken your leg," Mrs. Rust informed him.

"I have," admitted the gardener rather fretfully. "But then everything has its price."

"A good many other people have come off much worse," said Mrs. Rust. " I'm not complaining, mind, but any other woman would say you were disgracefully selfish. A lot of people are dead, and a lot of other people's people are dead . . ."

"The longer I live . . ." said the gardener, from the summit of his twenty-three years, " the surer I am that we make a fuss which is almost funny over death. We run after it all over the world, and then we grumble at it when it catches us up from behind. It's an adventure, of course, but then — so is — shaving every morning. Compare death with — love, for instance."

He felt ashamed of this after he had said it, and tried to cover it with a little laugh which shook him, and changed into a yelp. After breathing hard for a little while he went on.

"We who have survived this ordeal have gained much more than we risked. I know that anything is worth a risk, the risk in itself is the gain, and to risk everything for nothing is a fine thing. Why otherwise do we climb Alps, or hunt the South Pole? In theory, I would run in front of an express train to save a mou. In theory I don't mind what I pay for danger. That's why I love the suffragette; she would risk her life for a little vote, and her honour for a bleak thing like independence."

"Do you love the suffragette?" asked Mrs. Rust, who was at heart a woman, although she believed herself to be a neutral intelligence.

"I do, I do," cried the gardener, suddenly and gloriously losing his pose of One Who Evolves a New Scale of Values — in other words, the pose of a Paradox. But his emotion awoke his nerves, and for a while, although the suffragette obsessed his imagination, pain obsessed the rest of the universe.

When Courtesy and the doctor came in, they found the gardener with a temperature well into three figures. So for some time Mrs. Rust was not allowed to see the patient.

By the time the gardener felt better, the earthquake, in the eyes of the townspeople of Union, had become not so much of a horror as a disaster, a thing possible to dilate upon and even to lie about. The homeless were beginning to look upon homelessness as a state to be passed through rather than the end of things, the bereaved were discovering little by little that life may arise from ashes, and that sackcloth may be cut quite becomingly. Those ghosts of dead hope who still searched among the ruins were looked upon as " poor things " rather than companions in sorrow. Young nigger ladies, dressed in pink and silver, flaunted their teeth and their petticoats around the firemen who worked desultorily at the little gaseous fires that broke out among the lamentable streets. The one church that remained standing was constantly full. (The picture palace had met the fate it perhaps deserved.) There is nothing in the world so saved as a saved nigger. And nothing so lost as a lost nigger. After an earthquake it always occurs to these light and child-like minds that it is safer to be saved. The horse has fled from the stable, but the door might as well be attended to, and the padlock of salvation is not expensive. Fervent men and women throng the pews, shouting hymns down the back of each other's neck, and groaning away sins they do not realise, to the accompaniment of words they do not understand. Those who have lived together in innocent sin hurry to the altar for the ring, which, to these harmless transgressors, is as the fig-leaf apron of Eden, and heralds virtuous tragedy.

When the gardener became well enough to resent being ill, he was allowed visitors, among whom was one, by name Dallas Tring, Esquire. This was a very honest man who, in spite of having an excellent heart, believed that he always told the truth at all costs. The only lie he permitted himself, however, was constantly on his lips. It was: " I take your meaning."

It was obviously unnatural to him to be enthusiastic. It is to most very honest people. He came into the gardener's room like an actor emerging from stage fright on to the stage.

"You saved my children from being crushed to death," he said, and seized the gardener's hands. " Thank you, thank you."

"Oh, not at all," murmured the gardener. "I pretty nearly crushed them to death myself. Have a whisky and soda."

This last is the Trinity Island retort to everything, its loophole, its conversational salvation. The average Englishman takes several weeks to acquire the habit in the real Island style, but the gardener was always more adaptable than most.

Privately he did feel unreasonably conceited about the rescue. He would have admitted that the impulse to gather Aitch and Zed beneath his prostrate form had been unconscious, but he considered that unconscious heroism proves heroism deeply ingrained. Nevertheless, the people who voice your conceit for you are only a little less trying than the people who relieve you of the duty of being humble. One must do these things for oneself.

Mr. Dallas Tring was glad to have accomplished his duty, which was not spontaneous, but had been impressed upon him by his wife. Left to himself he would have said: "Say, that was good of you. I'd have been cut up if anything had happened to the kids."

His wife not having warned him how to proceed, he began now to talk about the banana crops. It was only towards the end of the interview that he risked himself once more upon the quicksands of emotion.

"Look here, you know, it's altogether unspeakable — what I owe you. Those are the only children we have. Aitch is a fine boy, don't you think?"

"Fine," agreed the gardener, relieved to be allowed a loophole of escape from, " Not at all."

"You're a fine boy yourself," added Mr. Tring. " When you get well, will you come and help me?"

"What to do?"

"To start again."

"Oh, yes," replied the gardener. "I love starting again. What I never can do is to go on."

After this the gardener, considered to be stronger, was allowed to see Mrs. Rust again. She was now but little better than a fretful echo of Courtesy.

Some people seem born to walk alone, and others there are who are never seen without a group behind them. Courtesy was as far a leader of men as can be compatible with having no destination to lead them to. She never knew what it was to be without a " circle." Acquaintances were as necessary to her as air, and she used them, as she used air, innocently for her own ends.

Mrs. Rust never attained to the dignity either of being alone or the leader, of a group, though she worshipped independence. She believed she had bought precedence of Courtesy for £200 a year. And on the occasion of this visit to the gardener, she believed that she was about to shock and surprise that wise young man.

"Do you know what I have done?" she asked, when she had to some extent overcome the nervous cautiousness of behaviour impressed upon her by the absent Courtesy.

"I do not," said the gardener, whose gently irreverent manner towards her was his salvation in her eyes. "It's sure to be something that any one else would be ashamed of doing."

Mrs. Rust bridled. " It was partly to annoy you that I did it," she said. " Because you dared to advise me not to. I have sent my son Samuel a cheque, so as to launch his hotel."

"Rash woman," protested the gardener. " If you knew your son Samuel as well as I do "

"I know he is my son, so he cannot be altogether a fool."

The gardener bent his thick threatening eyebrows upon her.

"Do you know what else I have done?" she continued.

"I tremble to think," replied the invalid.

"I have advertised for your suffragette in the Union Paper. Courtesy said what a mercy it would be if she should have got safely away and wouldn't come back, so I advertised, just to show that I disagreed. I never knew her name, so I described her appearance . . ."

"Her little size . . ." he said eagerly. " Her small and hollow eyes. Her darling-coloured hair that always blew forward along her cheeks . . ."

"Well, I didn't put it like that," said Mrs. Rust.

"She had such wonderful little hands," said the gardener, upon whom a sick-bed had a softening, not to say maudlin effect. " You could see everything she thought in her hands. They were not very white, but pale brown. You might have mentioned them. But she is obviously mine. Nobody could overlook that. Nobody could overlook her at all."

"On the contrary," said Mrs. Rust, " she is a perfectly insignificant-looking young woman. And I am sure that she would strongly resent your describing her as though she were a dog with your name on its collar. She had sensible views about women."

You have been intended to suppose all this time that the suffragette had succumbed to the earthquake, but as she is the heroine — though an unworthy one — of this book, I am sure you have not been deceived. Loth as I am to admit that a friend of mine should have been so near to such an experience without reaping the benefit of it, I am obliged by tiresome truth to confess that she was never aware of the earthquake as an earthquake at all.

She was in the train when it happened, a little Christian the Pilgrim, making her way through many difficulties up to the Delectable Mountains. Far off they stood, defying the pale sea and the pale plains, shadowed mountains, each with its cool brow crowned by a halo of cloud.

The train service in Trinity Islands is not their chief attraction. First, second, and third class alike may watch the vivid country from the windows, otherwise there is no compensation for rich or poor. The price of a first-class fare is supposed to guarantee your fellow-passengers matching yourself as nearly as possible in complexion; it also entitles you to a deformed wicker chair in a compartment that a cow would appeal against in the Home Country. The wicker chair, unsettled by its migratory life, amuses itself by travelling drunkenly around the truck, unless you lash yourself to the door-handle with your pocket-handkerchief, or evolve some other ingenious device.

The suffragette was always without inspirations in the cause of comfort. She was a petty ascetic, and never thought personal well-being worth the acquiring. Her body was an unfortunate detail attached to her; she resented its demands, and took but little more care if it than she did of the mustard-coloured portmanteau, another troublesome but indispensable part of her equipment. She put her body and the portmanteau each into a wicker chair in the train, and promptly forgot how uncomfortable they both were.

(There is much fascination in the big world, but I think the most wonderful thing Tn it is the passing of the little bubble worlds that blow and burst in many colours around you and me every minute of our lives. In a 'bus or at a ball, in a crowd around a fallen horse, meeting for a moment as reader and writer of a book, or shoulder to shoulder in church singing to a God we all look at with different eyes, these things happen and will never happen exactly that way again. How I wondered at the cut of your moustache, O stranger, how I wondered at the colour of your tie. . . . But your little daughter with the thin straight legs and the thin straight hair pressed to your side, her glorying face filled with the light of novelty, and prayed that drive to heaven might never cease. And next to you was the girl who had just discovered the man by her side to be no saint, but a man. And he was trying by argument to recover his sanctitude. "But strite now, Mibel, I never dremp you'd tike it so 'ard. 'S only my bit of fun. . . ." There was the man in khaki, next to me, born an idler, brought up a grocer's assistant, and latterly shocked into becoming a hero. . . . There was the conductor, a man of twisted humour, chanting the words of his calling in various keys through the row of sixpences that he held between his lips, while the little bell at his belt tolled the knell of one ticket after another. ... A little oblong world glazed in, ready to my hand. But I got out at the Bank, and the world went on to Hammersmith Broadway. . . . These things are, and never shall be again. The finest thing about life is its lack of repetition. I hate to hear that history repeats itself. My comfort is that history is never word-perfect in so doing. Fate has always some new joke up her sleeve. Sometimes the joke is not funny, but certainly it is always new.)

There were two Eves and an Adam in the world which evolved from chaos under the suffragette's eyes, as the train moved out of Union station. Also a dog. We are never told about Adam's dog, but I am sure that he had one, and that it wagged its tail at him as he awoke from being created, and snapped at the serpent, and did its best to propitiate the angel with the flaming sword.

Dogs seldom ignored the suffragette. As a race they have either more or less perspicacity than ourselves — you may look at it as you will — and they seldom concur with the public verdict of humanity on its own species. And in the suffragette a confiding dog was never disappointed, for she knew the exact spot where the starched buckram of one's ear is sewn on to one's skull, on which it is almost unbearably good to be scratched.

This dog was the sort whose name is always Scottie when he is owned by the unenterprising. He wore his forelegs so short and so bent that he looked as though he were continually posing as being thoroughbred. When he drew himself up to his full height, the under outline of his figure was about three inches from the ground. When at leisure he walked broadly and foursquare, as a table would walk, if endowed with life; when speeding up, he cantered diagonally — forefeet together — hind-feet together

— no one foot moving independently of its twin.

The sort of conversation that this dog and the suffragette immediately began did not prevent the latter's hearing the conversation that was woven by her fellow-passengers across the loom of the train's roaring.

The fact that the dog's name was really Scottie should give you a clue as to his mistress's character. It was perhaps malicious of me to describe her as an Eve; that would have made her blush. For she was very fully clothed in blue serge. It is almost impossible for the average woman to conduct the business of life except in blue serge. We travel in blue serge (thin for the tropics, thick and satin-lined for our native climate), we sit at our desk in blue serge, we meet our Deity or our stockbroker in blue serge, in blue serge we raid the House of Commons. Perhaps the root of the feminist movement lies in blue serge. If I were defended by a crinoline, or rustled in satin or gingham or poplin, I might have been an exemplary spinster in my sphere to-day.

The other Eve, attired (for she was obviously cosmopolitan) in fawn tussore, occupied an undue fraction of the little universe. She was the sort of person whose bosom enters a room first, closely followed by her chin. Black eyes and a hooked Spanish nose led the rear not unworthily. She intended to be looked at, and she hoped to be recognised as a notorious novelist. For she was a momentary novelist with a contempt for yesterday and no concern at all for tomorrow. A public of a hundred thousand housemaids was all she asked.

One of the virtues of men is that they are not intended for fancy portrayal. Why should one ever describe the outward surface of a man, unless he is the hero of one's book, or unless one is engaged to marry him? The particular Adam in this compartment comes under neither of these headings. He is copiously reproduced all over the world, but clusters thickest in Piccadilly. Possibly you see him at his best very far away from Piccadilly. There is something that transfigures the commonplace in the fact of having kissed the very hem of the Empire's wideflung robe.

"I say, Miss Brown, how's Albert?" asked the young man.

For the other occupants of the little world seemed mutually familiar. It occurred to the suffragette that Fate always threw her with people who knew each other and did not know her.

Miss Brown, the Eve in blue serge, bridled. To all women so flawlessly brought up as Miss Brown, there exists a sort of electricity in the voice of man which sends a tremor across their manners, so to speak.

"Albert, Mr. Wise, is still very weakly. I sometimes wonder whether I shall rear him. His mental activities, I am told, have outgrown his physical strength."

The young man fanned himself. And indeed mental activities sounded unsuited to the climate. The sun spilt square flames upon the floor through the window. The silhouette of the passing landscape scorched itself across the sky-line. Tattered bananas looked like crowds of creatures struck mad by a merciless sun.

The voice of the lady novelist seemed to reach the suffragette through a veil.

"That child will make his mark. He has the most marvellous mental grasp . . ."

Two hills to the northwest moved apart in the middle distance, like the curtains from a stage. And there was Union Town lying white beside her sea, white, but veiled by her green gardens. Port King George, on an attenuated isthmus, stretched its parallel form along to shield the mother coast from the Atlantic. Even from here you could see the white gleam of the ocean's teeth, as they gnashed upon the reef. A spike of calm steel water lay between Union Town and her defending reef. The suffragette thought: " A skeleton in the grass with a sword beside it . . ." She also looked at the toy figure of the Caribbeania, so close to land as to be disguised as part of the island. Her two funnels mingled with the factory chimneys by the wharf.

"But he is sure to have landed by now," thought the suffragette. She felt unsentimentally interested in the fact. It was too hot to feel more.

"I happened to mention the Book of Genesis," said the lady novelist. " And Albert produced a most ingenious theory about the scientific explanation of the fable of creation. I wish I had such a nephew. What a marvellous link with the coming generation!"

"On the other hand," said Mr. Wise, " I happened to mention Alice in Wonderland, and he said it was out of date, and, as a dream, most improbable."

"I am sorry he criticised the Bible in your hearing," apologised Miss Brown. "I am afraid he has a tendency towards irreverence."

"I wish he had," muttered Mr. Wise.

Acres of sugar filed past the window. High waved the proud crests of it, all innocent of its mean latter end as a common comestible. The suffragette's mind laboured under a rocking confusion of green tufted miles, — and somewhere on the outskirts of her thoughts, a little sallow Albert entrenched behind an enormous pair of spectacles.

"A glorious child," said the lady novelist, in her monopolising tones. " Simply glorious. Quite an experience to have met him."

"Good copy, eh?" grinned Mr. Wise.

"Excellent. You know I collect copy."

Now the suffragette collected copy, but she did it without self-consciousness. There are several kinds of copy-collectors. Some of us squeeze our copy into little six-shilling novels, or hack it into so many columns for the benefit of an unfeeling press. Some of us live three-score years and ten, and then wake suddenly to find our copy-coffers full. Upon which we become bores, and our relations hasten to engage a paid companion for us. But some of us carry our lives about with us sealed up in our holy of holies, and take pride in hiding the precious burden that we bear. Copy-collecting may become a religion; to the suffragette, who never put pen to paper for any one else's benefit, and who never told an anecdote, this pursuit was the great consolation for a bleak life. At the gate of death, or on the step of Paradise, such a soul may be found filling its pockets with the gold of secret experience. I think the mania is most acute when no thought of eventual print intrudes. Its most encouraging characteristic to the lonely is the sense of irresponsibility it brings. After all I may go and turn cart-wheels down the Strand, I may murder you, or throw my last shilling into the Thames, I may go halfway to Hell, and if I miscalculate the distance and fall in — it's all copy. To the lady novelist, however, copy was but a currency to spend. Every experience in her eyes formed a part of a printed page, surrounded by a halo of favourable reviews. She never wrote a letter without an eye on her posthumous biography, never met a notable individual without taking a mental note for the benefit of a future series of " Jottings about my Generation." Both she and the suffragette kept diaries, but only the suffragette's had a lock and key.

The engine was approaching the climax of its daily task. It faltered. Looking out of the window, Mr. Wise described its arrival at the foot of a pronounced hill. The engine gazed up the perspective of its duty, and panted prophetically, as pants an uncle before a game of stump-cricket

"This hill is always a surprise to the engine," said Mr. Wise. " Every day it has two or three tries, and yet it never learns the knack."

The suffragette's fingers tore at the arm of her chair. It was not only too hot to travel, it was also much too hot to cease to travel. She felt a crisis approaching.

Her window had stopped artistically opposite a little slice of distant world, carved out between the trunks of two great cotton trees. Union Town, perceptibly diminished since its last appearance, languished again around its bay. Against the white water you could see the cathedral and the factory chimneys, the spires of God and the spires of mammon.

The suffragette, as she looked, saw the cathedral spire cock suddenly awry and bend over, like a finger in three joints.

"The heat," she thought. "I believe I'm dying.

Almost at once after that the train suffered a great spasm, as though yearning for the top of the hill.

"She's going to try again," said Mr. Wise.

The suffragette's head cocked suddenly awry, she bent over in three joints like a finger, and slid off her chair in a faint.

A prostrated suffragette is a contradiction in terms. This one became a child, lying in ungraceful angles, in need of its mother.

"By Jove!" said Mr. Wise. Miss Brown, after lifting up her skirt carefully, knelt upon her petticoat.

An ebony ticket-inspector rushed into the compartment.

"Ull right! Ull right!" he shouted. " Ull ovah! Nobuddy killed!"

"Certainly not," said Mr. Wise. " Why should they be? Only a faint."

"Earthquake, sah, earthquake!" yelled the inspector. "Jes' look at the steeple daown in taown!"

There was no steeple to look at.

"My — what an eventful journey!" said the lady novelist.

"Poor little thing," said Miss Brown to the suffragette, in almost human tones. "Better now, better now?"

The suffragette began to struggle a little. Even had she been in her grave, I think pity would have aroused a spark of militant protest in her bones.

"Tell her to make an effort," said the lady novelist, who had never in her forty years been guilty of physical weakness. "Pretend not to notice her. Probably hysteria."

This well-worn accusation touches a familiar chord in the ear of any rebel. It opened one of the suffragette's eyes. She had black eyebrows which suggested that she might have fine eyes, but she had not. When her eyes were shut you only saw the hopeful suggestion.

"Come, come," said Miss Brown, handing Mr. Wise's brandy flask back to him, and becoming aware that her petticoat was bare to the gaze of an unmarried gentleman and a negro inspector. " Might I trouble you to lift the young lady on to a chair?" she added, as she rose.

Seven stone of political agitator takes but little time to move.

"A most eventful journey," said the lady novelist.

Miss Brown, now decently seated on a chair, stroked the suffragette's hand. " Are you going to friends, my child?" she asked.

"No, enemies, I expect," said the suffragette drearily.

"Where?"

"I don't know."

"You must know where you are going," said the novelist severely.

"Booked to Greyville," said the inspector, who had picked up her ticket, and was thoughtfully clipping it all over.

"Do you know any one in Greyville?" asked Miss Brown.

"No."

"Were you going to an hotel?"

"I suppose so."

"Some kind deeds are so obvious that they are impossible to escape.

"Albert can move into the back room," said Miss Brown.

And the train, as if relieved to have this affair settled, moved on up the hill.

By the time the chapel bell, which Island engines always wear, had begun to sound its warning to the pigs upon the line at Greyville Junction, the suffragette's independence was a thing dissolved. Her protests had no weight. Constitutionally she was unable to be politely firm. She must either be militant or acquiescent; she knew not the half measures of civilisation. And it was impossible to be militant in the face of Miss Brown's impersonal sense of duty.

"If only she had been a more interesting person this might have been like the beginning of a novel," murmured the lady novelist to Mr. Wise. That young man, who was wearing the sheepish look peculiar to the Englishman in the presence of matters which he considers to be feminine, shrugged his shoulders.

At Greyville station Miss Brown emerged like an empress from incognito. A black coachman, with so generous an expanse of teeth that you suspected them of being the only line of defence between you and the inner privacies of his brain, was on the platform. He seemed torn between acquired awe of

Miss Brown, and an innate desire to conduct the welcome heartily. The station-master bowed. The porter chirruped to Scottie.

"New visitor, missis?" gasped the coachman, looking at the suffragette. He had taken some time to assimilate the visitorship of the lady novelist. His mind was being educated at too great a speed.

"Gorgeous fellow," said the lady novelist, who considered all black people gorgeous because they were not white. The conversation of John the coachman had already filled two note-books, though he had never said anything original in his life.

There is so much superfluous sunshine in Trinity Islands that splashes of it have been lavished upon all sorts of unnecessary details, the lizards, and the birds, and the self-conscious orchids roosting in the trees. Some of it has even been rolled into the roads, making them white and merry and irresponsible. The buggy horses feel the tingle of it, for they seldom walk; although the Creator specialised in hills on Trinity Island.

Down from some lofty market came the peasant women; their children, their donkeys, their tawdry clothes, trappings and merchandise, soaked with sun.

Fantastic in outline, fairies of a midsummer day's dream, the little donkeys capered on spindle legs, bestridden by wide panniers, and by the peasant women, riding defiantly like brigands, with bandanas round their heads, and sun-coloured draperies.

It is curious that fashion has not yet decreed a mania for dyeing one's complexion mahogany, that one might wear flame-colour with impunity.

The buggy scattered the marketers. The Island horse, a plebeian creature of humble stature, seldom meets with the luxury of feeling superior. But the Island donkey is nothing but a door-mat on four legs, clogged red with the hectic mud of its mother land. A cheap-jack's pony would feel a prince beside it.

Mr. Wise, who had been met at the station by a very small brown boy with a very tall brown horse, had cantered away in another direction, with a message of greeting to Albert, the sincerity of which Miss Brown had possibly overrated.

A bungalow crouched behind a copper-coloured hedge upon the skyline. Two cotton trees surveyed it, one on each side. A drive of the violently ambitious kind shot at an impossible angle up to its doorstep.

"That is Park View, my home," said Miss Brown.

"Of course, as your dog's name is Scottie," murmured the suffragette.

Miss Brown looked surprised. The poor suffragette's attempts at polite interchange of fatuities never seemed to meet with the usual fate of such efforts. Her trivialities somehow always fell upon silence; if she ventured on the throwing of a light bridge over a gap in the conversation, it seemed to snap communication instead of furthering it. She was, of course, unlucky, but she was also, it must be admitted, too earnest in intention for petty intercourse. She tried too hard.

The buggy, commending its springs to the mercy of Providence, charged the drive of Park View.

On the door-step, carefully posed, Albert was reading a very large book. He started laboriously as the buggy approached, and placed the book under his arm, taking care that the title should be visible. An emaciated child, with manners too old, and clothes too young, for his years.

"I have dot bissed you at all, Ah-Bargaret," said Miss Brown's genial nephew. "I have been too idterested id by dew book od Chebistry. I ab quite sorry you have cob back."

"Chemistry," retailed Miss Brown to the lady novelist. " A child of ten. And — did you notice, he was so deep in his book, he got quite a start when we arrived."

Albert, at Park View, met with that appreciation of his poses which we all hope to meet in heaven.

"Albert, you are to move into the back room," said Miss Brown.

"Why?" asked Albert.

"To make room for this lady."

"Priceless child," said the lady novelist in brackets.

"Because she needs somewhere to rest," said Miss Brown in a voice of tentative reproof.

"But so do I."

"I had better move into the back room myself, then," sighed his aunt.

The suffragette began those hopeless protests which make the burden of an obligation so heavy. It is so very much easier as well as more blessed to give than to receive, that the wonder is that generosity should retain the name of a virtue. Up to a certain point we are all altruists, because it is too much trouble to be otherwise.

Albert, who, having gained his point, was once more comparatively genial, prepared to bring the suffragette to his feet.

"I expect you are wudderig what is the dabe of the bode I ab readig," he suggested to her as she stepped shakily from the buggy.

"No, I was not," she replied gently. " I'm afraid science bores me."

"Wha-t a lot you biss," observed the child. " You probably spedd your precious time id dancig, ad dressig yourself up, ad bakig berry. How buch better — — "

"Albert," said his aunt, " this lady is tired and waiting to pass."

"Yes, but I ab speaking to her."

The suffragette smiled at him, and gave him her portmanteau to carry.

The earthquake at Union Town had shot the most lurid rumours into Greyville. All the Park View servants had suddenly gone to church. The whole village was enjoying an impromptu half-holiday.

The triangular village green, which held Greyville together and formed the pedestal of the Court-house, echoed with news at every stage of exaggeration. One of the mildest rumours was that Union Town had fallen into the sea. It was said on the highest authority that the Devil had run along the streets, throwing flames right and left. No actual news arrived, the sources of news being wrecked, but towards evening all the Americans whose cars had survived the ordeal suddenly invaded the hills, suffering from nerves and a lack of luggage.

Miss Brown says she does not believe in doing a thing unless you do it thoroughly. She says this as if it had never been said before; she propounds it as one propounds a revolutionary theory. But unlike most theory makers, she always translates such boasts into action. She performed the feat of keeping a militant suffragette in bed for the rest of that day.

The suffragette lay and imagined the gardener and the earthquake at different stages of contact. She thought of him fighting to get out of a falling house, and her eyes shone. She thought of him with his head bound up, and wriggled where she lay. She thought of him unhurt, walking with his usual gait as though he were marching to a band, and this thought left her neutral. She never thought of him dead.

She never believed in death either as a punishment or a reward. She had either lost the art of faith, or else she had never found it. She pictured death as a blink of the eyes, as an altering of the facet turned towards life, never as a miracle. She was the only person I ever knew who honestly looked on death as unworthy of contemplation.

Of course if a friend steps round a corner, you lose sight of that friend. But you must get used to the windings of the road. If you are a suffragette, you have to be your own friend. You must not stretch out your hands to find the hands of another; you must keep them clenched by your side. On the other hand, even a suffragette is human — (I daresay you have doubted this) — and my suffragette was only a little less human than you or I. The fact must stand, therefore, that when she thought of the gardener in pain, she forgot to clench her fists.

It may still be a mystery to you why the suffragette should expend ingenuity in running away from her only friend.

If you are a rebel of thorough nature, you believe that your cause is such a good cause that no supporter can be worthy of it. And, in the effort to reach worth, you may possibly arrive, step by step, at the Theory of the Hair Shirt, to which my suffragette had attained. For in throwing her little weight on the side of the best cause she could see, she cowed: " All my life long to discard everything superfluously comfortable or easy. To despise peace, and to love loneliness . . ."

This is the texture of the Hair Shirt worn beneath the armour of a rebel. You may call it hysteria.

And perhaps you are perfectly right. But perhaps there are even better things than being perfectly right.

The night on the Island falls as abruptly as though he who manages the curtain had let go the string by mistake.

With the night came a trayful of supper for the suffragette, and with the supper came Albert, not of course in the useful role of supper purveyor, but only as an ornament.

"This earthquake id Udiod Towd seebs to have beed quite a catastrophe."

"Quite," agreed the suffragette.

"I caddot picture ad earthquake," continued Albert. "I suppose doboddy cad picture such ad urheard-of disaster."

"I can," said the suffragette. "I expect my picture is all wrong, but it's certainly there. I see it red and grey, which is the most vicious discord I know."

"Red ad grey?" repeated Albert. "Why red ad grey? What for idstadce is red, ad what grey?"

"Why," said the suffragette rather lamely, " I suppose the quaking is red, and the pain grey."

"You seeb to be talking dodsedse," said Albert, with creditable toleration. "I expect the flabes are red, ad the sboke grey. However, go od with your picture."

"I think the world would suddenly give a lurch to one side, and you would wonder what had happened, and why you felt so sick. Before you realised anything else you would notice a sort of dazzle of chalk-white faces all round you."

"The people are dearly all degroes Id Udiod Towd."

"Then you would understand, but still you wouldn't believe that this thing was really happening to you. You would see the houses curtsey sideways in a leaping dust, and a house front, with its windows, all complete, would shoot across the street with an unbearable roar, pricked by cracking noises . . ."

"Why would it dot fall od you?"

"Because things don't. And there would be a great chord of screams. And men running a few yards this way or that, and then back again, yelping, with lighted pipes still in their mouths . . ."

"What ad ugly picture. How cad you see it all so clearly?"

"I have been thinking all day — of a friend of mine, who must have seen it. I don't expect an earthquake is a pretty thing, although there is something beautiful about any curious happening."

"I doad't agree with you," said Albert. " There are oadly a few beautiful thigs. Roses ... ad sudsets ... ad love . . ."

"Really, Albert," protested the suffragette, " what do you know about love?"

"Well, if it cobs to that — what do you dow about earthquakes? I cad picture love, easily. A bad, kissing a girl, udder a cocoadut palb . . ."

"Nonsense," exclaimed the suffragette, bounding so violently in her bed as to cane a serious storm in her soup. " Kissing s not love. Everything that was ever said or written about kissing, I think, must have been said or written by a man. It's only another of their tyrannies, to which, for the sake of love, women have had to submit."

"You sowd like a suffragette whed you talk like that," mocked Albert.

"No wonder," she replied. "lam one."

Albert looked shocked to find himself in the presence of such a monstrosity. He went at once to warn his aunt. And she replied: " It doesn't matter, Albert dear, she's only staying a few days, till she is well enough to make other plans. "

The suffragette, left to her cooling soup, reviewed her theories and her practice.

"What's the good of being hard?" she asked herself, " if you are not hard enough? Either you are harder than the world and can bruise it, or the world is harder than you and bruises you. There is no point in just having a hard crust. As well be dough."

In the middle of the night there was a loud wail from Albert's room. The suffragette, whose room adjoined his, was the first on the spot.

"I seeb to have a bad paid," cried Albert, who was always cautious in his statements, " id the heart. It feels like cadcer, I thigk."

"I don't think so," said the suffragette. " Perhaps you are only in love."

She went and knocked on Miss Brown's door.

"But I doad't wadt Ah-Bargaret," said Albert, as his aunt came in. "I should hate to die looking at Ah-Bargaret. I ab sure I ab going to die."

"We'll see that you don't," said the suffragette, as she began to rub his side, his poor little ribs, furrowed like a ploughed field.

"But you are an invalid yourself," objected Miss Brown jealously. " You had better go back to bed."

"Doh, she is dot ad idvalid, she's a suffragette," whined Albert. "I doad't wish her to go back to bed."

Even Albert, with his wide range of scientific ways of being inconvenient, could scarcely have chosen a more impossible moment for an illness. Next day it became apparent that every doctor on the Island who had survived the disaster had plunged into the whirlpool of its after effects. Nursing on the Island is in a rudimentary stage at all times, but what nurses existed were not to be dragged now from Union Town.

The lady novelist said: " I know I must appear heartless, dear Margaret, not to be helping to nurse him, but the sight of suffering gives me such acute pain. . . . It's not heartlessness, you see, it's that my heart is too tender."

"I wish she would go to an hotel then," said the harassed Miss Brown to the suffragette. " She wants her meals so good and so regular, and I seem to hate the sight of food just now."

It was against the suffragette's principles to hope anything so desirable without translating her hope into action. It was also beyond her powers to be diplomatic.

"I think you had better go to the hotel," she said militantly to the lady novelist. " You would be better fed there, and we should be more comfortable alone."

"In that case perhaps I had better, not being welcome in my friend's house," replied the novelist. "I was going to suggest it myself, as the sound of that priceless child's cries wrings my heart."

The suffragette therefore gained her point at the expense of tact, which, as future historians will note, is a characteristic of suffragettes.

Albert's temperament was not that of the Spartan. He never ceased to cry for a week. As for the pain, it was as if the god — whoever he may be — who likes little children to suffer, sat beside him, and with a blunt shears sliced off the top of each breath.

There is a sword, a fatal blade,

Unthwarted, subtle as the air,

And I could meet it unafraid

If I might only meet it fair.

But how I wonder why the smith

Who wrought that steel of subtle grain

Should also be contented with

So blunt and mean a thing as pain. . . .

Albert clung to the suffragette, the straw in his sea of troubles. His constant wail rose an octave if she ventured from the room.

"The only holiday she had during that first week was half an hour on the second evening of the ordeal, half an hour spent in carrying the lady novelist's majestic suit-case to the hotel.

John the coachman could not do it, as the road to the hotel was infested with "duppies" after dark. The probability of meeting a " rolling calf " with a human head and green eyes, or the duppy of some regrettable ancestor, robbed even a tip of its splendour.

The carrying of the suit-case was a physical impossibility to one of the suffragette's lack of muscle. But to her impossibility was only an additional " Anti " to fight, a rather worthier enemy than the rest. She believed in the power of the thought over the deed, that was her religion, and one is tempted to wonder whether any more complex belief is needed. Has it ever been proved that the human will, if reverently approached, is not omnipotent?

At any rate the suit-case, borne by a thing that looked like the suffragette, but was in reality a supersuffragette created for the occasion, travelled to the hotel, unmolested by duppies, but followed by a literary lady poisoned by injured pride.

At the hotel were many Americans who said, " I guess " and " Bully " and " I should worry," and all the things that make a second-rate copy collector swell with copy and feel exquisitely cosmopolitan. This collector's diary began to overflow to three or four foolscap sheets a day, closely covered with dialogues on trivial subjects by very ordinary American husbands and fathers; all Americanisms underlined and spattered with liberal exclamation marks.

At the end of the second week of the lady novelist's stay at the hotel arrived a millionaire, who immediately became the gem of the collection. He was exactly modelled on the stock millionaire to be met with in the pages of the comic papers. He was lean, self-made, and marvellously dressed; he wore eyeglasses and a little stitched-linen hat tilted over them. Also the beard of a goat. At the very outset he expressed himself, " Vurry happy to meet you, madam, always happy to meet any of our neighbours from across the duck-pond." It was almost too good to be true. The novelist followed him about, so to speak, with fountain pen poised.

His conversation was almost entirely financial. Neither the lady novelist nor I understand such matters well enough to write them down, but only I am wise enough not to try.

"Do you mind if I say you are a treasure?" asked the lady novelist, after listening for an hour to a dissertation on Wall Street.

"Not at all, ma'am," replied the millionaire politely, and drew breath to continue his discourse. But he rewarded her by descending to the level of her intelligence.

"Say, talking of money, I guess there've been more fine opportunities lorst in Union Town this last fortnight, than ever I missed since I commenced collecting the dollars. Would you believe me — there's a fellow, by name Dallas Tring, who's inherited the only flour dee-pot in Union Town. Uncle's orfice crumpled in on Uncle during the quake, and left Tring his fill of dollars right there for the picking up, so to speak. Union Town wants flour at this crisis, and if it was mine I'd say that Union Town, or the British Government, had darn well got to pay for it. We don't calc'late in hearts, this side of heaven, but in hard dollars. Philanthropy's a fool-game."

"You are simply priceless," said the lady novelist " Please go on."

"I'm going right on, ma'am," said the treasure. " Would you believe me, this Tring e-volves a system (save the mark) by which he gives away this flour — gives it away, mind you, gratis, free, for nothing, with a kiss thrown in if required, to any nigger cute enough to rub his little tummy and say he's feeling empty. You may reckon I just couldn't quit Union Town without a call to see if the man was an imbecile or what. I found a young cub with' a curly smile playing around in the orfice. Say, what do you suppose he answered me when I told him 'Good-morning, and what's this sentimental moneychucking, anyway? ' "

"I am dying to know," said the lady novelist.

"Said it was the foyrst time he'd ever been led to think there might be something in sentiment after all. I was fair rattled."

The young cub with the curly smile, as you may, with your customary astuteness, have guessed, was the gardener. He had assumed the pose of philanthropist, which, when conducted at some one else's expense, is one of the most delightful poses conceivable. The pleasure to be found in helping the dirty destitute seems to need an explanation beyond the plea of altruism. There is a real charm in domineering to good purpose. To say unto one man Go and he goeth, and to another Come and he cometh, is at all times pleasant, but when such a luxury as autocracy becomes a virtue, there are few who disregard its glamour.

The gardener's broken leg recovered as quickly as any leg could have done. He had an enthusiastic and healthy attitude towards suffering and illness, an attitude which he took instinctively, and which mental scientists and faith-healers try to produce artificially. He was always serenely convinced that he would be better next day. He lived in a state of secret disappointment in to-day's progress, and unforced confidence in to-morrow's. He might be described as a discontented optimist; though often convinced that the worst had happened, he was always sure that the best was going to happen. Conversely, of course, you can be a contented pessimist, happy in to-day, but entirely distrustful of to-morrow.

To the gardener's methods may perhaps be ascribed the fact that in a fortnight he was able with the help of a stick, and with the encouragement of Aitch and Zed, to walk about his room. His first excursion was to the window.

The houses opposite had fallen in on their own foundations. One complete wall was standing starkly amid the mass. Portraits of the King and Queen and a text or two still clung to their positions against the stained and florid wall-paper.

"Do you see that house that you just can't see, the other side of that wall?" asked Aitch.

"Yes, I see," said the gardener. "I mean I just can't see."

"That's where dead Uncle Jonathan lives," said Aitch. " He's left Father the flour in his will."

"How good of him. I hope it was a pretty one."

"Father said, ' There's a fortune there.' And Mother said, ' Oh, Dally, it's as if it was left in trust for poor Union Town.' "

When the gardener next met Mr. Tring, he discovered how entirely sufficient for two are the opinions of one.

"Of course I'm awfully lucky, in a way," said Mr. Tring. "It's a big inheritance, and hardly damaged at all by the earthquake. But at present, of course, it's all responsibility and no returns. I feel as if it's sort of left me in trust for Union Town."

"That's one way of looking at it," said Courtesy

— surely the least witty comment ever invented.

I don't agree with you at all," said Mrs. Rust,

who now made this remark mechanically in any pause in the conversation.

"You consider that Mr. Tring should pile up a big bill against the British Government?" suggested the gardener.

"Stuff and nonsense," said Mrs. Rust. "I consider the niggers can eat — mangoes."

"I sometimes wonder," said the gardener, "whether one has a duty to oneself. One feels as if one has, but I always — in theory — distrust a duty that pays."

"Certainly one has a duty to oneself," said Courtesy. "Duty begins at home. That's in the Bible, isn't it?"

"Most of the texts tell you your only duty is to the man next door," said Mr. Tring, blushing.

"I entirely disagree with you," said Mrs. Rust.

Soon after this discussion Mr. Tring, inspired by his wife, produced a plan for the benefit of the gardener.

"When this business is over we shall — I mean I shall be a rich man and a busy man. I need somebody young around. I'd like fine to buy your youth (his wife's words). What about being my secretary for the present? It might give you a start in Island business."

"This is not a time for paid work," said the gardener, "with half the money on the Island gone to dust."

"I take your meaning," said Mr. Tring. "But in my opinion the rime's all right. Good work's good work, whether it's honorary or not. I never liked the idea that there's something heroic in refusing money, making out that there's something mean in accepting it. If you help you help, and the help's none the worse if it makes you self-supporting.

The word " self-supporting " was a sharp and accusing word to the gardener. Most of us privately possess certain words that search out the tender parts in our spiritual anatomy. The words " absolute impossibility," for instance, angered the suffragette to militant protest; the mention of " narrow-mindedness " ruffled the priest's sensibilities; as for me, the expression "physical disability" hurts me like a knife. It may or may not be out of place to add that the effect on Courtesy — that practical girl — of an allusion to "banana fritters " was to make her feel sick. You may know people better by their weaknesses than by their strength.

The word self-supporting, therefore, goaded the gardener into accepting Mr. Tring's offer.

His stock of poses, though very wide in range, had not as yet extended as far as practical business, in black and white, hours ten to five daily. He had — I report it with disgust — a contempt for the pen as a business implement. He was himself an artist without expression, a poet caged; a musician in desire, he suffered from a mute worship of all art. And he believed that the pen was as sacred an instrument as the violin, or the palette. To make money by the pen in business was equal to fiddling on a kerb-stone, or designing picture post cards. These theories are pose-theories, of course, and untenable by the practical man. But some of the gardener's poses had crystallised into belief. He was, as you may have noticed, anything but a practical man.

"Perhaps," said Mr. Tring, "you might be what my wife calls an 'out-of-doors secretary.' I have been officially asked to organise the distributing of the flour. Enquiries will have to be made. The niggers are awfully sly, you know; you'd have thought they'd be too silly to be sly."

"I have noticed that the silly seem to be protected by Providence. Slyness seems to be given as a sort of compensation. Otherwise, of course, we should stamp out the silly, and a lot of valuable human curiosities would become extinct."

"I take your meaning," said Mr. Tring. " That being so, if we found you a horse to ride about on, would you undertake the notification and examination of the necessitous cases, the pruning away — as my wife would say — of the dishonest applicants."

"I am a gardener," said the gardener. "I love interfering with nature. Mr. Tring, you are a most excellent friend to me. Thank you seems too little a word."

There are only a few people to be met with who can do justice to such a thankless task as the expression of thanks. Man under an obligation is always convinced that the conventional words are not enough, and tries to improve on them. This must always be a failure, however, as improving on convention is a work that only genius can undertake with success.

A horse was found for the gardener. He was what might be called an anxious rider, and Courtesy, after watching his first equestrian exhibition, went to some trouble to find him an elderly mare of sober propensities. Mounted upon this excellent creature, the gardener one morning threaded the little passes that had been made in and out of the crags of ruined Union Town. It was early. The Olympians had not yet begun to compound that horrible broth of sun and steam and dust which they brew daily upon the plains of the Island. The sun's eyes had not yet opened even on the most ambitious of the hills, but the sky was awake, and so clear that you might have thought you were looking through crystal at a blue Zion. The dew was laughing in the crushed gardens. Grey lizards with a purple bloom on them jumped from ruin to ruin over chasms of ruin. A humming-bird, looking as though its tail and beak had been added hurriedly out of the wrong box, stood in the air glaring into the open eye of a passion flower. The air was shining cool. The songs of the birds were like little fountains of cold water.

There is always a pessimistic gloom about the woods of the Island. The cotton tree, with its ashen blasted trunk, looks as if it had known a bitter past. Logwood gives the impression of firewood left standing by mistake. And the cocoanut palms, which are unstable souls, lean this way and that, as though glancing over their shoulders for their enemy the wind, against whom they have no defence. Only the great creepers throw cables of hope from tree to tree, and the orchids nestle blood-red against the colourless hearts of the cotton trees.

The huts for the homeless had been built in a wide clearing in the woods, only divided from the sea by the road, a belt of palms, and a frill of sand so white that the word white sounded dirty as you looked at it. The rocks leant out of opal water into pearl air. A pensive pelican, resting its double chin upon its breast, stood waiting on a low rock.

The gardener dismounted with great care. A person of three summers or so came to watch him do it. The only thing she wore that nature had not from the first provided her with was a hair-ribbon. Her head looked like a phrenologist's chart. It was mapped out in squares by multiplied partings at right angles to each other. From every square plot of wool sprang a rigid plait of perhaps one inch in length. On the highest plait was a scarlet hair-ribbon. The effect was not really beautiful, but suggested a beautiful maternal patience. The person thus decorated was gnawing a piece of bread.

"That bread," thought the gardener, who in flashes posed as Sherlock Holmes, " must have been made with flour. That flour probably came from Tring's. Where did you get that bit of bread, Miss?" he added.

The person, determined not to appear to overlook a joke for want of an effort, gave a high fat chuckle, and danced the opening steps of a natural tango. The gardener, unwilling to shatter the illusion of his own humour, did not repeat the question. He gave the elderly mare in charge of not more than a dozen little boys. It was an insult to the mare, a creature with a deep sense of responsibility, who could much more reasonably have taken charge of the little boys.

"Dat Mrs. Morra's pickney," said one of the older boys, with a polite desire to effect an introduction between the gardener and the dancing person. On hearing herself thus described, Mrs. Morra's pickney at once led the way at great speed to Mrs. Morra. Now Mrs. Morra's was the first name on the gardener's list of applications.

She was discovered outside the door of her hut, submitting the head of an elder daughter to that process of which the coiffure of the younger was a finished example. The conversation was punctured by wails from the victim. Wool does not adapt itself to painless combing.

"Good morning, Mrs. Morra," said the gardener, with his confiding smile. Mrs. Morra screamed with amusement.

"I hear the earthquake knocked down your home and didn't leave you anything to live on. You asked for some of the free bread, didn't you? The police gave us your name."

"P'leece?" questioned Mrs. Morra, who seemed amused by the mention of her necessity. "Whe' dat, please?"

"The police — the big man in blue," said the gardener, before he remembered that on the Island the police was always a little man in white.

"Fleece?" persisted Mrs. Morra.

"The policeman — the law," said the gardener desperately.

Every nigger is familiar with the law. Going to law is a vice that on the Island takes the place of drink. The nigger's idea of heaven is a vast courthouse, with the Almighty sitting at a desk awarding him damages and costs.

"Oh, de law — de polizman, please sah," said Mrs. Morra.

"Right. Now how did your little girl get this bread?"

"Beg a quattie from a lady, please," said the mother.

"Yes, but where did she buy the bread when she had the quattie. Bread is free now, you can't buy it."

"Bought it fim Daddy Hamilton, please, old man who live alone by himself across opposite. But he ha'n't got no more, please!"

"I'll go and see Daddy Hamilton," said the gardener. " How many children have you got, Mrs. Morra?"

"Please?"

"How many children?"

"Please?"

"How many pickneys?" said the gardener, inspired.

"Pickneys please thank you," said Mrs. Morra. "I got Dacia Maree Blanche Rosabel Benjum Teodor Lionel."

"Seven," panted the gardener, who had kept careful count.

"Tree, please sah," corrected the lady.

"Me Dacia Maree," explained the victim of maternal pride.

"Have you a husband?" continued the gardener.

"O la, no please sah."

"A widow?" he suggested.

Mrs. Morra shrieked with laughter.

"Nebber had no man mo' dan tree monts," she said. "Dacia Maree's fader — he on'y stop a week. Ben j urn's dad bin in gaol two yahs. Blanche Rosabel — her fader was a brown man, her grand-dad was a buckra."

The gardener blushed into his note-book.

The police had certified that the family's means of subsistence had been swept away by the earthquake, and the gardener, by one glance into an unsavoury hut, satisfied himself that no luxuries had been saved from the wreck. He therefore noted the case as needy, and asked his way to Daddy ton.

This gentleman, seated upon an upturned bucket, was studying a hymn-book through a pair of hornrimmed spectacles.

"God bless you, sah," he said in the loud unmistakable voice of a joyous Christian.

The gardener thanked him.

"I see, Mr. Hamilton, that you told the police you had two married daughters whose husbands had been killed by the earthquake, and seven grandchildren dependent on you."

"Yessah. De Lawd giveth, an' de Lawd taketh away."

"Certainly. And you had an emergency grant of several loaves of bread on Monday."

"Praise be to God, sah, I did. De Lawd giveth "

"On the contrary, in this case it was Mr. Tring that gave. Now, are either of your married daughters or any of your grandchildren at home?"

"No, sah. Dey all gone to chapel."

"Really? Now there seems to be an idea among your neighbours that you live by yourself. How is it they have never noticed your two daughters and seven grandchildren?"

"Dunno, sah. Deir eyes dey hab closed, lest at any time dey should see wid deir eyes, and hear wid deir ears "

"Do the whole ten of you sleep in that little hut?"

"No, sah, I sleep on de graound aoutside. Foxes hab holes "

"Now, Mr. Hamilton, can you look me in the face and tell me that the bread that was given you was really eaten by yourself, and two daughters, and seven grandchildren?"

"Yes, sah. To tell you de troot, sah, dey wasn't ezackly blood-grandchildren. All men are brudders, we are told, sah, and derefore grandchildren, an' daughters, an' nieces too, sah. All de pickneys call me Daddy Hamilton. Suffer de little children to come unto me, saith de Lawd, so I suffer dem gladly"

"Yes, but do you ever charge anything for suffering them? Have you ever sold any of the bread that was given you?"

"Well, sah, a man mus' live."

"Yes, but the bread was given you to live on."

"Well, sah, money is better dan bread. You ask for bread and dey give you a stone."

124

"Not in this case. The bread was excellent. Do you know, Mr. Hamilton, I believe you are liable to be prosecuted for obtaining Mr. Tring's gift under false pretences."

"No, sah, not false. I am a faitful sojer in de Lawd's army, sah, faitful an' joyful. Old Joybells dey call me."

"Still, this time I'm afraid you stepped aside.

I will ask Mr. Tring what he would like done about it. At any rate, you won't get any more bread given you for the present. I'll see to that"

" God bless you, sah. De Lawd giveth, an' de Lawd taketh away."

All novelties are interesting to One Who is Seeing Life, but novelty is unfortunately an elusive phantom to pursue. After a fortnight spent in inquiry, the gardener began to feel his heart sink at the mention of flour. He suffered from the gift of enthusiasm, in place of the gift of interest, and enthusiasm is like the seed that fell upon stony ground, the suns of monotony scorch it quickly. To do the gardener justice, it must be admitted that there was very little left to do. Union Town was not very long in adjusting itself to the emergency. Nigger huts are quickly built, and even the villas of the coffee-coloured aristocracy, the most serious sufferers from the disaster, are not the work of ages. The Post Office continued to lie upon its face in the High Street, but the bare feet of the people soon trod a path around it. Government House remained huddled in a heap upon its own cellars, but Governors, after all, are not human, and it makes but little difference to the population to hear of its viceroy sleeping under canvas.

In the gardener's mind, during the past fortnight, the suffragette had had Union Town as a serious rival. His vanity was a little hurt by her continued lack of appreciation of a great man. He would have liked, while still on crutches, to have met her searching among the ruins for him. So for a little while he posed as being in love with his work. But when Union Town began to retire into the background, the suffragette stepped forward into insistent prominence. She triumphed finally one night in the verandah of the St. Maurice Hotel, after dinner. It was a night without a flaw, every star spoke the right word, and the moon was a poem unspeakable. Fireflies starred the garden.

The stars and fireflies dance in rings,

The fireflies set my heart alight,

Like fingers, writing magic things

In flame upon the wall of night.

There is high meaning in the skies

(The stars and fireflies — high and low),

And all the spangled world is wise

With knowledge that I almost know .

"I'll have to return to the search' said the gardener.

"What for?" asked Courtesy, who always liked everything explained.

"For the suffragette," he replied. " I'm tired of being respectable and in doubt."

Luckily the priest had changed his table since

Courtesy had changed her company. He sat at the far end of the verandah, with his back to every one.

His righteousness had subsided to some extent since the earthquake, but he still looked on the gardener as a hopelessly lost lamb. Such a shepherd as the priest may yearn towards the lost lamb, but would rather not sit at the same table with it.

"If you start that silly game again, gardener," said Courtesy, "you'll have to throw over Mr. Twing's job. Why can't you leave the girl alone? She can't have been killed, because there are no white people left unidentified. Why can't you stick to one thing?"

"I have no glue in me," replied the gardener. " I'm glad of it; there could be nothing duller than sticking to one thing. Besides, there's nothing left to stick to. There was only half an hour's work to do yesterday, although I spent three hours over it."

Mrs. Rust shot a fountain of tobacco smoke into the air as a sign that she intended to speak. The priest liked Mrs. Rust, because his own tolerance of her vagaries made him feel so broad-minded. He liked to smile at her roguishly when she took a small whisky and soda; he liked to hand her the matches when she smoked; he liked to write to his sister at home: " One comes in contact with a worldly set out here, but if one is careful to keep one's mind open, one finds points of contact undreamt of at home in one's own more thoughtful set." If the gardener had been a drunkard instead of being in love, the priest would have liked him better. But the gardener posed as being a non-drinker and a non-smoker on principle. Really the taste of spirits or of tobacco smoke made him feel sick.

"I am going to leave Union Town myself," said Mrs. Rust. "I know of a car I could hire to-morrow. I will help you in your search, gardener, although she strikes me as being a totally unattractive young woman."

"We had arranged to go to the hotel in Spanish City next Wednesday by the nine train," said Courtesy in a reproachful voice; " and from there to Alligator Bay, and then in a car round the Island. I daresay other plans might be made, but you should have let me know sooner."

"No plans need be made," said the gardener rebelliously. "We might just get the car, and start now in the cool."

"Ass!" observed Courtesy simply. "Mrs. Rust's lace scarf won't be dry enough to iron till tomorrow. I will see whether we can start the next day."

To disobey Courtesy was unthinkable. The gardener gritted his teeth at the stars, because he would have to see them again before he could start on his search. Now was the only time for the gardener; then hardly counted; and presently was a word he failed to acknowledge.

"Anyway, you don't either of you know where to look for her," said Courtesy, that practical girl.

"She'll be at Alligator Bay," said Mrs. Rust. "They've got a picture gallery there."

"She'll be somewhere in the hills," said the gardener. "She would always go up."

"I entirely disagree with you," retorted Mrs. Rust.

"Anyway, it seems hot on sea-level," said

Courtesy. " We'd better go up to where it's supposed to be cool. I'm told the Ridge Pension, High Valley, has a good cook, but the New Hotel, at Greyville, is also well spoken of."

Fortunately thirty-six hours, though they may stretch half-way to eternity, never succeed in covering the whole distance. A moment arrived when the three, bristling with travellers' trifles, met the waiting car at the nearest spot in the ruined High Street to which cars could penetrate. And then followed a long series of dancing moments. Little village ports strung like beads along the coast; thatched huts thrown together by a playful fate; waterfalls like torn shreds of gauze draped on the nakedness of the hills; logwood plantations, banana plantations, sugar plantations, yam plantations . . . Then as the approaching hills began to usurp more and more of the sky, the road cut through a high and low land; hand in hand with a very blue river, it threaded a great grey crack in the island; high cliffs yearned towards each other on either side; a belt of pale sky followed the course from above. Then out into the sun and wild woods, with ferns and flowering trees beckoning beautifully from all sides. And then long hills, a road that doubled back at every hundred yards, with a great changing view, growing bigger, on the right hand or the left, as the course of the road decided. Little brown villages clung desperately to the hill-side; gardens of absurd size balanced themselves on almost perpendicular slopes; paths of red mud, disdaining the winding subterfuges of the road, sprang from angle to angle, like children playing at independence beside a plodding mother.

Towards the afternoon a blue-black cloud crept suddenly over a summit, and emptied itself with passion upon the travellers. In a minute the waterproof hood of the car was proved unworthy of its name; the screen in front became less transparent than a whirlpool; the road went mad and believed itself to be a mountain torrent. The wet wrath of heaven began to make itself felt even down Mrs. Rust's neck.

"This is disgraceful," said Mrs. Rust. " Courtesy, do something at once."

No doubt Courtesy would have risen to the occasion, but for once Heaven was quicker. The sun suddenly shouldered its way round the intruding cloud, and made one great shining jewel of the world. Park View, that forward house, residence of the retiring Miss Brown, stood bold upon the skyline.

The gardener's heart did not leap within him when he saw Park View. Only in books does Fate disguised stir the heart to such activity. In real life, when I stumble on the little thing that is to change my life, I merely kick it aside, and hurry on.

In case you should think that by bringing my travellers to Greyville I make the long arm of coincidence unduly attenuated, I must add that there are only two tourist centres on the hills of the Island — Greyville and High Valley — and that almost everybody visits both.

The gardener was now posing as a Seeker, and instinctively his eyes took on the haggard look that belongs to the pose. As he mounted the steps of the New Hotel verandah, the lady novelist thought, "What an interesting young man!" When, however, she saw Mrs. Rust's hair, her notebook trembled in her pocket. The Treasure had left, and as to the other Americans, she had practically drunk their cup of copy dry.

"Charles," she said to the woolly black waiter when he brought her tea, " will you put those new people at my table?"

"No, please, missis," replied Charles, who, being a head waiter at seventeen, was suffering from the glamour of power. " Shall sit dem wid Mistah Van Biene."

A fraction of the proceeds of the lady novelist's last novel, however, soon silenced the authority of Charles.

And after all it was Mrs. Rust who sought acquaintance first, at breakfast in the cool verandah next morning.

"There was a lizard in my bath," said Mrs. Rust. " Disgraceful! Why can't you exterminate your vermin?"

This was hard on the lady novelist, who screamed for Charles whenever she saw anything moving any where, but she bore the injustice with a beautiful patience.

"What do you think of the Island in general?" she asked. "I can tell by your face that your opinion would be worth having."

She might have added that she could tell this, not so much by Mrs. Rust's face as by her hair.

"I don't think of the Island if I can help it," retorted Mrs. Rust after some thought, during which she sought in vain for some adequately startling reply. " That earthquake — on my first day — a revolting exhibition."

"Oh, were you in Union for the earthquake? I am collecting the reports of intelligent people who were there. I am sure your adventures must have been worth recording."

"On the contrary," replied Mrs. Rust, "the whole thing was absurdly overrated. My nerves remained perfectly steady throughout."

The gardener, the only person who might have cast a doubt upon this statement, was not present. Still posing as the strenuous seeker, he had gone for a walk before breakfast.

There is a great glitter about morning in the hills which drags the optimist for long walks in the small hours upon an empty stomach, and causes even the pessimist to attack his grape fruit at breakfast with a jovial trill. The little tables on the verandah of the New Hotel have a glamour of heaped bright fruit upon white linen. In the garden the tangerines grow radiantly among their shining sober green, the butterflies blow across the pale young grass. There is a salmon-pink azalea, whose smile attracts the humming-birds, and a riotous clump of salvia. There is a benevolent John Crow, who strikes attitudes upon the roof of the annex, and stands for hours with his ragged wings spread open to the sun, as he surveys the diamond world. Really he is hoping that you will fall dead over your breakfast, but you lose this thought in the glitter of a hill morning. For the sake of your own peace of mind, never get close enough to a John Crow to see his gargoyle face. Content yourself with admiring his barbaric grace from a distance, and forget why he is there.

Courtesy was characteristically still in bed. She never was one to hear the call of a singing world.

The gardener came in with eyes crinkled by the sun, and his hair standing up in a spirited way all over the top of his head. Did you know that it is possible to be a specialist in posing without giving thought to the appearance?

"You look as if you had been fighting," snapped Mrs. Rust. " Disgraceful state of hair."

"I wish I had," replied the gardener. "I could fight beautifully at this moment. I never knew what it was to breathe until this morning."

"Air is indeed a blessing" said the lady novelist.

"I have a passion for air. I sometimes think I should die without it. How interesting to meet any one who loves fighting. You ought to be a soldier.

I myself am a peace-loving woman, but I often have quarrels forced upon me."

"Let me conduct them for you," suggested the gardener, wrestling with his grape fruit. " Show me the enemy."

"I wish I could. I think I will," said the lady. "I came to Greyville to stay with a dear friend, and a young woman, of no standing whatever, picked up anyhow and anywhere, not only turned me out of my friend's house, but now insists on my moving two of my trunks from the sick-room."

"Oh, there is a sick-room, is there?"

"Yes, my friend's little nephew is ill."

"But didn't your friend protest? Has the young woman a hypnotic power over her?"

"My friend is very weak. The young woman is only a sort of second-rate children's nurse, apparently."

"And do you want to go back there?"

"No, I prefer to be here. But it is so undignified not to be consulted."

"That's very true," said the gardener, whose interest was beginning to wane.

"That road below is as crowded and as noisy as Piccadilly," said Mrs. Rust. " Disgraceful."

"Market day," replied the novelist rapturously. " Such a blaze of colour. Such a babel of tongues . . ."

"And so smelly, I am sure," said Mrs. Rust. "I am going to market."

"Let's all go to market," added the gardener.

An hour had to be allowed for Courtesy to have her breakfast, and for Mrs. Rust to don her panama. Mrs. Rust, though not averse to startling any one of her own colour, had a secret distaste for the naive criticisms of the niggers on her strange hair. The Islanders were not aware that dyed hair was the apex of modern fashion; they looked upon it, poor things, as a deformity, and a most amusing one. Mrs. Rust had been obliged to invest in a perfect beehive of a hat for wear in such ignorant parts.

So four more units joined the stream of marketers along the red road. In spite of Mrs. Rust's panama, the niggers laughed. Niggers always laugh unless they cry, and the lunatic ways of white women provide a source of amusement that never fails, although white women have been on the Island for three hundred years. Some of the marketers actually had to remove their baskets of fruit — crowned with boots — from their heads, to give free play to their sense of humour. Every nigger wears his boots upon his head. It is, I suppose, as much a disgrace not to own them as it is a discomfort to wear them.

The appearance of the market was like a maniac garden, and the sound of it was like a maniac rookery. By way of compensation to the niggers for their individual ugliness, Providence has granted to them an unconscious beauty in the matter of grouping themselves. A nigger by herself looks like a comic picture post card, a lot of niggers together look like the picture that many master-hands have tried to paint.

My senses tingle even now with the welter of sun and sound and smell and colour, that constitutes an Island market.

"You meet every one in Greyville here," said the lady novelist to the gardener. "I will introduce you to the enemy."

The gardener agreed absent-mindedly. He was helping Courtesy to buy baskets. The Island is the paradise of basket lovers. Those hearts are rare which do not thrill at the sight of a plaited basket in many colours, and I believe that nobody ever left the Island without succumbing to the charm. I suppose the reason why Island baskets never get on to the market at home is that everybody loves them so much, they never part with them. Courtesy, who always loved the popular thing, had been very busy buying baskets since the first moment of her arrival.

Mrs. Rust was busily occupied in refusing to buy anything. " Buy a pine? Why should I? I loathe pines. Lace? No, I won't buy lace, my underclothes are already overcrowded with it. What's that? A basket to keep my letters in. I keep my letters behind the fire. Why, gardener — look — here's "

"Mr. Gardener," tittered the novelist, " here is the enemy behind you."

"You dream," said the gardener, "I've been looking for you everywhere."

With an amiable smile the suffragette allowed her hand to be shaken an enormous number of times. She was looking plainer than the gardener had expected. With the pretty obtuseness of men, he had in his dreams forgotten that brown hat with the weary flowers in it. He had imagined her dressed in blue, he had thought her eyes were blue to match, he had created a little curl in her hair. Yet somehow he was not disappointed. For he had also forgotten in his dreams the comfort that lies in lack of ornament. It isn't love that makes the world go round, it's the optimism of men.

"Why, it's quite nice to see you again," said the suffragette in a voice of surprise.

"Courtesy," shouted the gardener, " from this moment I'm not a fit companion for Mrs. Rust. Courtesy says I'm not respectable when I'm with you," he added to the suffragette.

"I don't see anything very disreputable in your behaviour with me," she replied. "But it's only for a little while, Courtesy."

"Oh, Lor', no," said Courtesy. "He's come to stop."

"I haven't," said the suffragette.

The gardener would never have put into words the appeal that came into his eyes.

"Yes," said the suffragette, cc you are thinking that I am growing more and more militant every time you see me."

"I was not," he answered, " I was wondering how I could manage to see you apart from all this noise."

"Quite easily. You can walk back to Park View with me now. I have got the oranges for Albert."

So they squeezed out of the market-place, and side by side paced the avenue of donkeys which on market days lines the village street.

"What are you waiting for?" asked the gardener. " What's wrong with me? When will you want me?"

"It isn't you I don't want. It's what you stand for. Possibly I haven't mentioned to you that I am a suffragette of a special kind. A cat that walks by itself ... Or rather perhaps it is presumptuous of me to lay claim to cathood. I have only walked such a little way. I am an elderly kitten, say, walking by itself."

"But if all suffragettes were like you, it would certainly be an argument against the franchise. For what would become of England?"

"God forbid that all suffragettes should be like me. I am a fanatic, a rather silly thing to be."

"I know what you are waiting for," said the gardener. " Heaven! you want so much beside the Vote, and you'll never get what you want this side of heaven."

"God forbid that I should want heaven," said the suffragette. "Heaven is not made for women. Why, the very archangels are men."

"Why won't you have me? We could get married to-morrow. Why not?"

"Because I am too busy. Because there is a superfluity of women, and as I am not a real woman — only an idea — I'd better sit out. Because I am conceited and couldn't bear my pride to have a fall — at your expense. Because you don't know me and I don't know you. Because it's better to live alone with an ideal than coupled with a fact. Now I'm sick of talking about myself, it makes me feel sugary, as though I'd been swallowing golden syrup neat."

"But before you retire into your militancy, tell me," said the gardener, " do you think you will ever recognise this bond between us?"

"There is no bond between us."

"There is love between us."

"I'm sorry, but it's not mutual."

"Love is an automatically mutual thing."

"Then I'm afraid that proves that whatever may be between us is not love. Here is Park View."

"Damn Park View!"

Words are supposed to be a woman's luxury, but it always seems to me that men put a more touching faith in argument than ever women did. I believe the gardener thought that if Park View had been five miles farther on, he might have made a woman of the suffragette.

"And what do you expect me to do now?" he asked pathetically.

"Get busy," advised the suffragette, " somewhere else. Dear little gardener, remember that this road has been trodden before. Being young is a devastating time, anyway. It always comforts me to think that there are crowds before and behind me, and that even a cow has had a delirious calfhood. After all, the past is such a little thing, one can drown it in a drop. And the future is so big."

"That's what I complain of — the size of the future."

"Oh, no, don't. Size is space and space is growth. Good gracious, what a prig I am becoming!"

"For God's sake, come and fill up a little corner of my big future, then. You little thing, I could hold you in my hand . . . And you can hold me with no hand at all, but only with your heart."

"Good-bye."

"But why? Why?"

She was climbing the steep drive. She never looked round. She always looked up.

With excellent intentions the suffragette had, I think, succeeded in killing her heart. She was so heartless that even the hole where her heart should have been was a very shallow one. Some rudimentary emotion turned in her breast as she walked up the drive, and if she could have had the gardener as friend, she would have turned even then and tendered him the friendly mailed fist of the independent woman. But if one is a fanatic, one cannot also be a lover. She suffered from the cold humility that sometimes attacks women. Every morning she occupied three minutes in the thankless task of pinning her hair into a shape conformable with convention's barest requirements, and was then confronted with her own thin short face, white — but not white like a flower as the face of a beloved woman should be; her small eyes, grey —

but not grey like the sea; her straight and drooping hair, made out of the ashes of the flame that burns in real women's hair; her thin pressed lips, her hard set chin, the little defiant wrinkles over her brows ... It was impossible for her to believe that such a thing could be indispensable to any eyes. Her attitude towards the paradox was always sceptical, and the idea that there is nothing a woman can offer as a substitute for such a small gift as herself was beyond her. The little ordinary fiery things of youth had been shorn out of her life, she had been crushed by the responsibility of being a woman and a devotee.

No man would believe that such a woman exists. The pathetic vanity of man would never be convinced that any woman could prefer her own independence to his kisses.

By the time the suffragette had reached the front door of Park View, the interview with the gardener was but a pulse beating at the back of her mind.

Miss Brown, looking as nearly dishevelled as a persistently Real Lady could possibly look, was standing in the hall, ankle-deep in her own prostrate property. Trunks yawned on every side, highly respectable dresses, like limp ghosts of Miss Brown herself, embellished every chair.

"And I haven't even begun on Albert's books yet"

"The more of Albert's books we leave behind the better," replied the suffragette. "I have got him Treasure Island to read on the boat, and he might take that one on Chemistry for Sundays."

"I'm sure I don't know how you manage Albert," said Miss Brown. "I could never even get him to read the Bible. It really looks as if Providence had sent you to us at this crisis."

"Providence would never have chosen a militant suffragette."

"Well, but really one wouldn't notice your opinions," said Miss Brown in an encouraging voice.

"What about Scottie?" asked the suffragette. "Has anybody thought what is going to happen to him?"

"I haven't thought of any details," answered Miss Brown. "The doctor's orders were so sudden, they altogether upset me. I suppose Scottie can be left with John."

"I hope he won't," said the suffragette. "I caught John using Scottie as a target yesterday. He scored two bull's-eyes before I got there."

"I can't think what to do with him. There is nobody but Mr. Wise, and he already has a fierce bulldog. Have you any ideas?"

"Yes, one. I have a sort of friend on the Island. If I left Scottie with him, he would act as a brake in the pursuit, because of the difficulties of quarantine."

"I don't quite follow your meaning," said Miss Brown, not unnaturally. "I didn't know you had a gentleman friend on the Island."

"I haven't. But I'm sure he will be kind to Scottie."

Very late that night, when Courtesy, Mrs. Rust, the gardener, and an unknown young man picked up at the club by the gardener, were playing Bridge in the verandah, a very young boy with a very fat dog appeared, asking for Mr. Gardener. The boy was too well educated to be afraid of duppies. The solid Scottie, too, was felt to be a sound defence against the supernatural.

"What is this?" asked the gardener, who had assumed the melancholy pose of the Rejected One, and had unconsciously acquired a sad sweet smile to correspond. Even on his death-bed the gardener will pose as a dying man.

The young boy put a note into his hand, and dragged Scottie from the shadow where he had modestly seated himself.

"By Jove," said the unknown young man, who happened to be Mr. Wise. "It's Scottie, the Park View dog."

The gardener literally burst the envelope open. The enclosure said: " Dear Gardener — Will you please keep Scottie until I ask you for him again. — Your fairly sincere suffragette."

The note went round the Bridge Table.

"I have always wondered," said Mrs. Rust, "whether politics were really good for women. Now I am sure that they have an unhinging tendency. What does it mean?"

"It means that they are going on an expedition," said Courtesy. " They want the dog looked after for a day or two."

"Why, but Park View is a regular palace in Greyville," said Mr. Wise. " There are three servants in it, all competent to look after Scottie for a day or two."

"I shall have to do what she says," said the gardener. " The suffragette's only fault is that she leaves almost too much to the imagination."

The boy had vanished.

"Better go round and ask for an explanation," said Courtesy.

"He must play out these doubled lilies," said Mrs. Rust.

"It must be nearly twelve," said Mr. Wise. "The cocks have been crowing for an hour."

The Island cock proclaims the night rather than the day. Not even a cock can feel much enthusiasm for such a tyrant as the Trinity Island sun.

"I can't go now," said the gardener.

But next morning at breakfast he said, " I daren't go now" He had hardly slept at all, and looked white. The light of the Seeker had gone out of his eyes, there had been no wish in him for a wild walk in the early sun. He was not even posing. He had been pathetically late for breakfast, and Mrs. Rust and the lady novelist had disappeared to read the English Review and the Lady's Pictorial respectively on the front verandah.

"Why daren't you?" asked the Courtesy.

"Oh, Courtesy — she's beaten me. She's left me without hope."

Courtesy took several mouthfuls of porridge before she replied, " You're young yet, gardener. And she isn't so extra unique, after all. If you like, I'll go round and ask for an explanation of the dog."

"You don't know the way," said the gardener tragically.

It was lucky that Mr. Wise at that moment arrived in his buggy to invite Courtesy and Mrs. Rust (if she wasn't too tired) for a drive. The buggy was a single one, and held two only, so there was a transparency about his motives which did him credit. Courtesy never even passed on the invitation to Mrs. Rust, and the owner of the vehicle failed to repeat

Armed with her inevitable box of sweets, Courtesy set forth on her romance.

"Ripping woods," she said, as the sun winked through the delicate lace of the forest.

"Ripping," agreed Mr. Wise. "But full of ticks."

Courtesy suffered that beautiful shock that attacks a woman when she first realises that the man by her side is an uncommon person, and that he holds the same view about herself. She offered him a chocolate cream.

They went to Park View by the longest way possible, but I think the nearest approach to romance that they reached was when Courtesy said, "Oh, Lor', I am enjoying myself!"

And Mr. Wise replied, " So am I. I hope you'll come again."

When they reached Park View they were neither of them observant enough to notice the forsaken look of the house.

"I'll just go and tackle that funny little suffragette," said Courtesy. "I won't be half a mo.

She looked back and smiled at him as she climbed the drive.

"Dey all gone, missis," said John, who was sitting in the hall, reading the letters out of the waste-paper basket.

"Gone? Where to?"

"Gone to Lunnon Town to see a doctah man, please, missis."

"Union Town, you mean."

"No, please thank you, missis. Gone lars' night to catch a big steamboat."

"How many of them went?"

"Missis Brown, and Mars' Albert, an' de visitor missis'

"Do you know their address? Where are you forwarding their letters to?"

John laughed shrilly at this joke.

"Carn't say, please, missis. Post-missis wouldn't send me de letters, now de fambly gone."

The Island is the home of elusive information.

"What's the matter with the woman, anyway?" said Courtesy, as she remounted the buggy. "I never can understand a woman that doesn't know her vocation."

"What is her vocation?" asked Mr. Wise.

"Ou, I don't know," giggled Courtesy.

"I think all women ought to marry," said Mr. Wise. " Somehow it keeps them softer."

"It wouldn't make a hard woman soft," said Courtesy. " Only all the soft women do marry."

"Do you consider--"

"Ou, Lor', this is a killing conversation!" interrupted the lady. "Let's talk about something else."

"All right. That's a very pretty dress you've got on.

They found the gardener sitting on tenterhooks on the verandah, pulling Scottie's ears.

"What did she say?"

"She didn't. She's gone to London."

"I hope they'll take care of Westminster Abbey," said Mrs. Rust.

The gardener said nothing.

By this time the suffragette was putting romance behind her by means of a little boat limping across a heavy sea. Compared to the Caribbeania, this boat was like my suffragette compared with Mr. Shakespeare's Desdemona. There was rust on the little boat's metal, and her paint still bore memories of London smuts. The purser was occasionally to be seen in his shirt sleeves, and the Captain had a button off his coat.

The priest was on board, returning to his flock, overflowing with material for sermons. By mutual consent he and the suffragette ignored each other. He made an attempt to approach Albert, with his special children's manner, but that cultured youth quickly silenced him. So he occupied himself in trying to save the soul of the second officer, a docile youth, of humble and virtuous tendency.

Within two days the little boat reached the Isthmus which has lately been converted into one of the wonders of the world.

"My poor Albert," said the suffragette. " I'm afraid the doctor says you mustn't go to see the Canal. It's so dusty. And you know such a lot about it, don't you? It is disappointing."

"I dow quite edough about it," replied Albert. "I have do wish whatever to see it. I dow every detail of its codstructiod."

"That's all right, then. The doctor says when it's cool after dark, you may walk as far as the gardens behind the quay, and listen to the band."

"I do dot wish to hear the badd. I wish you ad Ab-Bargaret to go away for the whole day, ad let the youggest stewardess cob ad sit with be. She is a charbig persod, ad it would be very good for you to see the CadaL"

In Albert's eyes the halo of the suffragette was to some extent evaporating. Her attitude towards science alienated him in his capacity as an educated man, although as a child in pain he still clung to her. And she had that morning offended him by buying him a bottle of sweets from the barber's shop.

"I really thigk you sobetibes forget I ab do logger a baby," he observed, and forthwith began to lay great stress on the charm of the youngest stewardess.

Miss Brown was delighted at the fall of her nephew's latest idol.

"You'd better come away," she said. " Let's go and see the Canal. If you stay with Albert when he is displeased, you get on his nerves."

So they landed on the quay of one of the two terrible towns that guard the entrances of the Canal. They paid a great price and manned a train that cost humanity a very great price indeed to create. That train is built of dead men, the embankment on which it runs has largely peopled purgatory, the very sleepers might as well be coffins, yet the train moves with the same callous rhythm as the train from Surbiton to Waterloo. In it you may see the calm inheritors of the fatal past sit upon spread handkerchiefs upon the smutty seats, and stick their tickets in their hats that the passing of the conductor may not disturb their train of thought; and all as if there were no ghosts to keep them company. Only outside the windows you can see the haunted land, white water enveloping a dead forest, ashen trees suffering slow drowning, tall grey birds standing amid floating desolation, and the Canal, a strip of successful tragedy, creeping between its treacherous red banks. The train leaves the Canal for a while, and returns to find it in a different mood. The First Lock is the crown of that great endeavour. I am assured that much more genius has been spent on the Cuts than on the Locks, but to you and me, ignorantly seeking copy, the First Lock triumphantly dominating the weary waterway, seems like the seal of success, as if Man had built this stupendous thing as a barrier between him and failure.

When you see the Lock you feel like an ant seen through the wrong end of a telescope. The suffragette, as she stood on the iron way that goes along the top edge of one of the gates, had to think of all the biggest things she had ever imagined to keep herself from dwindling out of existence. Even Women's Rights grew small in the light of this manmade immensity. She was standing on the highest gate, and she could look across a perspective of three empty cube-worlds, at the white Canal and the white sea beyond it.

"Really," she said, " there is very little to choose between God and Man."

"Good gracious me, what a thing to say!" said Miss Brown, bridling. " God could knock all this down with one stroke.

"He couldn't knock down the spirit that would make man build it up again. Why do we pray to a Creator, if we can ourselves create?"

"I think you had better come out of the sun," said Miss Brown coldly. "I am feeling a little sick myself."

But on their way across the gate back to the white paving that borders the Lock, they found their way blocked by the priest, who was advancing in the opposite direction.

It is impossible for a stout Miss Brown and a stout priest to pass each other on this route. Two suffragettes might have passed, but fortunately for the Isthmus there was only one present.

"I will retire," said the priest. " Place aux dames, yerce, yerce."

"Oh, how good of you!" said Miss Brown, bridling. "I am sorry to put you to such inconvenience."

With a jocular reference or two to goods trains at a shunting station the priest retired from the dilemma. But when they had all reached the safety of the broad paving again he seemed to have shed his desire to cross the gate. He was by himself, which he detested; there were countless morals to be humorously drawn from the Canal, and nobody to point them out to.

"This is a marvel of workmanship, is it not?" he said to Miss Brown, pointedly excluding the suffragette.

Miss Brown agreed, and asked whether he had felt pretty well on the voyage so far. Thus the Canal introduced them, and when the acquaintance was safely formed, Miss Brown strove to introduce the suffragette.

"Yerce, yerce," said the priest hurriedly. " We have met before. An introduction is unnecessary."

Fortunately for the suffragette she saw a dog at a little distance, and hurried to speak to it. The dog is blessedly cosmopolitan. Wherever you may meet him he speaks your home tongue to you, and his eyes are the eyes of a friend in a strange land.

The suffragette and the dog walked along the side of the Lock some twenty yards behind their elders and betters, and the suffragette watched her character falling in shreds between them. Some people like safe hunting, and there is no prey so defenceless as prey that is not there. The priest's conscience had been for some time accumulating reasons why the modest Miss Brown should be warned of the true character of her immodest companion.

The suffragette allowed them half an hour to finish the destruction, and joined them at the train, when the dog reluctantly remembered another engagement.

The party returned to the town in dead silence.

At the station the priest left them, with promises to come and read to Albert. The suffragette and Miss Brown made their way across the gardens to the quay. Under a great palm, Miss Brown stopped tragically, and spoke to her companion for the first time since leaving the Lock.

"I trusted you" she said, rather dramatically, though, of course, she was too ladylike for melodrama. "I gave you my hospitality, I succoured you when you needed help (this was an echo of the priest) , and all the while you deceived me, you took advantage of my kindness."

"Certainly you were all that to me," said the suffragette mildly, " and certainly I am very grateful for all your kindness. But I don't remember deceiving you."

"You are an immoral woman," said Miss Brown, with a great effort, "and you never told me."

"It is hardly expected that I should have told you that. Partly because it would have been silly, and partly because it would have been quite untrue."

"No one could dislike gossip more than I do," said Miss Brown, who loved it. "But a priest is a priest, and this one is such a truly nice man, so goodhearted, never said a word yesterday when the steward upset the soup into his lap. Why did you never tell me that you travelled from England in company with a man who was not your husband?"

Now the suffragette, though she was distrustful of the reasoning of men, seldom failed to see the point of view of a woman, even though that woman was an anti. She specialised in feminism, and in her eyes to be a woman was in itself a good argument.

"Of course I ought to have told you, Miss Brown," she said in a warmer voice than was usual with her. " As a matter of fact it never occurred to me that the thing was worth telling, but that, I admit, is no excuse. I do see that I have been accepting your kindness under false pretences. It is perhaps useless to say I am sorry, and worse than useless to tell you that I would rather die than be married, and that I would rather be hanged than live unmarried with a man. Still I admit I allowed all the fools on the Caribbeania to think I was also such a fool as to be married. I will not bother you again, Miss Brown, I will keep out of your way as much as possible on the boat. It's only a fortnight."

Miss Brown was mollified, and when she spoke again it was like the angel Gabriel sympathising with the difficulties of a beetle. " Of course if you are penitent," she said, " I should like to help you to retrace as far as possible the false step you have taken. I believe there are Homes. . . . But perhaps you had better not come near Albert."

The little boat was indulging in a two days' rest at the Isthmus. It is a problem worthy of the superwoman to avoid a fellow-passenger on a small boat in port. The bearable space on board becomes limited to inches. The side nearest the quay affords nothing but coal-dust to breathe, the other side allows a small percentage of air to dilute the coal-dust There is no scope for choice.

After-dinner, however, Miss Brown settled down to play chess with Albert. Chess with Miss Brown is a most satisfactory game, a crescendo of " Checks " leading to a triumphant " Mate " in a delightfully short time.

So the suffragette went on shore to listen to the band.

The Isthmus band is as gaudy in attire as it is sombre in complexion, and it plays to a stratum of society as striking to the eye as any in the world. The Isthmus is the centre of nigger fashion. Here, under the glare and the flare of a hot night in the season, you may see the effect of a layer of civilisation on an aboriginal worship of colour. Crimson, gold, and silver are the prevailing motifs. As to the coiffure of the ladies, for every plait to be found on a Trinity Island head there are half a dozen on the Isthmus. There is something uniquely wicked in the appearance of rouge and powder on a mahogany ground. The look of vice which the Parisian or London lady strives to attain by means of a shopful of cosmetics can be acquired by the lady-nigger with one dab of the flour-dredger. Once more I pause to ask when we may expect the decree that we must further conceal our incurable virtue by means of a complexion dyed copper colour.

There was a moon, and there were stars standing aloof in the sky; and there were many lights about the garden. There were shrill brass voices everywhere, and the band was playing that tune of resigned sentimentality, "My Old Kentucky Home."

The suffragette felt slightly drunk. She had had a day of emotions, and it was an unusual and intoxicating experience for her to find her emotions escaping from the iron bound cask in which she kept them. She felt totally irresponsible, and when the priest came along, looking as conceited as the moon, and as sentimentally benign as the stars, she discovered a lunatic longing to tear the hat from his head and stamp upon it, to make him look a fool, to prick his pride; not because of any personal enmity — or so she thought — but because he seemed eternally on the side of sanity and of yesterday, and barred the path of young and mad modernity. She approached him.

The priest suddenly perceived in front of him a soul dangerously in need of salvation.

"My dear young lady, I have been seeking an opportunity for a quiet chat with you, yerce, yerce. Whatever you may think of me, I assure you that I am not the hard and inhuman man you think me. I should be only too thankful to be of service to you. Let us sit on that quiet seat, away from the crowd."

"It is good of you to risk contamination," said the suffragette.

"My calling leads me among the publicans and sinners," said the priest. " It is not my business to divide the sheep from the goats."

"Not your business, but your pleasure" suggested the suffragette'

The priest stiffened.

"I wish you had not hardened your heart against my help" he said " Believe me, I have every sympathy with a young and unprotected woman in your position. I think sometimes life seems hard on the weaker sex, yerce, yerce."

"It is a great honour to be a woman," said the suffragette. " Your God certainly turns his back on the individual, but he is very just to the mass. The day of women is just dawning."

"There may be something in what you say," observed the priest, feeling that she was somehow erasing all that he had meant to say. "I am sure we shall all be glad to see Woman come into her own. But . . ."

"Men may possess the past, but women have the future," continued the suffragette, who was certainly very much excited. " We have suddenly found what you have lost — the courage of our convictions. The art of being a fanatic seems to me to be the pivot of progress; but men have lost, and women have caught that blessed disease."

"I do not see how all this applies to the matter in hand," said the priest. " Unless you are trying to convey to me, by way of an excuse, the craving which I am told possesses most women of your persuasion — the craving for fame, the morbid wish to be talked about."

" I did not hope to convey anything at all to you. And certainly not fame, for there is no such thing. I have seen pigeons sitting on the heads of statues of great men in London, and I have seen little critics sitting on their fame. This is a world of isolated people, and there can be no fame where there is no mutual understanding."

"You are oddly pessimistic, and you are also wilfully evading the point. When I saw you just now, I hoped that you had repented of your sin and needed my help."

"I have committed no sin that would appeal to you," said the suffragette. "But that is, of course, beside the point. What you want is that I should repent of being myself, and become a sort of inferior female you."

"Indeed you have come to hasty and mistaken conclusions about my intentions," said the priest, whose principal virtue was perseverance. " Regarding your political opinions, I have every sympathy with your cause, though none for your methods. There is something so very coarse about militancy."

"Have you ever tried denying a creature the food it needs? I think you would find that even a white mouse would be coarse if you starved it."

"You may be right. My sister is a member of the Church League for Women's Suffrage. Perhaps you also belong to that sisterhood?"

"No," she answered. "I belong to the Shrieking Sisterhood."

"It seems useless for me to try and help you in this mood," sighed the priest. "I can only pray that I may be shown the way to your heart . . . "

"I have none," she said.

In a garden not five hundred miles away from the garden in which she sat was the Fact which she had Forgotten, set in a silver light among the silver trees. The gardener stood among the pale grape-fruit trees, with his head back in his usual conceited way, with his hands in his pockets and his feet in the wet grass.

"This is nonsense," he thought

"She is only half human."

"Love for a thing only half human is only half love."

"You can't build a world out of words, as she tries to do."

"In a thing like love, there is fact and there is theory. Theory is only falsehood disguised as fact."

"She is not a bit pretty."

"I believe she would rather make an enemy than make a friend."

"Something has gone wrong with the woman of to-day. She has left the man behind, but she has not gone forward."

"What have I been about to allow such a woman to disturb me? I came to this island a king, and I have made myself a slave."

"It is youth that has burnt me. I am done with youth. It is fine to have reached age in theory, and yet in practice still to have one's life ahead. My youth has been a fire in my path, and she has stamped it out."

The moon explored the spangled sky. The fireless interwove with the pale purring noises of the night. The mad still shadows of the palms blotted the grass.

The gardener went into the verandah firmly posed as He Who has Passed through Fire, and has emerged, cured of the silly disease of youth, into a pale silver light.

For the gardener made his theories, while the suffragette's theories made her.

The gardener was awakened next morning by the loud noise of Scottie chasing lizards across the room. Scottie was a bristly Northerner, and never became really used to the conditions of tropical life. To this day he labours under the delusion that lizards are only bald or naked mice, that have deceitfully changed their smell and their taste.

The gardener thought that he awoke perfectly light-hearted. He did not recognise the curious thing that throbbed in the back of his consciousness as his heart.

He whistled in his bath. He whistled as he came out on to the verandah for breakfast.

Courtesy had risen for early breakfast by mistake.

"Stopped brooding?" she asked. " Brave boy."

"Two and two is such a poor formation after all," said the gardener. "One and one is much more comfortable."

Courtesy giggled. " There are times," she said, " when two and two is ripping. Mr. Wise is coming up to lunch."

" He came up to lunch yesterday. And he's coming up to tea to-morrow."

"Yesterday and to-morrow are not to-day," said Courtesy, that practical girl

The gardener had not time to ponder, for Mrs. Rust then appeared. Her complexion was even more of a contrast to her hair than usual.

"I had a letter last night," she said. "I didn't tell you at once, because it's such a vulgar habit to blurt out news. I don't know whether I have mentioned my son Samuel to you?"

"You have," said Courtesy.

"So have I," added the gardener.

"His house has played him false — I knew it would. One of the ceilings gave way — on to Samuel. Him and his house — he always was a fool. I believe he thought the Almighty built his house for him."

"Yes, but what happened to Samuel?"

"I told you — the ceiling fell on him."

"Yes, but what is the result?"

"Oh, the rest of the house is still standing. It was only one of the ceilings. He put the billiard table upstairs, and probably had his rafters made of bamboo."

" Yes, but I mean what was the result as far as Samuel was concerned?"

"He was concussion. There have been one or two people staying in the house since he started the atrocious practice of advertising, and they had him taken to a hospital. My letter is from the matron."

"Poor Mrs. Rust," said Courtesy, " you must be terribly worried. I suppose you'll be wantin' to get home by the next boat."

"Stuff and nonsense," snapped the mother. "Haven't you noticed by now that I have iron nerves. Next boat — indeed."

"But I should have thought " began Courtesy, and the gardener kicked her under the table.

"There is only one perfectly obvious thing to do," said the gardener, "and that is wait till the next mail, a fortnight hence. Knowing Mrs. Rust as I do, Courtesy, I am sure she will follow this obvious course."

"Obvious course — indeed," said Mrs. Rust, much relieved. " Stuff and nonsense. I shall do exactly as I please, whether it's obvious or not. Suppose I decide to go home by Wednesday's boat, what then, young man?"

The gardener shook his head. "You won't, I know," he said. "You are too reasonable."

"Reason be blowed," said Mrs. Rust with spirit.

"You don't know me very well, young man, if you think I'm like all the other old cats, to be persuaded by that sort of argument."

The gardener was now an expert at saving Mrs. Rust from herself. Although she entangled herself habitually in contradictions, her real mind was not subtle enough to be well hidden, and to guide her action into the path of her desire was a matter that only required a little delicacy. The gardener, being a gardener, was always ready with tactful guidance and unseen support in such matters. In this case, he would have been surprised if you had told him that his secret desire pointed the same way as Mrs. Rust's. He thought he had killed desire. But he was tired of the Island, and he had by that mail received a quarterly instalment of his income.

"Courtesy," said Mrs. Rust, "we sail for home next Wednesday. Unreasonable — indeed. And none the worse for that."

"We have engaged the car for a week from Friday," said Courtesy. " Mr. Wise is lunching with us on Thursday. And the hotel insists on a week's notice."

"I am paying you two hundred a year," said Mrs. Rust brutally, " to save me from these vulgar details."

"Oh, Lor'," said Courtesy.

"But what about Scottie?" asked the gardener.

"Scottie's your affair, not mine. I'm not paying you £200 a year to follow me about."

The gardener is a very difficult person to snub.

"Scottie and I are coming gratis."

And Mrs. Rust said, "Good."

"But the little boat, with the suffragette on board of her, fled across the Atlantic, as if aware of the projected pursuit of the great mail steamer.

The suffragette, a morose unit on a desert island of her own making, stood separated from the world by a gulf of gossip. She used to sit on the poop, where nobody else would sit, with the wind in her hair and the sun in her eyes, building theories.

There are some people who can never see a little cloud of fantasy float across the horizon of their dreams without building a heavy castle in the air upon it, and bringing it to earth. Whenever the suffragette thought of the gardener, she broke the thought with a theory. It is sad to be burdened with a brain that must always track illusion to disillusionment. She had one consolation, one persistent and glorious contradiction, one shining truth in a welter of self-questioning: — " I'm alone — I'm alone — - I'm alone. . ."

It was not until they had passed the Azores that a voice from the outer world spoke to her. They had reached those islands late one moonlit night.

The little square houses, climbing up the hill-side hi orderly ranks, looked like silver bricks in a castle of dreams. There was a white fringe of breaking waves threaded between the black sea and the black land. From the boats that hurried between the shore and the steamer, little lamps swung and thin voices cut the darkness. Thundering silence seemed to invade the emptiness left by the ceasing of the propeller. The ceaseless loom that always sang behind the turmoil of the suffragette's consciousness spun the moon into a quiet melody. The still lap of the sea against the ship's stern struck the ear like a word never spoken before. You could hear the gods creating new things. You could hear the tread of the stars across the sky.

"I am sorry to disturb you," said Miss Brown; "It's Albert I knew something would come of his going to the fancy-dress dance as Galileo, with such a thin tunic on; but he is so wilful. And now he has a high temperature, and a worse pain in his side than ever. He is crying for you."

It was a strange sensation for the suffragette, after all these days of loneliness, to be cried for. Tears, like all things that belong to women, appealed to her beyond words.

She found Albert beating on the wall of his cabin. When he cried — it hurt. When he breathed — it hurt. When he moved — it hurt. And yet he had to cry and pant and struggle. There was something in the suffragette's plain and ordinary face that acted as an antidote to Albert's hectic personality. She was a poor nurse; her only experience of the sickroom had been from her own sickbed. But she had a cold hand, an imagination which she only allowed to escape at a crisis, and nerves very difficult to excite. All that night, while the ship climbed the steep seas of the Bay, she and the doctor kept something that was very big from invading the little cabin. The battle was, of course, a losing one. There is something almost funny in the futility of fighting Heaven on an issue like this.

I said there should be no death-bed scenes in this book, so I will only add that after much battling Albeit managed at last to get to sleep, and he died before he woke.

The suffragette was there, but she was not needed. She went away and cried because no one would ever cry for her again.

She marconied for Miss Brown's brother to meet the bereaved aunt at Southampton. And when the boat reached home, she carried her mustard-coloured portmanteau up the gangway, and, by disappearing, closed the incident.

In this wonderful age we do our disappearing by machinery. Fairy godmothers prefer Rolls-Royce cars to broomsticks, the pirate employs a submarine instead of a gallant three-decker, the black sheep of the piece, instead of donning a mask and confining the rest of his career to

Maidenhead Thicket, books his passage to a Transatlantic sheepfold on a thirty-knot liner.

The suffragette disappeared by the London train.

By travelling third, she hoped to escape the majority of her fellow-passengers, and it was not until the train began to leave the station that she identified a hitherto unnoticed person opposite to her as the priest.

The priest was always overcome by a feeling of virtue when he travelled third.

"So our modesty is mutual," he said jovially to the suffragette. " Yerce, yerce, in England I travel third on principle. My parish, you know, is in a poor part of London, and I think a shepherd should as far as possible share the circumstances of his flock"

The suffragette hovered for a moment over a very crude flower of repartee dealing with cattle-trucks, but discarded the idea. She was always cautious, when she allowed herself time for caution. Her principle in conversation was, "When in doubt — don't." But being a militant suffragette, she was seldom in doubt.

The priest was aggrieved with the suffragette, partly because he felt obliged to speak to her. He would have preferred to ignore her, but she had behaved too well during the last few days. She had tried as hard to save a life as ever he had tried to save a soul, and had failed with equal dignity. Inconsistency annoyed him very much. You must be one of two things, a sheep or a goat, preferably the latter until the priest himself had had time to lead you to the fold. For a confessed goat suddenly to don wool without any help from him looked very much like deliberate prevarication. He did not now know how to classify the suffragette, and not knowing how to do a thing in which he had specialised was naturally exasperating.

"You were asking for my advice about the problem of your future," he said, leaning confidentially towards her. "I have been thinking much about you, and I believe I have solved the problem."

I need hardly say that the suffragette never asked for advice. When circumstances obliged her to follow the advisable course, she hid her docility like a sin.

"My future always looks after itself, thank you," she said in a polite voice, " and so does my past. It's old enough."

The priest stiffened for a moment, but when on the track of a goat he was hard to check. Besides, the suffragette's voice was so low and calm that her words seemed like a mistake, not to be taken seriously.

"My idea is that you should join in the glorious campaign against poverty and sin in the slums," he continued. "I assure you that peace lies that way. My sister once had a love affair with a freethinker; she lost a great deal of weight at the time, and became almost hysterical. But she followed my advice, and now runs several social clubs in connection with my Church in the Brown Borough, North London, where the poor may buy cocoa and cake and listen to discourses by earnest Christian workers."

"And what does she weigh now?" asked the suffragette, after a pause.

"She is a splendid example of a Christian woman," said the priest, " a woman of unwavering faith, indefatigable in charitable works."

"I think I shall come down to your parish as an antidote," said the suffragette, "the only sort of And I ever could tolerate."

Certainly my suffragette is not worthy to be the heroine of a book. I must apologise for presenting a nature so undiluted by any of the qualities that go to make good fiction. A pun, I admit, is the last straw, but it is unfortunately a straw occasionally clutched at by erring humanity, though rarely admitted by the novelist.

"I should not advise you to choose the Brown Borough for the scene of your endeavour," said the priest hurriedly. " There is little scope for workers unconnected with a church there. I had in my mind for you the neighbourhood of Southwark, or Walworth, South London. Much more suitable, yerce, yerce. The Brown Borough is very unhealthy for those unaccustomed to London slums."

"Yet your sister gained weight and lost hysteria there," said the suffragette maliciously. "I myself might be said to have room for improvement on both these points."

"I strongly advise you to choose another parish," said the priest, bitterly repenting of his zeal. " So much excellent work has been done in the Brown

Borough that the majority of the people ought by now to be on the way to find salvation, both in body and soul."

"That's why I propose to come as an antidote" said the suffragette.

The conversation closed itself. They opened the Spectator and Votes for Women simultaneously.

London provided the sort of weather it reserves for those who return from sun-blessed lands. It was a day with rain in the past and rain in the future, but never rain in the present. The sort of day that makes you feel glad you thought of bringing your umbrella, and then sorry to find you left it in the last bus. The streets looked like wet slates splashed with tears.

The suffragette kept a lonely flat not far from Covent Garden, apparently with the object of ensuring herself the right to exercise a vote when she should have procured that luxury. For she very seldom put the flat to the ordinary uses of flats. It contained a table and two chairs, as a provision against the unlikely event of its owner's succumbing to social weaknesses. It also contained a bed. Curtains and carpets, and any cooking arrangement more elaborate than a gas-ring, are not included in the Theory of the Hair Shirt, the motto of which is, " I can very well do without."

The suffragette deposited the mustard-coloured portmanteau at this Spartan abode, and went to report herself to her Society. She was not a famous suffragette. If I told you her name, you would not raise your eyebrows and laugh facetiously and say, "Oh — that maniac . . ." She was nominally one of the rank and file, although, being rebellious even against co-rebels, she seldom acted under orders.

There are, broadly speaking, two kinds of workers in the world, the people who do all the work, and the people who think they do all the work. The latter class is generally the busiest, the former never has time to be busy.

The Chief Militant Suffragette, who believed that she held feminism in the hollow of her hand, was a born leader of women. She was familiar with the knack of wringing sacrifices from other people. She was a little lady in a minor key, pale and plaintive, with short hair, like spun sand. She dressed as nearly as possible like a man, and affected an eyeglass. She probably thought that in doing this she sacrificed enough for the cause of women. She had safely found a husband before she cut her hair. I suppose she had sent more women to prison than any one magistrate in London, but she had never been to prison herself.

The cause of the Suffrage, while attracting the finest women in the country, also attracts those who consider themselves to be the finest. It has an equal fascination for those who can work but can never lead and for those who can lead but never work.

"I have written to you three times," said the Chief M.S. pathetically to the suffragette. "I do think you might have answered."

"So do I," admitted the suffragette, "only that I have been abroad. What did you write to me about?"

"Abroad?" said the Chief M.S., and raised her eyebrows. She had none really, but she raised the place where they should have been. "Abroad? Enjoying yourself at such a time as this?"

"What do you mean?" asked the suffragette. "What has happened? Have we got the Vote?"

The eyeglass of the Chief M.S. fell out with annoyance. " Of course not," she said, "But it's the great massed procession and deputation tomorrow, and I wanted you to help with the North London section."

The suffragette loathed processions. She loathed working or walking with a herd. She would rather have blown up Westminster Abbey than stewarded at a meeting. A less honest woman would have flattered herself that these are the signs of a great and lonely mind, but the suffragette knew them as the signs of vanity. And to cure vanity is, of course, the business of a hair shirt.

"When have I got to be there? And where?" she asked.

In the eyes of the Chief M.S. punctuality in other people was the ideal virtue. The moment she named to her assistants was always an hour before the correct time, and two hours before the one she chose for her own appearance.

The suffragette had long been a servant of the Society. By an instinctive calculation she managed to arrive at Little South Lane next day punctually at the moment when help began to be needed. She collected some of the native enthusiasts who were adding fuel to their ardour on the door-steps of neighbouring public-houses. She quelled the political antagonism of a bevy of little boys who were vocally competing with a Great Woman's preliminary address. She soothed the objections of the paid banner-bearers, who had not been led to expect the additional opposition of a high wind. She eliminated from the procession as far as possible all suffragists below the age of four. She lent a moment's friendly attention to the reasons why Woman's Sphere is the Home, expounded by a hoarse spinster from an upper window. She courageously approached an enormous dock-hand, who had snatched a banner from its rightful bearer, and was waving it with many oaths.

"Might I trouble you for that banner?" said the suffragette.

The gentleman's reply was simple but obscene.

"Might I trouble you at once to move out of my way, and let the procession join up?" said the suffragette in a red voice.

"Gaw-love yer, me gal, I'm comin' along," said the gentleman. " Wot price me for a ... suffragette? You'll need a few fists, if you git as fur as the Delta way."

How very rare it is to mistake the staff for the broken reed. The suffragette recovered herself quickly.

"I beg your pardon," she said. "I ought to have known from your face that you were a sensible man. How good of you to carry a banner!"

The procession, like a snake, reared its head and moved. In the van a marching song was begun, in the rear — a ragtime. The police, looking dignified, but feeling silly, marched in single file on either flank, and kept an eye on the interests of the traffic. The one mounted policeman obviously regretted the prominence of his position, his horse was an anti, and showed a man-like tendency to argue with its hoofs.

The suffragette walked between a little woman in a plush coat with a baby and a person who might have been a poetess, or a philosopher, or a Low Church missionary, but was certainly very earnest. The long brown streets swung by. The flares on the coster's barrows anchored to the kerb, danced in the yellow air. A hum of barbaric voices, and the large firm pulse of many feet marching, made a background to the few clear curses and the fewer clearer blessings from the pavement.

"I wish to Gawd my kiddie 'ed been a gel," said the little mother beside the suffragette. " Bein' a woman — mikes yer proud-like. . . ."

The suffragette put her chin up and laughed. " As a man, your kiddie'll make you proud. There's sure to be something splendid about a man whose mother was proud to be a woman."

" Men . . ." said the little mother, with more alliteration than refinement "are . . . brute beasts,"

"'Ere, draw it mild," said the dock-hand, who was just in front.

" There's men, wytin' for us, somewhere down the Delta wy now, Wytin' to mike us yell an' run, wytin' to 'urt us — jus' becos we was proud to be women."

" Waiting for us? " gasped the poetess. " Why — how dreadful ... I wasn't told there would be any fighting."

"You might have known there would be," said the suffragette. "You can't assert facts without fighting for them."

The poetess, obviously wishing she had left such dangerous weapons as facts to themselves, gave a hoarse giggle, and said, " I declare, I'm quite frightened..."

"It is frightening" agreed the suffragette. " Not the bruises, but the stone-wallness of men. I'm always frightened by opposition that I can't see through at all. I am frightened of Delta Street hooligans. I am also frightened in exactly the same way by a polite enemy. You go into the law courts, for instance, and watch those men wearing their wigs like haloes and their robes like saints' armour "

"You do talk nice, miss," said the little mother.

"I wish you'd come down to the Brown Borough, an' jaw my young man."

The suffragette, though a trifle damped, continued, " It isn't that their arguments are strong, nobody minds that, but it's that they don't bother to have any arguments. Just like the hooligans, only in different words.

It's no more an argument than it is one between God and Satan. One side is established, the other doesn't exist. It makes you see that tomorrow is never strong enough to fight to-day. It would take an angel to admit tomorrow as a fact at all, and unfortunately it's men we're up against."

"Then what's the good of all this?" asked the poetess, who was naturally becoming more and more depressed.

"Oh, a losing battle's fine," said the suffragette. " I'd rather wear a black eye than a wig, or a crown, any day."

"'Ear, 'ear," said the dock-hand.

"Wiv Parliament, for instance," said the little mother, who was evidently accustomed to fill her sphere with her voice. " They sits an' argoos about Welsh Establishment, an' all the while I 'ed my little gel die of underfeeding, becos I wuz carryin' this one, and couldn't get work."

"Thet's all very well," said the dock-hand; "But wot do you expec'? You carn't expec' the lawyers to frow up their wig an' say the Law's a Liar. (Not but wot it ain't.) You carn't expec' the Prime Minister to tell 'isself l There's Mrs. Smiff's biby dyin', I mus' go dahn an' see abaht it.' (Not but wot it ain't 'ard.")

"There are lots of things you can't kill," said the suffragette. " But you can always try. Men don't try, because impossibility is one of the things they believe in."

"You carn't kill Votes fer Women," shouted the little mother, with a burst of enthusiasm. She waved her baby instead of a banner.

At that moment a yelling horror dropped like a bomb upon the level street. The suffragette saw the mounted policeman, complete with his horse, fall sideways, like a toy. She saw a chequered crowd of perspiring faces come upon her like a breaking wave. She saw the banners ahead stagger like flowers before a wind. She saw the poetess fall, and some one stamp on her shoulder. She saw a man with a fiercecoloured handkerchief knotted round his throat seize the little mother's chin and wrench it up and down, as he cursed in her face. The suffragette, who never could be angry in a dignified way, gave a hoarse croak and snatched his arm. Possibly she felt like the child Hercules during his interview with the serpents, but she did not look like that at all. The man jerked his arm up, the suffragette's seven stone went up too. She was waved like a flag.

The tears were shaken out of her eyes. Her feet kicked the air. And then she alighted against a wall. She saw a chinless and unshaven face heave into her upper vision, and a great hand, like black lightning, cleft the fog. The knuckles of the hand cut like a blunt knife. In North London we always repeat our arguments, when we consider them good ones. The suffragette, who was a person of no muscular ability at all, gave up hoping for the chance of a retort in kind, after the third repetition. So the argument went on undisputed, until the dock-hand perceived it, when it was successfully overborne.

The suffragette picked up her hat. She hated it because it looked so dirty. She hated her heart because it felt so sick. She picked up the poetess and hated her because she was crying. She was crying herself, but she thought she looked courageously wrathful.

"What do we do now?" sobbed the poetess.

"We walk on," said the suffragette, and took her, not very gently, by the arm.

"But I can't, I can't. It may happen again," wailed the poetess. " Policeman, can't I go home?"

"Yes, miss," said the policeman, wiping his brow.

"But there are no taxis."

"No, miss," said the policeman.

You never can tell what strange thing you may do at a crisis. The poetess slipped a confiding hand into that of the policeman, and walked meekly by his side.

"Murderers . . ." exclaimed the little mother. " They might 'ev done biby in. Your 'ead's bleedin', miss. So's my gum, but I kin swaller that."

The suffragette felt as if she had been divided in two. Her militant spirit, clothed in its hair shirt, seemed to be moving at a height, undaunted, monopolised as usual by the splendour of its cause. And below, very near the dust, a terribly tired woman, a unit among several hundreds of other terribly tired women, put one foot before the other along an endless road.

You must stride over a gap here, as the procession did mentally. For a very long time I don't think anybody thought anything except — "How long, O Lord, how long?"

When I am very tired and see the high and friendly smile of St. Paul's curved across the sky, I feel as if I am near home. I always think St. Paul's is like a mother to all London, while Westminster Abbey is like a nun, the bride of heaven, with an infinite scorn of you and me. St. Paul's stands at the top of the hill of difficulty, and after that your feet walk by themselves down Ludgate Hill.

There was a burst of song from all parts of the procession as it passed that friendly doomed milestone. The burst was simultaneous, but the song was too various to be really effective.

"Votes for Women," shouted the little mother. "I sy, miss, when are you comin' dahn to the Brown Borough to 'elp wiv votes for women? We ain't got nobody there as kin talk like you."

"Am I coming down?" asked the suffragette, who had a vague idea that she had said many things, now forgotten. "I never speak at meetings now. My brain is always wanting to say the next thing but one, and my tongue is always saying the thing before last.

»"There's too much to be said about Votes for Women."

"Meetin's . . ." said the little mother in a voice of scorn. " Tain't meetin's we want. It's somebody jus' to talk ornery, as if they was a friend-like. Somebody to live up the street — if you unnerstan' me — an' drop in, an' be interested. When my little gel died, lars' October, an' 'ole lot of lidies made enquiries, an' got me a few 'alfpence a week to git on wiv till I could get back to the box-miking. I useter 'ave to go to an orfice an' answer questions, an' the lidy useter sy she was sorry to seem 'quisitive, but she ses — If some on yer cheat, you mus' all on yer suffer. . . . Bless you, I didn' mind answering questions, but I was very low then, an' I useter tike it 'ard that none o' them lidies never seemed interested. Nobody never as't wot was the nime o' my little gel that died, nor 'ow old she was, nor nothink about 'er pretty wys that she useter 'ave. . . . 'Tisn't that they ain't kind, but it's being treated in a crowd-like as comes 'ard, an' there's many feels the sime. . . ."

"What do you expect?" asked the poetess, who was now detached from the policeman. "I am myself a C.O.S. secretary, so I know something about it. None of us have time to do more than is really necessary. And when there's public money in question — well, it's all very well, but one can't be too careful."

"When there's money in question you may be right, miss," said the little mother. "But it ain't alius a question of money, an' It seems to me as 'ow, wiv votes fer women, if some on them suffragettes 'ud stop talking about women's wiges at meetings, an' come an' look at wiges at 'ome, they'd 'it a lot of women wot thinks now as 'ow votes for women is only a public thing an' don't matter outside Trafalgar Square. It seems to 'it you 'arder if a person's friendly than if they're heloquent. . ."

"Something is happening in front," said the poetess, looking wildly round for her policeman.

"The police have turned on us," said the suffragette. " They always do in the Strand. Downing Street gets nervous when we get as near as this."

It was too true. The police, relieved to be at last freed from the burden of their false position, were characteristic of their profession.

"But I was told I was to walk to the Houses of Parliament," said the poetess, finding her quondam protector's hand on her shoulder.

"You may walk to Jericho, miss," replied the policeman with a wit as heavy as his hand. " Only not more than three in a group, if you please."

A great crowd of little groups trickled on to the Embankment and followed the tide of the river towards Westminster. There was a moon. I think the moon is really the heroine of this unheroic book. Half the blessing of London belongs to the river, and half the blessing of the river belongs to the moon. Do you know how beautifully a full moon bends out of her sky to trail her fingers in the river?

Do you know how faerily she shoots shavings of her silver under the bridges, and how she makes tender the blackness of the barges and the shadows of the little wharves? I always think the moon has in her quiver of charms a special shaft for the river of London. She never smiles like that elsewhere.

It was no surprise to Westminster to see the deputation and procession arrive, albeit in a less neat form than that in which it started. The police force has moments of wonderful insight into the psychology of law-breakers, and in this case it seemed aware that a procession of women disbanded and told to go home in the Strand is nevertheless likely to appear sooner or later in Parliament Square. The great space resounded to the tramp of the feet of the law. A detachment of mounted police strove to look unconcerned in the Whitehall direction. I always think it is unjust to drag dumb animals into these political questions. I wonder the S.P.C.A. doesn't step in. Imagine the feelings of a grey mare, for instance, on being called upon to charge into the ranks of a female deputation to Downing Street.

Neither the suffragette nor I are familiar with the great ways of deputations. We are of the humble ranks which suffer physical bufferings in the shadow of St. Stephen's, while our superiors suffer moral bufferings in the shadow of the English Constitution. There is very little sport in being a shuttlecock anyway, but while the head gets the straight hit, the feathers feel most the stress of adverse winds. The object of the police in a crowd is to keep it moving. The direction in which it is to move is never explained to it Whether you move to the right or the left you are sure to be wrong in the eyes of the law. If you weigh seven stone, your tendency is to move either upwards or downwards. Correctly speaking, the suffragette never set foot in Parliament Square for some time after she arrived there. She was caught in a gust of crowd, and borne in an unexpected direction. She did not mind which way she went, but she was human enough to mind whether her ribs got broken. Even in a good cause, matters like these touch you personally. The shoulders of partisans and martyrs, packed closely against your ribs, feel just as hard as the shoulders of the less enlightened. The suffragette began to feel a cold whiteness creeping up from her boots to her heart. She began to take a series of last looks at the moon and the spires of the Abbey. She reached the earth just when she had decided that she had reached the door-step of Heaven, and found herself cast by an eddy into a tiny peace. There, in an alcove, was the Chief M.S., protected by a stout husband. The Chief M.S., whose hair was too short to have been dragged down, and whose eyeglass was trembling on her breast with pleasurable excitement, was looking cool and peaceful.

"You do look a wreck," she said brightly to the suffragette. "I have been wanting to talk to you about something I want you to do for me."

This was such a frequent remark on the lips of the Chief M.S. that, as a rule, it made no impression on her followers and acquaintances. But the suffragette was incredibly tired, and the power of kicking against pricks was taken from her. She had no spirit in her except the ghost of her hair shirt theory, that fiend which croaks — "Go on, go on. . . ." She made a great effort. She pulled her hat down on her head, she put her chin up, she wrapped her cloak of endurance more closely round her. " Talk on," she said.

"Oh, not now, child," said the Chief M.S. " Come and see me next Wednesday. I shall be away for a long week-end after this."

It seemed like making an appointment for a hundred years hence. The suffragette agreed, because it seemed impossible that she could live so long as next Wednesday.

At that moment the mounted police charged. The careful husband of the Chief M.S. whisked her away. The forelegs of a horse entered the suffragette's alcove. The safest place in a police charge is under the noses of the horses. These animals, usually anxious to preserve neutrality, have mastered the art of playing upon the fleeing backs of agitators as gently as the pianist plays upon the keys. I have had a horse's hoofs fanning my shoulder-blades for minutes on end, and yet only suffered from the elbows of my fellow-fugitives.

The suffragette, alone on the strip of pavement between the rearing horses and the recoiling crowd, conceived the sensational idea of charging the chargers. This is the sort of idea that comes to one after a five-hour march and a series of street fights. I have never been drunk with liquor, but I know what it is to be drunk all the same. The suffragette determined that those horses should never see her coattails. She heard a voice shouting, "Women . . . women . . . women . . ." and on finding it was her own, added, " Don't run back — run forward." And she flung herself on the breast of the nearest horse.

A foot-policeman caught her on the rebound. She was not in the least hurt, but he picked her up and carried her across his shoulder. She hit her fists against his helmet; it sounded like a drum. It seems hard to believe, but I assure you that even on that high though humble perch, she was revelling in the thought that it concerned nobody but herself that she was going to prison.

My poor heroine, I am afraid, has stepped beyond the limits of your toleration, but if you look, you will find I never asked you to admire her.

The policeman lowered her, and stood her like a doll on the steps of the Metropolitan Railway. That excellent institution, shocked at the doings outside, had drawn its grill modestly across its entrance, and its employes, like good lions at the Zoo watching the rampant behaviour of the public, were gazing through the bars.

"You're not the right size for this job, young woman," said the policeman.

The suffragette's reply was a further struggle. The policeman held both her arms.

"You go 'ome," he said. " The deputation's goin' 'ome now, like a good gel. What's your station?"

A terrible exhaustion drooped like a weight released upon the suffragette. The only retort that came to her mind was, " Leicester Square, please."

"Change at the Embankment," said a railway official, and opened eighteen inches of the gate. The policeman pushed her in. She took her ticket, and went home as meekly as any Anti.

You may be surprised to hear that the suffragette spent the next day in bed. A day in bed is not, of course, part of the Hair Shirt Theory, but this was a Sunday, and Sunday is a day of weakness, though it seems politer to the Old Testament to call it a day of relaxation. The suffragette always spent Sunday as she liked, with the hair shirt doffed and neatly folded on a chair beside her. She smoked as many cigarettes as she pleased, instead of the strict two of ordinary life, she occasionally ate as many as three large meals, she had been known to invest in nougat. Sundays were the oases in her desert, and if the gardener had chanced on one for the scene of one of his luckless spasms, this story might have been much prettier. It is very tiring to be yourself with such ardour as the suffragette employed, and to be somebody else for twenty-four hours once a week almost a necessity'

Besides, she had court plaster on her forehead, and the publicly court-plastered pose was one that the suffragette loathed.

If the Chief M.S. had had the luck to catch a painless black eye in the Cause of the Vote, she would have flaunted it like a flag up and down Piccadilly. But the husband had been almost too effective. She had not even broken her eyeglass.

One of the most striking differences between the suffragette and the gardener was that the gardener told himself: " When I die, they will be sorry, and they will perhaps understand." But the suffragette thought: "When I die, nobody except the charwoman will know."

The suffragette went to see the Chief M.S. on Wednesday.

"How curious you should come this afternoon," said the Chief M.S. " Some one was here asking for you only this morning."

The suffragette hardly ever explained herself. She did not remind the Chief M.S. that she was there by appointment. Nor did she ask who had been inquiring for her. Perhaps she knew.

"He asked for your address," said the Chief M. S. "But as he was a man, I didn't give it to him. He didn't leave his name, but he asked me to tell you that your dog was now in the hands of the quarantine officials. I attacked him on the suffrage question, as I always do strange men."

"What did he say?"

"He had nothing to say. I pointed out to him how ludicrous was the argument that just because a person wore two tubes on his legs instead of one, he was competent to rule."

"I have never heard that argument used," said the suffragette soberly. "I didn't know that even men--"

"Why, you're as dense as he was," snapped the Chief M.S. "Of course they don't put it like that. He asked me which M.P. was responsible for the tubular argument. I saw it was no use going on. He left his address for me to give you."

"What was it you wanted to see me about?" asked the suffragette.

"Did I want — Oh, yes . . . Well, I have been thinking you have done nothing for the Cause lately, have you?"

The suffragette fingered a sore dint under the shadow of her hat "Hardly anything," she admitted.

"I think the slum districts want working up," said the Chief M.S. "Somebody who walked behind you in the procession said you hobnobbed wonderfully with the North London women. How would it be if you were to undertake a series of informal meetings—"

" It isn't meetings they want, they told me so themselves," said the suffragette.

"It's meetings everybody wants," retorted the Chief M.S. "I thought also that you might start a soup kitchen or a turkey club, or one of those things that one does start in the slums. You can't educate the poor without feeding them, I'm sure."

"Nonsense!" said the suffragette, who was certainly no more accommodating as a follower than as a woman. "I don't believe the anatomy of the poor is one bit different from the anatomy of the rich. And I don't believe the way to anybody's soul lies through their stomach. Only if one is hungry, one naturally pretends that blind alley is a thoroughfare."

"How do you suggest that the slums should be worked up, then, may I ask?" said the Chief M.S. coldly. There is no point in being a born leader, if the rank and file refuses to behave suitably.

The suffragette loathed the wording of this remark, but kindly refrained from further criticism. " If you like . . ." she said, " I'll try an experiment on the Brown Borough. I'll give no meetings and I'll give no membership cards, but if you leave me time I'll bring as many women to the Cause as ever did a dozen meetings in Trafalgar Square."

To hear of other people busy always cheered the Chief M.S.

"You will have done a good work," she said warmly.

The suffragette went out with those words singing in her head. A thing that very seldom happened to other people's words in the ears of this selfabsorbed young woman.

"To have done a good work ..." she said, on the top of a west-bound 'bus.

"To have done a good work . . . But if it were a good work it could never be done. The way of good work goes on for ever. And that's why I swear I'll do this work till I die . . ."

It was fine to feel busy again. The suffragette had always liked to have the measure of her day pressed down and running over, but she had never yet known the luxury of having enough of what she liked. In the home — which is Woman's Sphere — there is always time to think how little time there is. Even the career of an incendiary, though hectic, often fails to give the illusion of persistent industry. The suffragette was so lost in enthusiasm over the discovery of a good long road under her feet at last, that she presently found herself at Kew.

If you must drift, there are few places better to drift to than Kew Gardens. Only if you go there just when the months have reached the bleak curve of the hill that runs down into spring, you must know where to find the best and most secret snowdrops. The suffragette knew. She was very familiar with the art of being alone in London.

You will perhaps not be surprised to learn that never once in her life had her leisure meant some one else's pleasure. There had never been any one who would have been in the least interested to know that the suffragette had a few hours unbooked. She never regretted this fact, because she never noticed it. With the exception of Excursion Agents, I should think no one ever knew the holiday resorts around London better than she did. She could enjoy herself very much indeed sitting seriously on grass, watching a world dotted with sentimental cockneyism. It gave her no pang to be one among many twos.

Today she found the seat that sits forever looking at the place where the snowdrops should be, and only really lives when they come out. And when she got there, it was most annoying, she thought of the gardener, to the exclusion of everything else. After several minutes she found that she had been occupied in committing the address she had been given to memory.

"Number Twenty-one Penny Street. Twenty-one Penny Street"

I cannot account for the occasional inconsistency of this woman except by reminding you of a certain well-known natural phenomenon. Just as a man whose arm has been amputated may still suffer from a phantom finger-ache, so a woman who has killed her heart must, at certain points in her life, feel the pain of a heart, as if the dead thing turned in its grave. One of the most tragic things about loss is that it is never annihilation.

"This is absurd," thought the suffragette, pulling herself together. "I must make a plan of campaign, as the M.S. Society would say. How am I going to start?"

Brown Borough popularity is a slippery thing to seize. You must have a handle to grasp it by.

A robin appeared, like a fairy, between two snowdrops. He did not notice the suffragette, nevertheless he looked self-conscious. He re-arranged a perfectly neat feather, and glanced at his waistcoat to see whether its curve was correct. He even tried to glance over his waistcoat at his feet, but this was physically impossible. The suffragette loved him until she realised that he was in love, on which she wearied of him. A chirrup behind her drew her attention to the lady in the case.

"I believe I'll have to get hold of the priest," said the suffragette. I have told you that she was devoid of tact She never took enough notice of the world to sulk when the world was unkind, she was not human enough to quarrel. I have seen her give great offence to the Chief M.S. by borrowing a cigarette in the middle of a tempestuous scene of mutual reproach. She never reviewed the past when arranging for the future, and this, in human relations, is a fatal mistake.

She had an apple and an oatmeal biscuit in her bag. In spite of the robin's sentimental drawbacks, she shared the biscuit with him and gave him the apple core. He finished the biscuit, and when about three-quarters through with the apple core, he remembered his affair of the heart. With the laboured altruism of the man in love, he tore himself away, and embodied the apple core theme in a little song, by way of informing the lady. She came, she began. Looking up with her third mouthful, she noticed the suffragette. With a hoarse chirp, she shot over the horizon.

"He forgot to want her," sighed the suffragette, " Men are to unimaginative."

The gentleman came back and finished the apple core.

The suffragette's mind, which was rather sleepy, turned to the occasion when she too had shot away from destiny, over a blue horizon.

"But I left Courtesy as an apple core" she said. " Men ought to be as good philosophers as robins, any day."

You and I are getting tired of this scene. And so was the suffragette. She shook herself.

"I must wake up," she said. " The incident is closed. I'm glad it's closed. But I'm very glad it was once open. By mistake I came alive for a little while. I don't believe in God, and I don't believe in love. But I thank God I have met love — in a dream."

She might possibly have been referring to the robin drama. But I don't think she was.

She put her chin up, and buttoned up the hair shirt, and exchanged the snowdrops for a 'bus.

It was the day after this that the priest was addressing his sister's Girls' Club in the Brown Borough. He was supplying food for the soul while his sister prepared food for the body. The girls were listening with the polite though precarious attention which Brown Borough girls always bring to bear on the first three hundred words of any address, especially if the addresser be a man. Factory girls are amiable creatures with something inborn that very closely resembles good manners. Unless you are so unfortunate as to stumble upon their sense of humour, they will always give you a hearing. Their sense of humour is broad, but only touched by certain restricted means. If you have a smut on your nose, or if your hat is on one side, or if you stammer in your speech, or if it is obvious that you have just sat in a puddle on alighting from your 'bus, you need cherish no hopes, but be sure that every word you say is only adding to the comedy of the situation.

The priest was extremely neat, as usual. His piercing eyes under his grey hair looked dignified, and he was concealing moral quack remedies in gilded anecdotes with marked success. He had reached the critical point in a comic story about his recent adventures in the tropics, and was just preparing to lead the roar of amusement, when, over the heads of his audience, he saw a face that seemed terribly familiar. He finished the story with such gravity that nobody dared to smile.

"How unwise I was to put the idea into her head," he told himself, and, descending from his eminence, went to meet her.

"This is indeed a surprise, yerce, yerce," he said, shaking her coldly by the hand He thought that she would be cut to the heart by the fact that he failed to qualify the surprise as pleasant She did not notice the omission. She was not accustomed to being made very welcome.

"I have followed your advice," she said. "I have come down to ask you for work."

"How very well-timed," said the priest's sister just behind him. " Christopher, introduce the young lady."

"We will talk of that later," said the priest. "I have not finished my address."

But he virtually had. For he could find nothing else to say, although he continued speaking. The girls lost interest, and began passing each other letters and photographs from their chaps. A little plain girl, beside whom the suffragette had taken her seat, handed her one of these documents.

I have said that the suffragette had a hard face — it is worth noting that no beggar ever begged of her unless he was blind. But I suppose she had loved women so long and so fiercely that there was something in her look that established confidence in the women she met. Nobody would have handed a love-letter to Mrs. Rust to read, within five minutes of her first appearance.

"The cocoa is ready, Christopher," said the priest's sister audibly, from an inner room.

A remark like this, though trivial, will throw almost any orator off his track. The priest stopped, with the resigned sigh of Christian irritation.

The suffragette handed the letter back to her neighbour. " What a nice chap yours must be," she said.

"Are you the young woman wot's come to ply the pianner?" asked the girl.

"I'm not sure," replied the suffragette, with a guarded look at the priest. "I rather think I am."

This was luckily considered amusing, and over the cocoa the comments on the new young woman were favourable.

The priest's sister came out from the inner room, whence proceeded the loud bubbling squeaks of cocoa-drinkers.

"Now, Christopher," she said, " why didn't you tell me you had found a new helper?"

"I do not know that I have, my dear," replied the priest. " This young lady has misinterpreted something I said to her."

"It's very lucky that she did, then," said the priest's sister. " We are so badly in need of a new voluntary helper."

"You oblige me to put the matter baldly, my dear," said the priest, keeping his temper with a creditable effort. " This is the young lady I mentioned to you last night in the course of conversation.

All our helpers hitherto have been of the highest moral character."

"From your face . . ." said the priest's sister to the suffragette. "I am sure you mean well. I am sure you are not wicked. And if you have slipped, there is nothing like hard work in the Brown Borough to make you forget"

The suffragette was so much startled to hear herself addressed in this unusual rein that she very nearly cried. It is rare to have tears so near so horny a surface as hers.

"My dear . . ." said the priest. "I think you forget my position of authority in this parish. You also forget the pure young souls committed to your care in this club. Yerce, yerce."

He actually imagined the factory girls to be as innocent as himself. To him the words youth and innocence were indivisible.

"Oh, nonsense, Christopher," said his sister. " She doesn't necessarily want to help with this club, and even if she did she can't convey infection to the girls by playing the piano to them."

"I do not expect she does play the piano," said the priest lamely.

"You do play, don't you? You have such pretty hands."

After that, of course, the suffragette felt as though she could have played Strauss to please her. As a matter of fact she had little real articulate gift for music, but she never forgot a tune she had heard, and found no difficulty in rendering the songs that always sang in her head, outwardly instead of inwardly.

The priest's sister was not musical. Nor was she critical. She considered that the Brown Borough had in this newcomer found something it had lacked. The suffragette, who possessed certain secret springs of conceit, was to some extent of the same opinion. And by the end of the evening the majority of the girls shared this view.

"Do you know a Mrs. Smith?" asked the suffragette, as she said good-bye.

"I know perhaps five hundred Mrs. Smiths," said the priest's sister.

"She wears a plush coat, and a baby, and a little girl of hers died in October."

"About two hundred and fifty out of the five hundred wear plush coats, and babies, and little girls that die."

"I wonder what surnames are for," said the suffragette pettishly, " since they have ceased to distinguish one person from another?"

"If you come to me to-morrow," said the priest's sister, " I will give you the names of various women who want visiting. If your Mrs. Smith needs you, you will soon find her, if you live in the Brown Borough."

The suffragette was a rash woman. She always abode by her own first choice. Before she went to see the priest's sister in the morning, she found herself a Brown Borough. lodging. She did this by the simple device of knocking on the door of the first house she saw that displayed a notice, "Apartment."

" Now then, wot's the matter? " asked the lady who opened the door.

The suffragette, though impossible to silence, was easy to abash. And there is certainly something disheartening in such a salutation. However, she suggested that the notice in the window might excuse an intrusion.

But the suffragette had, by mistake, knocked on the door of the most respectable house in the most respectable street in the district. She found a clean, though dark room, with a window blinking against the sun at a back yard tilled with snowdrops. The wall-paper talked in a loud voice of tulips: winecoloured tulips trampled on each other and wrestled for supremacy over every inch of it. The tablecloth and carpet were the colour of terra-cotta, and firmly disagreed with every word the wall-paper said. Two horse-hair chairs, in sullen brown, looked moodily at each other across the table.

The suffragette never asked more than that her body might live in a clean place. She kept her mind detachable from colour schemes. After all, what is my body for but to enclose me?

"I'll have the room," said the suffragette, as if it had been a cake of soap.

It was like a dream to the landlady, a dream she had never been sufficiently feverish to indulge in.

"You'll have it?" she gasped.

"Yes. Why not? What's the rent, by the way?"

The landlady, by means of a rapid mental process of multiplication, rose manfully to the occasion.

"All right, fifteen shillings," said the suffragette. " I'll come in to-morrow."

She went to see the priest's sister, but to her mild annoyance found the priest instead.

"My sister suggested that you should visit the Wigskys," said the priest, who never bore malice, as far as one could see. He never allowed you for a moment to forget that he was a Christian. " Mrs. Wigsky's latest baby hasn't been christened. Also I think the eldest girl must be getting into bad ways; she has left the excellent place I found for her."

"And must I persuade the baby to be christened?"

"Not the child itself. You had better do your best to persuade the mother."

'But supposing she refuses on principle?"

The priest fixed her with his piercing eye. " There can be no principle contrary to the Right," he said. "The opposite to Right it Wrong."

"How simple!" said the suffragette. "But won't Hell be terribly overcrowded?"

The priest sighed, and certainly with reason. But he remembered that he was very broad-minded, and that he had often said that everybody had a right to their own opinion. He remembered that toe soft answer that turneth away the fatuity of women had found a place even in the New Testament,

"No one would be more loth than I . . ." he said, "to classify as condemned all whose views do not coincide with the dictates of the Church. Let us rather call them mistaken."

The suffragette shut in a renewed protest with a snap of her jaws. Although she badly needed a handle by which to seize the Brown Borough, surely there must be other handles than the Church. She determined secretly on determination as her unaided weapon.

But she went to see the Wigskys. She found them — a large family, red and mutually wrathful in an atmosphere of hot smells ancient and modern.

When she got inside the door she wondered why she had come. The baby screaming on its mother's breast looked incorrigibly heathen, the eldest girl looked wholly unsuited to any " excellent place " discovered by the priest. "Wooder you want?" asked the harassed mother, a drab and dusty creature, with the used look of cold ashes.

"I've come from Father Christopher . . ." began the suffragette, wishing she had come from some one else.

"'N you can go back to Farver Christopher," said Mrs. Wigsky. " Becos I ain't goin' to 'ave no more bibies christened. It's 'eaven 'ere, an' 'eaven there, this biby's goin' ter grow up 'eeven fer a chinge. It carn't get us into worse trouble nor wot we've 'ad."

"I haven't come to bother you," said the suffragette. " After all, it's your baby, not Father Christopher's."

"That's wot I ses," said the mother, slightly mollified. " Well, if you 'aven't come abaht Biby, wot 'ave you come for?"

"I've come because I want to find friends in the Brown Borough. If you don't want me, please tell me to go."

The Brown Borough never protests if you surprise it; and in any case, Mrs. Wigsky's soul was too dead for consistent protest. Also it was certainly a change to be visited by one who lacked the visitor's apprising eye, who seemed unaware of an unswept floor and an unmade bed.

"As Father Christopher talked about the Brown Borough women . . ." said the suffragette, " I wanted more and more to know them, because it seems to me so splendid to keep going at all in the Brown Borough. I must tell you I always love women. So you must forgive me for coming."

"'Tain't often as lidies come to admire us," said Mrs. Wigsky. " They alius comes to show us 'ow wrong we are."

"I'm not a lady," said the suffragette.

"Ow, yus you are," said the eldest girl, speaking for the first time.

"Are you the girl that's out of a job?" asked the suffragette.

"Yus. Farver Christopher got me a job as general to the lidy oo keeps the post office. She give me three-an'-six a week an' no food, an' mother ain't earnin' now, an' Tom's in 'orsbital, so it weren't good enough. I run awiy. She 'it me too, an' mide me cerry up the coals. But 'er bein' a lidy, I couldn't siy much — I jus' run awiy."

"I wish you'd hit her back," said the suffragette. " And I wish the word ' lady ' had never been invented."

"Lidies is lidies, an' generals is generals," said Mrs. Wigsky. " Gawd mide it so, an' you carn't get over it."

"I'm sure God never made it so," said the suffragette. " He made men and women, and nothing else. He made man in His own image, and left woman to make herself. And she's doing it. That's what makes us all so proud to be women."

"I'm not proud of bein' a woman. I'm sick of it," said Mrs. Wigsky; but the girl said, "You do talk beautiful, miss. I b'leeve I'm a little bit proud. Anywiy, I wouldn't be a man for somefink."

"Men," sniffed Mrs. Wigsky. "It's men wot does all the 'arm. An' yet you carn't get along wivout 'em altogether. They're so 'elpless."

(I hope you notice this truth, one of the few unposed truths in this book. Man is potentially a son, and woman is potentially a mother;

176

woman depends on the dependence of man. The spinster, if pathetic at all, is pathetic because she has no one to look after, not because there is no one to look after her. Bear in mind that the conventional spinster keeps a canary as a substitute for a husband.)

"All the same," said the suffragette, " men are proud of being men, and that is one of the greatest virtues. I don't suppose there is a man in London who would be general to a Post Office lady at three and-six a week and no food."

This was thought to be supremely witty, and the suffragette rose to depart on the crest of a ripple of popularity. The girl followed her half-way downstairs.

"You fink that I was roight then to chuck that job, miss?"

The suffragette at that moment parted company with Father Christopher.

"Certainly I think you were right. It's very wrong to take less money than you're worth. I'd rather lend your mother money to get on with until you can get a worth-while job than let a friend of mine go so cheap as three-and-six a week. You can give your mother this address, and tell her I'll come to see her again very soon."

As she reached the first landing, she became aware of a fresh twist in the maze. I think drama of a rather sombre variety is the very life of the Brown Borough, and I defy you to thread its streets or climb its stairways for half a day without meeting some Thing you never met before.

The doorway on the first landing was practically filled by a woman, whose most surprising characteristic was that her right eye was filled with blood. The blood was running down on to the breast of her dress.

"I'm feelin' that queer," said the woman. "It's the sight o' blood alms mikes me queer."

""You must let me help you," said the suffragette. "You must let me put you on your bed."

The woman laughed and remained swaying in the doorway.

"Bedder standen' . . ."she mumbled hysterically.

She was an enormous woman, and effectually blocked the doorway. For one mad moment the suffragette meditated climbing over her. An obstacle always had an irresistible fascination for her.

"Don't be so silly," said the suffragette. " Let me come in at once. I am here to help. Stand aside." k\ The woman laughed again, and her head suddenly lolled down upon her breast. A little drip of blood ran down upon the floor.

"You are making a mess on the floor," said the suffragette.

There was a magic in the words. I suppose their power lay in their utter futility. The woman stood aside.

"Now let me get you to bed," said the suffragette as she entered. But there was no bed.

There were a dresser, a small table, and a chair. There was also a man, noisily asleep upon the chair.

"Ran me eye agin the corner of the tible," said the woman.

"How very unlucky," said the suffragette, " considering the table's practically the only thing in the room. Except the man."

She took the back of the chair and tipped it forward. She tilted it to such an angle that nobody in their senses could have remained seated in it. But a guardian angel seems to look after the drunk at the expense of the sober. When because she was not a professional weight-lifter, the suffragette had to let the chair revert to its natural position, the man was still comfortably asleep.

The woman fainted in the corner.

"Wake up, you damned pig I " said the suffragette, with the utmost strength of her soft voice, and she struck his shoulder with all the weight of a perfectly useless fist.

" Shall I fetch a policeman ?" asked Miss Wigsky.

"The Law's no good" said the suffragette frowning. " I don't believe there is a law against a man being drunk in the only chair. Do you think you could borrow a cushion or two from your mother, so that we could make the woman comfy on the floor?"

By the time Miss Wigsky returned with the relic of a pillow, the suffragette had bathed the blood from the eye.

"Woz this?" inquired the woman, opening the surviving eye upon the appearance of Miss Wigsky. "Woz this? Pillers? Tike 'em awiy. I 'aven't bin to bed in the diytime for twenty years, nor I ain't goin' to begin now . . ."

"You must lie down," said the suffragette. " And I will fetch the doctor to sew up your eye."

"Bless yer . . ." crowed the invalid. " S'long as I've got legs to walk to the doctor on, you kin bet yer life 'e won't walk to me. I'll go'n see 'tm, soon's as I stop bein' all of a tremble."

"I'll come with you."

"As you please."

Miss Wigsky escaped.

"Why do you allow that man to be drunk in here?" asked the suffragette after a pause.

"'E don't arsk my leave."

"Is he your husband?"

"No. 'E is in a manner of speakin'. But I wouldn't really marry a soppy bloke like thet."

"Then why do you have soppy blokes crowding you out of your own furniture?"

"Ow, one must 'ave a man about the plice. Feels more 'omely-like."

"Does he work for you?"

"I don't fink."

"Is he very good to you?"

The woman, not unnaturally, began to get restive. "'Oo ye're gettin' at? Nat'rally a man ain't soothin' syrup when 'e come 'ome as my young man come 'ome an hour ago. 'E's better'n some."

There was a long silence. Then the suffragette said, "Women seem to be extraordinarily cheap in the market. They hire themselves out to the man who hits the hardest. It makes one almost tired of being a woman."

"Look 'ere . . ." said the patient wrathfully, but she stopped there. Presently she sat up and said, "I'm goin' to doctor's now. And if you ain't still too tired, miss, perhaps you'll see me as fur as the 'orspital . . ."

So the suffragette laid hold of the Closed Door of the Brown Borough, by the handle of her fanatic determination. She never saw the impossibility of victory. It was the earliest of the early spring, and there was hope in the air. For many weeks hope was her only luxury. With it she sweetened her bread and margarine when she rose, to the tune of it she munched her nightly tripe and onions. She saw the mirage of the end in sight, and with her great faith she almost made it real She was a blind optimist where women were concerned.

On the initiative of the priest's sister, she attended the Church Girls ' Club three evenings a week. On her own initiative she played the Church false, and established in its own field of labour, behind its back, the foundation of her task.

It was originally Miss Wigsky's fault. Miss Wigsky was a girl of practical energy, a warring spirit, a potential suffragette. She had long been a militant resister of the Church Club ideal, but when the suffragette became one of its regular adherents, Miss Wigsky joined it at once. Hers was the active responsibility for what followed, and 'Tilda's the passive. I think I have mentioned 'Tilda before, though not by name. She was a small white creature who had committed the absurdity of losing her heart to the suffragette at first sight, and had sealed her admiration by laying bare the letter of her chap at their first meeting.

The moment of cocoa-drinking was always the moment of confidences. It was during this comparatively peaceful time that the suffragette made friends, and it was at this point that 'Tilda one evening approached her.

"Jenny Wigsky's a funny gel," said 'Tilda. " She's bin talkin' about you, miss. I got a new job the other day, very little money — piece-work — on'y shillin' a diy if I work ever so 'ard. I ses to Jenny, I'ma good gel I am, to tike less money than I'm worth just to 'elp my muvver.' But Jenny ses I'm a very bad gel — she ses you ses as it's wicked to tike bad money."

"I didn't say it was wicked — I wouldn't use the word," said the suffragette. "But I do think it's selfish. Every time a girl takes too little money, she may be forcing another girl to take less. You know it's partly your fault that women's wages are so bad. You can feel now that you've had a share in the work of sweating women, 'Tilda."

"Didn't I tell you?" said Miss Wigsky. " Why don't you do as I do, an' stick out for ten?"

"But you're not gettin' it," objected 'Tilda.

"I'm goin' to get it, I am. I'm goin' back to my ol' tride — box-miking. I left it becos the work was so 'ard, but the money's better."

"I don't mind how hard people work, as long as they get paid for it," said the suffragette. "Of course, you have to do good work for good money. What I mean is that I think it's just as dishonest to take too little money as it is to do too little work."

"But wot's the good of one standin' out?"

"Very little good. But more good in a dozen standing out and more still in a hundred."

"Le's start a sassiety," suggested the strenuous Miss Wigsky. "You could be the Preserdink, miss, n' I'll 'elp yer. We'll call ourselves the ' Suffragette Gels, an' we won't allow none of us to tike less money than ten shillin'."

" Gam . . ." said 'Tilda. " Thet's a Tride Union, thet is. A man's gime. If I chuck my job, 'oo's goin' to keep me til I get a better one. Murver? I don't fink . . ."

" I will," said the suffragette. " If there's anybody here earning less than ten shillings a week, I'll give them seven-and-six a week for a fortnight if they have to chuck their job, and I'll also give a prize of seven-and-six at the end of the fortnight to the girl who's increased her wages the most."

No plan could ever have been less planned. She thought of it as she spoke of it, a most rash method. But Miss Wigsky immediately set to work to hew tt into shape.

"You'll 'ave to arrnge for piece-work, miss," she said. " Anybody on piece-work could increase their wiges by working for twenty-four hours a diy, but it wouldn't be fair."

"Nobody must work after eight at night," said the suffragette.

"An' if two or three gets the sime rise?" suggested Miss Wigsky.

"I'll give them each seven-and-six," said the suffragette.

Of the twenty girls present, three were earning over ten shillings and entered a different class of the competition, working for the prize without the maintenance, if a rise should be found possible without loss of employment. Of the remaining seventeen, two refused to compete, and one was too small to be worth more than her present earnings. The other fourteen determined on an immediate attack on their employers. Chances were discussed instead of dances for the rest of the evening.

"My boss'll siy — the money's there — you kin tike it or leave it. 'E's said that before."

"My boss'll smile — 'e alius calls me 'Tip-a-wink, becos I'm the smallest gel there. 'E's never cross — my boss ain't."

"I think I'll win the prize easy — don't know why I never thought of it before. Buster — my boss — ses I've got the 'andiest 'ands wiv the bristles as ever 'e see."

"My missus'll siy — there's 'undreds of sluts in the Borough twice as good as you, an' I like yer imperence, an' you kin tike the sack wivout notice. She alius calls me a slut — we won't be sorry to part."

"I shall stick to the fewer work, an' tike up curlin' an' sewin', as well as the knotting. I bin too lizy up to now, but I've got an aunt in the tride as 'ud learn me in no time."

At closing time the priest drew the suffragette aside.

"I heard Jane Wigsky's voice constantly raised in the dining-room this evening. I want your opinion of that girl. Yerce, yerce. She seems to me rough and coarse, and I am tempted to think she is a disturbing influence in the Club."

"She's not so disturbing as I am," said the suffragette, with a spasm of conscience.

" Oh, don't say that," said the priest, whose sister had been readjusting his manners. " Don't be disheartened, you will soon get into our ways, yerce, yerce. But to return to Jane Wigsky, I do not like the girl. She is impertinent and self-assured. I feel sure she puts ideas into the girls' heads."

"I shouldn't think an idea more or less would make much difference."

The priest sighed. I am not surprised. I quite admit that the suffragette was an infuriating person. I yield to none in my admiration for any one who could manage to keep their temper with her.

"You know I mean harmful ideas. She has no staying power. She left excellent employment, apparently simply through a whim. Her mistress, the postmistress, is a great friend of mine. In short, I consider the girl undesirable, and we are thinking of asking her to leave the Club."

The suffragette became red.

"I'm sorry the postmistress is a friend of yours," she said. " Because she can't be a very admirable friend. She herself admits that she only paid the girl three-and-six a week, with no food except a cup of tea at midday."

"Poor wages, yerce, yerce. But far better than idleness."

" Infinitely worse," said the suffragette.

A rather feverish silence fell for a moment. I think the priest said a prayer. At any rate he thought he did.

"Surely you have some sympathy with our aims in this Club. Surely you agree that it is a worthy ideal to try to raise the level of the young womanhood of the Borough. Surely you see that we cannot do this unless we keep the girls in good uplifting company. Jane Wigsky is a bad girl. One must draw the line between good and bad."

"One may draw a line, but one needn't build a barrier. And even to draw a line, one should have very good sight."

"I think I hardly need your advice on the management of a parish I have served for twentytwo years. If this were my Club I should request you to find some other outlet for your energies. But my sister is very obstinate. Good evening."

A certain amount of success attended the efforts of the Suffragette Girls. By the end of that week, three girls had been given a rise for the asking, the extent of it varying from sixpence to two shillings. Several had got a promise of a rise when work should be less slack, only three had taken the drastic step of leaving their employment. The piece-workers with few exceptions were working for a wage which seemed unalterable. An envelope-folder raised her earnings from three halfpence a thousand to twopence. But as a rule there is no labour groove so deep as the piece-worker's.

It was on the Thursday night before Good Friday that the suffragette, dressed in a dressing-gown, sat before her fire remembering the simplest character in this simple book — Scottie Brown.

"It's dog-stealing," she thought, " no less. Miss Brown may return to the Island any time crying out for Scottie to come and comfort her. And Scottie will be languishing in England, undergoing quarantine. We are dog-thieves."

The " we " sent a little heat-wave over the place where her heart should have been.

She had been working very hard all day, walking about the Brown Borough collecting its worries. She was so tired that she could not rest, could not go to bed, could not do anything except sit on her hearthrug and think feverishly of things that did not matter.

Outwardly the suffragette, when in her dressinggown, and with her hair drawn into a small smooth plait, approached more nearly her vocation than under any other circumstances. She was a nun, dedicated to an unknown God.

"A person to see you," said the landlady, and flung open the door. The suffragette shot to her feet, with a momentary terrible suspicion that the landlady had said " parson." Visions of a bashful curate brought face to face with a militant suffragette in her dressing-gown, were, however, swept away by the entrance of Miss Wigsky.

"It's a --- shime," remarked the visitor loudly, discarding the convention of greeting.

"Sure to be," said the suffragette, sinking down upon the hearthrug again. " Nearly everything's that kind of shame. Sit down and tell me."

"I tol' you I'd got a job, you know, at Smiff's — boot-uppers. A lucky find it were, I thought, ten shillin' a week an' I was to be learnt 'ow to work a machine. 'E ses 'e thought I was a likely sort on Monday when I went, but 'e ses as 'e was goin' to learn me somethink, an' 'e wanted a special sort of gel, like, 'e ars't for references. Knowin' as 'e was a religious sort of gentleman, an' give 'eaps of money to the Church, I toľ 'im Farver Christopher for my reference, because Farver Christopher's known Muwer sence she married, an' alius said 'e would 'elp 'er whenever 'e could. So when I went agine yesterday, to Smiff's, 'e ses as 'ow Farver Christopher 'adn't spoke well of me — said I was unreliable, an' never stuck to one job. So Mr. Smiff ses in thet cise I wouldn't suit, but 'e ses as I looked likely 'e'd give me a job as packer at six shillin'. I ses as I couldn' afford to tike so little money, an' I toľ 'im about you an' the Suffragette Gels. 'E ses you oughter be ashimed of yoursel', an' 'e'd write an' tell Farver Christopher as 'ow 'is Club was an 'otbed of somethink or other. I 'ites Farver Christopher — curse 'im — an' 'e miking belief to be so 'elpful.

I was in my first job free years, an' jus' because I chucked the job 'e found for me, 'e does me dirty like this. Curse 'im."

"Don't," said the suffragette. " Suffragettes don't waste breath in cursing — even when there seems to be nothing to do but curse."

"This evenin' . . ." continued Miss Wigsky, " I went to the Club to see if you was there, though it wasn't your night. Farver Christopher turned me out, 'e did. 'E's turned out fifteen of the gels, an' tol' them never to come back no more. 'E found out from the others which was the suffragette gels, an' turned 'em out. I stood up to 'im, and arsk' 'im wotever we've done that's wrong, there ain't no 'arm, I ses, in tryin' to get a livin' wige. I arsk' 'im 'ow 'e'd like to live under seven shillin' a week. 'E ses as 'ow God 'ad called us to this stite of life, an' it was wicked to try an' alter it 'E ses as women are pide what they're worth, an' God mide rich an' poor an' men an' women, an' never meant the poor to be rich, or women to be pretending they was as good as men ... I spit at 'im, miss, I 'ope you'll excuse me."

"I'll excuse you," said the suffragette, "though I don't think it was a very artistic protest. I am most awfully sorry for you, Jenny, but I'm not surprised. For you know when you became a suffragette you agreed to fight, and now you've found out what you're fighting, that's all.

Suffragettes are just soldiers — only more sober — and when they meet the enemy, they just get more determined, not more excited. If you were a soldier and got wounded, we should be sorry for you, but also rather proud of you. We must collect the suffragette girls somewhere else, and make the army grow."

"I don't believe you can, miss. I went to see 'Tilda, an' she was pretty near soppy about it. She's piece-work, an' earn' get 'er boss to rise 'er, so she ain't done nothink to be turned out of the Club for, she ses. She ses as 'ow she won't never 'ave nuffink more to do wiv them suffragettes. Then I met Lil, the tow-'aired gel — she was drunk — at the corner of the Delta. She puts it all on you, miss."

"Do you feel like that?" asked the suffragette.

"Ow well, in a manner o' speakin', it wouldn' 'ave 'appened if it 'adn't bin for you, miss. But I don't feel sore against you, not really. You did it for the best. You miy be right about fightin' the enemy, on'y the enemy's too strong. P'r'aps Farver Christopher's right, an' God mide women to starve till they marry, an' get beaten till they die . . ."

"If there is a God," said the suffragette in a low voice, " the only possible conclusion is that he is an Anti. Still, even a God can be fought."

"Ow, I'm sick o' fightin'," said Miss Wigsky. "I shall go orf wiv my chap, though 'e is out of work . . ."

The gardener was at 21 Penny Street, waiting for an answer to his message. To pass the time he had found work, or rather work had found him, for he was a man of luck. Eventually, instead of an answer, Mrs. Paul Rust called on him.

"How's your son?" asked the gardener, who was pleased to meet some one who had met the suffragette.

Beneath his superficial " unscathed " pose, there was a layer of deep faithfulness. He knew by now that the suffragette was not worthy of the love of a sober Assistant Secretary to a Society Which Believed Itself of Great Importance (one of his latest practical poses). But the thing one knows makes no difference to the thing one feels, if one is young. The gardener was under the impression that his wisdom had dethroned the suffragette from her eminence, but his heart, with the obstinacy peculiar to hearts, continued to look up.

"My son is bad. He gets no stronger. There is no reason why he shouldn't get up, except that he isn't strong enough to walk."

"I'm sorry."

"I'm not," said Mrs. Rust automatically, and stood checked by such a decided lie.

"What annoys me is Courtesy," she said after a pause. " Courtesy indeed, she hasn't treated me fairly. She had the impertinence to tell me last week that she was engaged to that ridiculous young Wise she picked up at Greyville. Engaged indeed, it's stuff and nonsense, pure defiance. She's treated me as a sort of matrimonial agent. I wasn't paying her £200 a year to look for a husband."

"No," agreed the gardener. " Then why don't you forbid the banns?"

Poor Mrs. Rust's helplessness in the hands of Courtesy rose vaguely to her memory. " Stuff and nonsense," she said. "I haven't yet decided what steps I shall take in the matter. There is no immediate hurry. She has suggested letting the matter drop until Samuel is better. She has many failings, but I think she is fond of me."

"That's a very attractive failing," admitted the gardener.

"I didn't come here to discuss Courtesy with you," snapped Mrs. Rust, suddenly remembering her temper. "I came because Samuel wanted me to come. He seems to be under delusions about you, he thinks he owes you gratitude. In fact — probably under the influence of delirium — he once said you financed his hotel. As a matter of fact I financed it myself, it owes its present success to me."

"It's awfully good of you to come all this way to bring me misdirected gratitude," said the gardener.

"Stuff and nonsense," said Mrs. Rust. "I wouldn't stir an inch out of my way to make you more conceited than you are. But that is the worst of having a son, you have to pay occasional attention to his wishes. Besides, Courtesy brought me up to town and gave the address to the chauffeur, so I really wasn't consulted. Samuel wishes to see you. All the time he was ill he was asking for the Tra-la-la young man, and now I find he means you. I might have said that right at the beginning, and not have wasted all this time listening to your chatter."

"I'm very glad you didn't," said the gardener. "I couldn't bear a caller who came straight to the point in five words and then left."

"Staff and nonsense," said Mrs. Rust " Are you coming?"

It was half-past three on Good Friday afternoon. There is something about that little Easter cluster of Sundays that weighs your heart down, if you are in postless London, and expecting a letter.

"Where is your son?" he asked.

"In Hampshire, in the Cottage Hospital, near the Red Place. You could put up at the Red Place. Samuel, being a fool, said you might have the big black and white room on the first floor. He might have let it for five guineas over Bank Holiday."

"What time is the train?" asked the gardener.

"My car is at the door. The chauffeur is a dangerous lunatic, and there seems to me to be every likelihood that the back wheel will come off before we get out of London. But — are you coming?"

So the gardener came. Seated behind the dangerous lunatic, over the dangerous back wheel, and beside a hostess in a musical comedy motor bonnet, he followed once more the road that led to the gods.

He had left his address with Miss Shakespeare for forwarding of letters. The great surprise of spring awaited them outside London. There were lambs under a pale sky, and violets under pale green hedges. Gnarled trees, like strong men's muscles, curved out of roadside copses, lit with a green radiance. There was lilac smiling across the cottage gardens, there were wall-flowers blotted dark against whitewashed walls. But when they reached the pines and heath they left the spring behind. Only the larches preached its gospel.

"You had better come and see Samuel first," said Mrs. Rust. " He is anxious to see you. He always was a fool."

So they passed the Red Place. It flared out at them along a sombre ride that cut the woods in two.

"Samuel says his gods look after the place as well as any manager, while he is away. But of course he has a chef now, and a competent bureau clerk."

"I suppose you couldn't ask the gods to dish up the dinner, or make out the bills," admitted the gardener regretfully. "But I wonder if there's room for the gods as well as the chef and the competent bureau clerk."

"Stuff and nonsense," said Mrs. Rust. " A good dinner's worth all the gods in mythology."

They drove up to their destination.

The cottage hospital had only recruited to the service of the sick in later life. For a hundred years or so it had been the haunt of the wicked landowner. Worldly squires' wives had given tea in its paved pergola to curates' wives in their best hats. But at the home grew older it reformed. Its walls, steeped in the purple village gossip of s century, now echoed only to the innocent if technical prattle of nurses. The only person who walked in its garden was Sister: she threw crumbs to the goldfish as severely as though the crumbs were for their good. For the blessing which the house inherited from its past was its garden. A small garden, like a cot emerald, but reflecting all other jewels. It was a garden that tried to enshrine sombre peace amid the vivid riot of spring. Its high clipped hedges drew decorously angular reflections in the pools. Brown wallflowers hid the feet of the hedges. The lilacs seemed somehow turned to half mourning by the proximity of a copper beech. A veil of tree seeds spinning down the wind fell diagonally across the garden. The pink horse chestnut was very symmetrical. Only the little saxifrages protested against the geometrical correctness of the paving-stones, and forget-me-nots sang a shrill song in blue from the restraining chaperonage of red pottery tubs. A little cupid with a dislocated hip played a noiseless flute from a pedestal. The garden was a prig, but it was the sort of prig that makes you wonder whether after all it is worth while to be so exquisitely sinful. They found Samuel Rust, who was the only patient in the hospital, the centre of a mist of nurses. He was lying in the shade of a great smooth yew pyramid with a military-looking bird fashioned on the top of it. Samuel Rust, that unusual young man, could never be much paler than he had been when in health, but he was grey now, rather than white, and his round sequins of eyes were set in a deeper setting.

"The Tra-la-la young man," he said as the gardener approached. "I have been wondering why I wanted to see you."

"So have I," said Mrs. Rust, who, after a momentary lapse into a maternal expression, had turned her back on the invalid.

"Let's pretend I'm just an ordinary sick-bed visitor, then," suggested the gardener. " One never knows why — or whether — one wants to see that sort of visitor. In that case I have to begin: — Dear Mr. Rust, I hope you are much better."

"Still posing," said Samuel. " What is your latest attitude?"

"I never pose," said the gardener. "I have a horror of the pose. My mind's eye sometimes changes the spectacles it wears, but that's all. I now find that all along the gods were intending me to be a business man."

"Hard luck," said Samuel.

The nurses had melted away, and Mrs. Rust followed them into the house. The sun was making ready for his triumph in the west and a diffident moon perched on the peak of the pink horse chestnut.

"Perhaps one ought to have foreseen the gods' intention of making you a business man," said Samuel, "for you certainly carried out the unscrupulous deceiver part with wonderful success — That is — jolty well — what? My Red Place now sings a hymn of praise to you, to the tune of ten pounder a week --- clear."

"Don't mention it," said the gardener. "It didn't need much unscrupulous deceiving; to persuade your mother to get her heart to work. And, to tell you the truth, the end was rather drowned in the meant on that journey. I got so busy living — I only thought of you when absolutely necessary."

"I didn't expect you to wear my image graven on your heart, what?" said Samuel. " You are young, and living- should certainly be your business. Is that why you said you were a business man? I have often thought that being young and only lately set up in business, you had no business to saddle your' self with a wife."

"No business whatever," admitted the gardener.

"Then why did you?"

"I didn't."

"Good heavens," said Samuel fretfully, " why was I born in such a cryptic age?"

"The truth is — I spoke in a futurist sense when I called her my wife."

"In other words, you lied," suggested Samuel.

"You just took a little tame woman on a string for a trip, as many better men have done before you?"

I dragged a woman by force across the Atlantic, and then she ran away. She ran back home."

" The silly ass," said Mr. Rust irritably. " Why did she do that?"

"The attitude of women towards force . . ." said the gardener sententiously, " is not what psychologists make it out to be. By some of the books I've read, I would have thought that women worshipped brute force; I would have thought that they kept their hair long specially in order to be dragged about by it."

"I have known very few women really well," said Samuel; " and the ones I knew didn't wear hair that they could be dragged about by. I should think the final disappearance of your post-impressionist wife was rather a good riddance."

"It was neither good nor a riddance. In the same futurist sense I still call her my wife. It's an effort, I admit, to continue to be fond of a militant suffragette, and yet somehow it's an effort I can't help making."

Courtesy appeared, her hair an impudent rival to the sunset.

"I've brought your book from the library," she said. "I couldn't get any books by Somethingevsky, as you asked, so I brought The Rosary.

"I ought to congratulate you on your engagement," said the gardener. " In fact — Mrs. Rust being out of earshot — I do."

"Thank you," said Courtesy, looking wonderfully pretty. "I wish everybody in the world was as happy as I am, though of course marriage is an awful risk. How's your young woman, gardener?"

"As militant as ever," said the gardener. " I'm expecting a letter from her any day, or a telegram any minute."

"Why, is she coming down here?"

"Probably," said the gardener. He had absolutely no grounds for his confidence except the ground of youth, and that, of course, is only a quicksand.

But the funny thing was she came.

For she cried all her current stock of militancy away on Thursday night, and by three o'clock on Good Friday afternoon she was on the door-step of 21 Penny Street.

"Even if slavery and polygamy become the fashion," she argued characteristically, " Scottie Brown will still be wrongfully detained in quarantine."

It was not to Scottie Brown that her thoughts turned when the maid told her that Mr. Gardener had gone to the country for Easter.

"But I must see him," said the suffragette, who was a little drunk with the bitter beverage of tears.

"It's impossible," said the maid. "I tell you — he's away."

The word " impossible " as usual acted as a challenge.

"Might I have his address?" said the caller.

After consultation with Miss Shakespeare the address was produced, and the suffragette's decision made. " The Red Place . . . His friend lives there — Mrs. Rust's son. Anyway there's no harm in going to a country hotel for Easter."

It was quite an advance for the suffragette to be human enough to consider whether there was any harm or not.

So she went home and had a ten minutes' interview with the mustard-coloured portmanteau, and then she put it and herself into a third-class carriage marked Girton Magna.

At sunset she arrived at the Red Place, and by luck extraordinary managed to procure a small attic which the tide of holiday-makers had passed by.

She saw the gardener first at dinner-time, and he looked almost as incredible to her as she did to him. It always surprises me to see a person looking exactly like themselves after absence.

When the gardener first saw the suffragette, he swallowed a spoonful of soup which was very much too hot, and rose. Courtesy was in the middle of a remark, and looked surprised to see him go.

"I knew I should hear or see something of you soon," said the gardener, shaking the suffragette's hand as usual an excessive number of times. " And yet I'm awfully surprised too," admitted the suffragette.

"Just an Easter holiday?" suggested the gardener carelessly. "But what luck you chose the Red Place."

"It wasn't exactly luck. I knew you were here."

Tears had been trembling in the gardener's eyes since the swallowing of the soup, he very nearly shed them now.

"Waiter," he called, " move that lady's place to our table."

The suffragette was excited and flushed. She looked almost pretty.

'I can't imagine why I came," she said when the change was effected and greetings had been exchanged. "I think I must have come in delirium. The woman I used to be never comes into the country except on business, and, in the case of friends, makes a principle of ' out of sight, out of mind.' "

"I hope you left that woman behind — permanently," said the gardener.

"No. That's the worst of it. They're both here. Each acts as conscience while the other one's in power. Why wasn't one brought into the world by oneself?"

"Why, weren't you?" asked Courtesy; " were you twins?"

"I still am. One of me is quite a good sort, really, almost an ' Oh, my dear ' girl. She is the one who was described in the paper as ' Boadicea Smith, a young woman of prepossessing appearance.' The reporter went on to say that the name was probably assumed — (which it was) — and that he knew who I really was — (which he didn't). He hinted that I was a deluded patrician incog. Do you know, I treasure that paragraph as if it were a love-letter. It's the only compliment I ever had."

"I should like to shake the hand of that reporter," said the gardener.

"But after that he referred to me all through as 'Smith,' without prefix, which is the sign of a criminal."

"The puppy!" exclaimed the gardener.

"What were you doing to get into the paper?" asked Courtesy sternly. "I never get into the paper."

"It's inconceivable that you should get into the paper, Courtesy dear," said the gardener, " except when you get born or married or dead."

"It'd be like a sultana in a seed-cake," said the suffragette, " or like a sunrise at tea-time. Or as if a Forty-nine 'bus went to the Bank."

I really think she was a little delirious, and perhaps she felt it herself, for she added apologetically, " I always think Forty-nine is such an innocent 'bus, it never knows the City."

Next morning it was raining in the persistently militant sort of way reserved by the weather for public holidays.

"A pity," said the gardener at breakfast. "I meant to take you over to the village to introduce you to Mr. Rust. And there are no 'buses or taxis here."

"Let's dispense with the 'buses and taxis," suggested the suffragette. "Let's forget London and get country-wet"

" You'll catch your death of cold," said the gardener delightedly, and presently they started.

" I don't really want to be introduced to your friend," said the suffragette. " Only I wanted a chance to speak to you alone. Do you know, beneath a militant exterior I am horribly shy? "

" It's obvious," retorted the gardener.

"Is it?" asked the suffragette, annoyed, and relapsed into silence for a moment.

"I wanted to tell you . . ." she began again presently, " that I beg your pardon for coming here. It's unforgivable of me. You know, as regards men, I'm not a woman at all; I haven't the unselfish instincts that other women have. I came because I had — reached the limit — and I wanted a friend..."

"Well, you didn't come far wrong," said the gardener. "I love you."

"I didn't think of your feelings at all, which is only another proof that it is no good your loving me."

"May I take the risk?"

The suffragette stopped, and stood leaning against the rain-whipped wind. Rain was trapped in the mesh of her soft hair. She clenched her fists upon her breast.

"Won't you believe me..." she said, " when I tell you it would be best to break up that poor little dream of yours — as I have broken mine. I told you once that I had somehow been born the wrong side of the ropes in the race. One can't love across a barrier."

"Love is not a dream," said the gardener. "It's your barrier that's a dream. Why don't you try breaking that?"

"You are a man, little gardener, and I am a thing. Not a bad thing, really, but certainly not a woman. And even a thing can reach the point which I have reached, the point at which there seems nothing to do but grope and cry ..."

They walked a little way in silence.

"I seem to have come to the edge of the world by myself," she went on. "And I can't go on — by myself. Oh, gardener, couldn't we be friends without being lovers?"

"That has been suggested before," said the gardener slowly. "And it has never succeeded. But — we — might — try..."

All the rest of the way to the village I suppose they were practising being friends and not lovers. For neither spoke a word.

"So this is the militant suffragette," said Samuel Rust, who was sitting in the hospital sitting-room. "I am most interested to meet you. I have long wished to meet a suffragette to ask her why she wanted the vote."

"Why do men want it?"

195

"Personally I don't."

" Personally I do," said the suffragette. " And mine is as good an answer as yours."

"Both answers are very poor," admitted Samuel " You want the vote so badly that you think it worthwhile to become hysterical over it"

"There is not much hysteria in the movement, only hysteria is the thing that strikes a hysterical press as most worthy of note. What hysteria there is, is a result — not a cause. Women never invented hysteria. How should we be anything but irresponsible, since you have taken responsibility from us? If we are bitter, you must remember that somebody mixed the dose. If the womanliness you admire is dead, bear in mind that nothing can be dead without being killed."

"But who is your enemy? Who are your murderers? I have never noticed that the majority of men are fiends incarnate. You may not believe me, but I do assure you that at frequent intervals in my life I have met honest, just, and moral men. Have you met none?"

"In the Brown Borough I meet excellent men. Older and wiser men, who sit on committees and behave like one conglomerate uncle to the poor; young lovers too hopelessly out of work to marry, and yet always gay and good-hearted; large tired fathers who come in after a day's work and sit under dripping washing and never slap the children . . . But that such just men are not in a majority is proved by the fact that women continue to suffer."

" Yes, but perhaps they suffer at the hands — not of men — but of circumstances."

"Circumstances always favour people with a public voice."

"And do militant suffragettes really think that by smashing windows they will attain to a public voice?"

"In what we do, we're a poor argument for the Franchise. In what we are, we're the very best. It's not possible for the community to be hit without deserving it. It must look round and find out why it is hit — not how. Punishment is no good to a smasher of windows. Any woman can see if she's wrong without punishment. If she thinks she's right, punishment can never alter her opinion."

"Smashers must be punished. It would be impossible to allow even the righteous to take the law into their own hands."

"In whose hands should we leave it? In the hands of those who declare themselves to be our enemies? A fair question from a woman never gets a fair answer. Windows are smashed — not as an argument, but as a protest."

"A protest strikes me as a futile thing. No one ever does anything that looks unfair or tyrannical without being perfectly sure that was the thing they meant to do. If a protest is successful it creates discord without altering what is done. If it's unsuccessful, it leaves you with a high temperature and bruised hands, and what is gained by that?"

"Protest isn't a thing you argue about," said the suffragette. "It's a thing you do when you see red. You seem to think that men have the monopoly of the last straw."

"It is hard to believe that you have reached the last straw," said Samuel. "It is very hard for men to picture women as an oppressed race. We are miles and miles away from each other. I can still think of a lot of things to say, but I can't say them without a moral megaphone. Shall we call a draw?"

"Let's," said the suffragette, relaxing her militant expression. "Only let me have the last word — a rather long one. Of one thing I am certain — when we have the vote, men will see what a small gift it was, and future generations will ask why it was grudged so bitterly. Only to us who have fought for it and suffered for it, it will always seem high and splendid — like a flag captured in battle . . ."

"The country is looking pretty just now, isn't it?" said Mr. Samuel Rust.

The gardener was standing at the window, watching the clipped yew bird outside curtseying to the wind. He had been pathetically silent, like a snubbed child, ever since he had consented to be a friend and not a lover. His white keen face was a striking illustration of enthusiasm damped. His jaw looked as if he were clenching his teeth on something bitter. I think he was regretting the days when gold hair with a ripple in it as laboured as the ripples in an old Master's seascape, wide blue eyes alight with matrimonial instinct, and the very red lips of a very small mouth, were all that his heart needed.

And I wonder what the suffragette saw in his face that made her say in a very non-militant voice, " Come, gardener."

They both shook hands in rather an absent-minded way with Mr. Samuel Rust. They started from the door with the wind behind them. It was with her hair blowing forward along her cheeks that the gardener always remembered the suffragette most vividly. It brought a brave idea to his mind, connected vaguely with a picture of Grace Darling with which he had been in love fifteen years ago.

"Gardener," said the suffragette hurriedly. " Can you imagine me sitting by the fire bathing a baby?"

"Easily," he replied. "I can imagine how the firelight would dance upon your hair."

"That doesn't sound like me at all," she said, with a catch in her voice. " Can you imagine me, looking sleepy and cross, giving you early breakfast before you went to work?"

"I can imagine you with the sun behind you, saying good-morning, so that the word seemed like a blessing through the day."

"It's a lie — you poet," she said. " Why don't you open your eyes and see me as I am?"

"I've had my eyes open all along. It's you who are blind."

"Then --suppose we become both lovers and friends... Suppose we get married on Tuesday..."

>
> To-morrow I will don my cloak
> Of opal-grey, and I will it and
> Where the palm shadows stride like smoke
> Across the dazzle of the sand.
> To-morrow I will throw this blind
> Blind whiteness from my soul away
> And pluck this blackness from my mind,
> And only leave the medium — grey.

To-morrow I will cry for gains
Upon the blue and brazen sky:
The precious venom in my veins
To-morrow will be parched and dry.
To-morrow it shall be my goal
To throw myself away from me,
To lose the outline of my soul
Against the greyness of the sea.

CHAPTER II

The suffragette went up to London on Monday — Bank Holiday — to contemplate finally the ruin of her work. For it was dead. I suppose if she had not felt so old and tired she might have thought of a fresh beginning, but she was always more passionate than persistent.

I don't think the Brown Borough ever made her suffer so much as it did the day she came back to it and found no place for her. You must remember she had always put work before pleasure, and a new joy born had no place in her mind with the pain of work killed. The gardener of yesterday retreated from the foreground of her mind, and for a while she never thought at all of the gardener of tomorrow.

Henceforward we part company with that suffragette whom I have loved perhaps a good deal, and of whom you have wearied. Her heart seemed to take on a different colour as she returned for the last time to the Brown Borough. What she had preached for years conquered her beyond hope at last, the world she had fought became suddenly victor.

She went to Jenny Wigsky, and found her gone.

She went to see 'Tilda, who was out. But 'Tilda's mother spoke out 'Tilda's mind.

She went to see the priest's sister, and she was away for Easter. But the priest was at home.

"I had no wish ever to see you again," said the priest "But it is as well that we should meet, for I should like to make my position and that of my sister perfectly clear to you, yerce, yerce."

" It is perfectly clear," said the suffragette, who felt curiously numb.

"Excuse me, but I do not wish that you should go away under the delusion that you are in the right though persecuted, and in your self-absorption proceed to make havoc of another field of work. Setting aside the fact that you have been guilty of bad faith towards us, you have approached the work from a wilfully wrong standpoint. You have mixed your despicable little political jealousies with Christian work, to the serious danger of young and innocent souls."

"I worked for the honour of women, and you — possibly — for the honour of your God. Certainly your work sounds better — to men."

"If there is a thing mat women excel in, it is the art of evading the point," said the priest bitterly. " The affair, bluntly put, is this: Jane Wigsky, an idle, vicious, and immoral girl, had the impudence to go to my very good friend, Mr. Smith, of Smith, Bird and Co., and, presuming on her showy appearance, to apply for a responsible post, a post which is in every way suited to be the reward of virtue, rather than something for the covetous to grasp at Mr. Smith is, as I say, a friend of mine, and a most generous friend to the Church, having only last week presented a beautiful carved chancel screen. Naturally it was my duty to tell him all I knew about the girl."

"And what did you know?"

"I am not obliged to answer to you for my statements, but, as a matter of fact, I told him that the girl was not a ' stayer ' — in colloquial language — and that she was of immoral tendency."

"That was only what you fancied. What did you know?"

There was a swallowing sound in the priest's throat, a sound as of one keeping his temper.

"May I ask if you are aware that the girl has now disappeared, with her lover?"

"But that was since you wrote."

"I have not worked for twenty-two years among the poor without reaching a certain insight into character; I am not blind to such things, whatever you may be, yerce, yerce. But that is beside the point. I reminded Smith that he might be able to give her less important employment — I was willing to help the girl up to a certain point. I suggested a protege of my own for the better post, to whom the generous opportunity offered would be far more suitable, a very deserving young man, who is debarred from ordinary employment by the loss of a leg. Mr. Smith accepted my suggestion, and offered Jane Wigsky a post as packer, at seven-and-six a week, a much larger wage than the hat been getting lately. She refused, and pot the responsibility of her refusal on you. She also mentioned that other girls in the Church Club were under your influence on the question of wages. I made enquiries and found that my sister's club was in a fair way to turn into a female Trade Union, an abominable anomaly. I took the only course possible. I dismissed all the misguided girls from the Club. There is nothing more to be said."

"Nothing," said the suffragette, who had become very white, " except — what must your God be like to have a servant like you?"

"If you are going to blaspheme," said the priest, " kindly leave my house at once."

"If God is like that . . ." she said, " I pray the Devil may win."

She ran out of the house childishly, and slammed the door.

The gardener, on Tuesday morning, was parting his hair for the third time, when he received a telegram:

"Don't come. — Suffragette."

It startled him, but not very much. He looked at the third attempt at a parting in the glass, and saw that it was an excellent parting for a man on his wedding-day. He reflected that a militant suffragette would naturally tend to become ultra-militant on this final day. And if the worst came to the worst, it could do no harm to go up and find out how bad the worst was. So he went up to London by the eleven train.

He was to meet her at the little bun-shop that clings for protection to the Brown Borough Town Hall. There the suffragette had a fourpenny meal daily, and there they had arranged to have an eightpenny meal together, before assuming the married pose. There was a " wedding-shop " round the corner. I don't suppose any couple ever made less impressive plans.

And the gardener pursued the plan. He entirely ignored the telegram.

I don't know whether the suffragette was confident that he would obey it, or that he would ignore it. I am entirely doubtful about her state of mind on that day. But I know that when the gardener arrived at the bun-shop she was there, facing the door, already half-way through her fourpenny lunch. Which appears to show that — if her telegram was genuine — she put implicit faith in his obedience. In this case she was presumably displeased to see him. Her face, however, looked too tired to change its expression in any way.

"Didn't you get my wire?" she said.

"What is a wire to me?" asked the gardener, sitting down.

There was a long pause, during which he ordered a Welsh Rarebit from a waitress who, six months ago, would have furnished him with an ideal of womanhood.

" Why did you wire?" he asked presently.

"I have to go on a journey," said the suffragette, waving at the mustard-coloured portmanteau, which was seated on a chair beside her.

"In that case, so have I," said the gardener. " We'll get married first, and then go on the journey together.

No reply. Their talk was like broken fragments thrown upon a tea of ice. It harried! faltered, stopped, and then froze into a background of silence.

The gardener noticed that the suffragette was trembling violently, and with a great effort he made no comment on this discovery.

Finally she rose, leaving quite twopence-halfpenny worth of her meal hiding beneath her knife and fork.

"You'll have to show me where this registry office is," said the gardener, "and also what to do. I don't know how one gets married."

"Neither do I," said the suffragette.

"I'll carry your bag."

"I like carrying things. I hate being helped. You must always remember that I am a militant suffragette."

"I am never allowed to forget it," sighed the gardener, his ardour rather damped. "Are we getting near the place?"

"Very near."

They stopped at the steps of a church.

"We might have thought it our duty to be married in a church," she said. " What a merciful escape!" He was silent.

"I hate God," she added.

"Don't," said the gardener. " You're too excited. Don't tremble like that. Don't hate God. After all, He made the world — a green sane world — with you and me in it . . ."

"He made it with you in it. But I got in by mistake."

"What a happy mistake!" said the gardener. " Come into the church, my dear, and rest for a moment. Don't try to look too deep into the reasons of things, you'll only get giddy."

He took her hand, and they went up the steps together.

"It's a fine church," he said. "That screen's a fine bit of carving." He felt as if he had taken charge of his suffragette's nerves, and he busied his brain in the composition of cool and commonplace remarks.

"That chancel screen is dirty. It's the gift of foul hands, bought with foul money. Do you think me mad?"

"You are, rather, you know. Pull yourself together. Surely you're not frightened of getting married to me?"

The suffragette laughed. " You wonderfully faithful friend," she said.

The gardener was not a religious young man. He was not quite rare enough in texture for that, and he was a little too clever for the religion of his fathers.

The Christian pose had never appealed to him, it fit not unique enough. All his life he had seen prayer used as a method of commercial telegraphy. You wanted a thing, and from a kneeling position you informed Heaven of your order. If it was complied with, you knew that you must be appreciated in high quarters; if it was ignored, you supposed that your message had miscarried, and despatched another. At any rate it cost nothing.

But the gardener had a vague reverence inborn in him. During his everyday life he posed as an unbeliever. When in his own imposing company he passively believed in something he had never defined. But under stained-glass windows or the benediction of music, under arched forests and a sinless sky, under the passionate sane spell of the sea, under the charm of love, he knew that he worshipped. For he was a poet without the means of proving it, and to such God is a secret mouthpiece, and a salvation.

So, at the back of the church, beside the suffragette, he pressed his face into his hands, and his elbows on to his knees, and found to his surprise that his heart was beating violently. Between his fingers he could see the east window. Its blood-like splashes of red, its banners of unearthly blue, its blur of golden haloes glorified the sunlight. It seemed to have a colour for each of his days; he found his childhood in it, and his little ambitions, his pale Trala-Ia days, and the babyhood of his heart, red hair he found, and the ardour of the sea, and love . . . And presently he looked round and found his companion had gone from his side.

He could see her, with her chin up, looking defiantly at the altar. The sunlight dramatically touched her distant face, and it was like a pin-prick in the twilight of the church. It was but seldom that nature provided a good setting for my suffragette.

It was only when he saw her with the mustardcoloured portmanteau raised shoulder high that he realised what she was doing. The knowledge tore a gash across his dreams, and severed him from himself. He did not move. He watched her throw the portmanteau at the foot of the chancel screen. He saw her wrap her arms about her face and swing round on her heel. He hardly heard the explosion, but directly afterwards he realised how loud it had been.

Smoke danced across the altar, smoke blotted out the window, smoke threaded the lace of the shattered screen. Smoke . . . Silver in the sunlight . . . blue round the altar . . . and grey — dead grey — over the little crumpled body of the criminal. Smoke stood over her, a transitory monument — like a tree — like a curse.

Yes, I pose of course. But the question is — how deep may a pose extend?

THE END.

24615818R00119

Printed in Poland
by Amazon Fulfillment
Poland Sp. z o.o., Wrocław